BROKEN CIRCLE

ALSO BY MATT BROLLY

Detective Liam Kilshaw Series

The Lines

The Replacement

Detective Louise Blackwell series:

The Crossing

The Descent

The Gorge

The Mark

The Pier

The Bridge

The Solstice

Lynch and Rose series:

The Controller

The Railroad

DCI Lambert series:

Dead Eyed

Dead Lucky

Dead Embers

Dead Time

Dead Water

Dead End

Standalone novels:

The Running Girls

Zero

The Alliance

BROKEN CIRCLE

MATT BROLLY

This is a work of fiction. Names, characters, organizations, places, events, and incidents are either products of the author's imagination or are used fictitiously. Any resemblance to actual persons, living or dead, or actual events is purely coincidental.

Published by Thomas & Mercer, Seattle

www.apub.com

Amazon, the Amazon logo, and Thomas & Mercer are trademarks of Amazon.com, Inc., or its affiliates.

EU Product Safety Contact:
Amazon Media EU S.à r.l.
38, avenue John F. Kennedy, L-1855 Luxembourg
amazonpublishing-gpsr@amazon.com

ISBN-13: 9781662520464
eISBN: 9781662520457

Cover design by Tom Sanderson
Cover image: © Swen Stroop; © SuxxesPhoto; © afotostock / Shutterstock

Printed in the United States of America

For Gareth Starr

Prologue

He'd been here before.

The Merry Maidens were the perfect starting point: a stone circle created from nineteen maidens turned to stone for dancing on the Sabbath, with the two pipers in the adjoining fields – their guardians, in a way – suffering the same fate for providing the music.

All of them were trapped for eternity within their granite prisons as both a punishment and a reminder.

A cautionary tale, almost constantly ignored by everyone.

There had been a time when such things hadn't mattered to him. But they mattered now. He'd studied the texts, slowly coming to accept everything he'd once dismissed. Now he probably knew the intricacies better than anyone alive. The contrasting accounts, the belief structures, the power battles, the countless differing views that still existed.

It was up to him to make sense of it all.

Everything pointed to him being at the centre, and it had to start here.

He rested against the Piper Stone, which lay north-east of the stone circle, the granite already decorated in ochre. Although his plan was intricate, there were still some aspects he didn't quite understand himself. His ultimate goal was the circle, but there would be obstacles on the way, and he needed to create distractions. Side stories. Useless trails to fool those who wished to stop him.

As he doused the Piper Stone, he sensed a huge surge of energy which intensified with every touch of the granite, the ochre thick against his skin, easing his motions over the rough stonework.

But what truly gave him power was the sight in the other field.

It was still dark, but she glowed, and it wouldn't be long now.

He doused the stone a final time before making his way across the field.

It would be sunrise in a matter of minutes, and if he'd timed it right she would pass at that exact moment.

It felt important that it happened that way.

She was still alive, and he envied what was happening to her body. The eternity she would now get to experience, free from her petty concerns and distractions.

'Not long now,' he whispered as her breath became ragged.

He smeared the limonite across her face. 'From flesh to clay, from clay to stone. This is how we last,' he said, as her head fell and he left her praying to the rest of the maidens.

Chapter One

A wind had built up on Porthmeor Beach, four-foot waves crashing to the shore as Liam Kilshaw finished his sprint along the sand. It was an early Monday morning in April, and for now he was the only one there. He closed his eyes and savoured the sounds of the surf and the squall of the seagulls, the rattle of the wind and his own laboured breathing.

His running regime had increased over the last few weeks as he'd slowly recuperated from the injury he'd sustained before Christmas. Most mornings he made his way to the beach before work. Where once he'd spent time in the sea to clear his mind, he now ran for the same objective.

His exertions were such that it gave him little time to dwell on anything else, but as he walked the narrow streets towards Back Road West, his mind started conjuring unwanted thoughts.

He dwelt on his current workload, the unsolved cases and court appearances that were due. His son, George, who he never got to see as much as he would like. His dormant love life after the relationship he'd ruined with his ex-girlfriend – somewhat awkwardly, George's one-time teacher – Millie. And Liam's mother, now all but lost to him in her own little world of dementia.

Finally, he thought about the sea and how his fears of the open water were still unresolved. The sea had been his life since he was a child, but now the thought of being out in the ocean triggered physical and emotional responses that he had little control over. He still volunteered with the lifeboat crew but it never seemed to get any easier to control the instinctual fear he felt ever since the accident that nearly killed him. He'd come to acknowledge that it would remain a constant battle.

Stopping at the foot of the hill to stretch, he supposed his concerns were not that out of the ordinary. With his work as a police officer – and former life as a marine and SBS specialist – he knew better than most the troubles and secrets everyone carried with them. He was simply being maudlin, subjecting himself to the dark moods that sometimes crept over him. It would pass, but to help it on its way, he took a final sprint back to his flat.

The run up the hill was gruelling but was exactly what he needed. All negativity was banished as he sped forwards, receiving the occasional look from the early risers, as he moved his considerable bulk upwards, his only thought his aching lungs and the heat of muscles as he pushed himself further, forcing his knees higher until he reached the staircase to his flat, and bent over, blissfully overtaken by exhaustion.

The coffee machine he'd set had brewed in his absence, so he poured himself a cup and took it into the bathroom. Changing, he noticed he'd lost a little weight. He was six-two, with a completely bald head he'd had since childhood due to alopecia. He'd always kept in shape, having entered the military as a teenager, but it had been a long time since he'd felt this good, his muscles well defined in the bathroom mirror as he stepped under the steaming jets of the showers.

He heard his phone ring but ignored it, only for it to start ringing again immediately. Swearing, he reached out for it. 'Kilshaw.'

'Sir, it's PC Walker. There's an incident close to you – a body has been found. Response team is there and CSI are on their way.

DCI Hargreaves thought it might be best to contact you before you got to work.'

'Did he now? Send me the details. I can leave in five.'

He changed and filled a thermos of coffee before locating his car a few streets up from his flat. He wasn't armed with much more information beyond a body having been found in a field close to Lamorna, south of Penzance.

As he approached the scene, flashing blue lights guiding his way, he began to recognise where he was. Liam had been here on a number of occasions. The field contained the Merry Maidens stone circle – a tourist hotspot. From Liam's recollection, the circle contained nineteen stones. The legend had it that each stone represented a dancing maiden, turned to stone for dancing on the Sabbath. The same legend suggested it was impossible to count them all without losing your place, though he was sure he'd disproved that particular wisdom once as a child.

He pulled into the makeshift car park, and followed the grass track along the field to where the CSIs had started working.

The nearest granite stone must have been a little over a metre tall. The stones were spaced every three to four metres, and kneeling with her back to the stone opposite him was the victim.

He donned a protective CSI coverall and joined the team, stopping to speak to one of the CSIs, Giselle Cooper. 'What do we know so far?'

Giselle removed her mask as they both looked over to the victim, who was being photographed by the other CSIs. Giselle shook her head as if she didn't know how to explain the situation.

'You're going to have to look for yourself. She was found in this kneeling position but there is nothing holding her in that position. No binds around any part of her body. There are no signs of obvious trauma beyond the clay.'

Liam walked towards the body, the grass wet beneath his feet. 'The clay?'

'Her hands and feet are covered in clay.' Giselle paused as they reached the cordon of the crime scene. 'As is her face.'

Liam peered towards the victim. Her face was covered by a thick mask, the clay covering it dotted with what appeared to be yellow paint. 'That was what killed her?'

'We still need to determine the precise cause of death, but it appears as if she suffocated or choked on that substance. Looks like some kind of clay mixture. We think the yellow is an ochre-like substance.'

With her features still covered, it was as if the victim wasn't real. More like a mannequin than the human they knew her to be.

'The body was discovered at eight-thirty this morning. I would estimate she'd already been in position for a few hours.'

'ID?'

Giselle handed him an evidence bag containing a driver's licence. 'Found this by the stone.'

'Tess Penrose, aged eighteen,' Liam said, as he looked at the address – the nearby village of St Buryan.

'She was found naked apart from her underwear, as you can see,' Giselle said.

'Sexual assault?'

'Not evident so far.'

'No sign of the rest of her clothes?'

The CSIs shook their heads as Liam studied the clay on the young woman's hands and feet. 'What's that on her?' he asked, noting the film of fine yellow powder on her back.

'We think it's ochre dust as well.'

'Significance?'

'Historically, it's used for painting,' said the CSI holding a video camera. 'Body paint, that sort of thing.'

'Always yellow?'

'No. It comes from iron oxide in the earth. Usually it's red, brown, or this yellow. If it is ochre dust, then I think the yellow colour would come from limonite.'

Liam considered the relevance of the paint as he walked over to the first responder who was in conversation with the man who'd discovered the body. Already his mind was moving in a hundred different directions, from the mythological significance of the body being placed in the circle, to the religious connotations of the body being configured in a prayer state.

He thought about the clay placed over the victim's mouth and felt a tremor in his chest. He sucked in the cold air as he fought a little wave of panic, and gave himself a few seconds to control his breathing before continuing.

'PC Aldershot, sir. This is Kyle Sturridge,' said the uniformed officer.

'Mr Sturridge. DS Kilshaw,' Liam said.

'Mr Sturridge discovered the body on his way to work,' PC Aldershot said.

Sturridge was a square block of a human being. A little shorter than Liam, he had the same broad shoulders. Liam was never one to rush to conclusions, but the man seemed remarkably composed for someone who'd found a corpse, especially one in such a disturbing state.

'That's right,' Sturridge said in a deep Cornish accent. 'I was on my way to the farm where I work when something caught my eye.'

'Which farm is this?'

'Bosvellan Farm, sir,' said the uniformed officer, receiving a withering look from Liam for interrupting.

'That's right,' Sturridge said.

Liam checked the sightline to the main road, confirming that the body would've been visible if Sturridge had been making his way further inland to the farm.

'Quite a spot,' Liam said.

Sturridge scratched his deep-red beard. 'I always look at the stone circle. Why wouldn't you?' A smile formed and disappeared in an instant. 'I think the sunlight made her stand out, but it was easy to see something was off. I've seen people here before. The youngsters, they sometimes use this as a party town in the summer, but I can't remember the last time I saw a semi-naked girl on her own in the field,' said Sturridge, holding Liam's gaze steadfast.

Sturridge was a strange one. With his woollen jumper, beard and thick accent, he was probably the kind of archetype upcountry folk thought of when they considered the Cornish. He had a quiet confidence about him when he spoke, almost as if he was constantly issuing a challenge. 'Walk me through your movements.'

'I parked up over yonder,' said Sturridge. 'That's my jeep there. I have to confess, I almost didn't stop. I thought maybe the poor lass had got herself into trouble and drunk too much and been abandoned by some bastard of a boyfriend. But as I approached her, I knew something was definitely off. It was the way her body was positioned, you see. Of course you can see,' Sturridge said under his breath. 'I got to about ten metres of her and I knew she was dead.'

'Did you touch her?' asked Liam.

The police constable opened his mouth to speak, but Liam cut him off by raising his hand.

'I know you're not supposed to in these circumstances,' said Sturridge, 'but I wanted to make sure. I hoped . . . I don't know what I hoped. That she was drunk, high on drugs. I would've taken anything at that point, would've been happy for it all to be a joke, a scam. I searched for a pulse but I could see from what was on her face . . .' Sturridge shook his head. 'Her neck was like ice.'

Liam couldn't blame the man for touching the victim. He'd known officers make the same mistake, and if there was any chance of her being alive then it was more than justified. It did mean that if Sturridge had killed her, he would have a convenient explanation for his DNA being on her.

'We're going to have to request you come back to the station, Mr Sturridge. We need to take your prints and DNA as a matter of process.'

'I thought as much. I've already called work.'

'You say you've seen youngsters here before?'

'In the summer, mainly.'

'Locals or tourists?'

'Both,' Sturridge said, scratching his beard again. 'Locals don't like it and they sometimes leave a mess, but they're drawn to this place. So many people are.'

'You noted the colouring on the girl's body?'

Sturridge nodded, his right hand playing with a rose gold wedding ring on his left.

'Ochre. I've seen it before. This place attracts a certain type of person. In my day, we called them hippies, new-age folk, druids, whatever. It's all part of the ritual. They paint themselves for whatever reason. I guess they use ochre to be one with nature or something like that. Even the ravers used it back in the day.'

'Ravers?' Liam asked.

'I guess I must have a good twenty years on you. You don't remember the rave scene of the eighties and nineties?'

'Bit before my time.'

'They used to go further inland, but there was more than one rave organised here.' Sturridge stepped a little closer and put his hand by his mouth. 'If I'm being totally honest, I may have come here once or twice myself, but don't go telling anyone. Don't get me wrong. I didn't take no drugs. I was just there for the ladies. But they used to do that. Boys and girls paint themselves. Some would use normal face paints, but those more attuned would use the ochre.'

'Attuned?'

Sturridge ran his tongue through the inside of his mouth as if he'd been caught out, his eye contact never wavering. 'Attuned with nature,' he said.

'And why do you think that young woman has ochre on her?' Liam asked.

Sturridge pulled at his beard. 'Beats me. All I know is that a lot of weird shit goes on around these places. These types of stone circles are steeped in history. I don't know much about it, but there've always been stories, pagan rituals and what have you. And of course you know what these stones are meant to represent.'

Liam felt another twinge in his chest. He thought about the maidens turned to stone, and couldn't help but view it literally. He imagined the young women trapped within their granite prisons, in an eternal struggle for breath.

He knew Cornwall as well as anyone, understood the legends and ritualistic beliefs that lay just beneath the surface. He'd travelled the world in the armed forces, but there was nowhere like the place. He wasn't one to fall for supernatural nonsense, but he couldn't deny there was a certain sense of power to the land, a pull he'd felt much stronger inside the circle. It was probably all in the mind, but he wasn't sure that made any difference.

'Enlighten me,' Liam said, wanting to hear Sturridge's take.

'They're the Merry Maidens,' said Sturridge, warming to his subject. 'It's believed they were caught dancing on the Sabbath and were turned to stone for their crimes as a warning to others. Can't get any weirder than that, can you?'

'No, I suppose not,' said Liam, considering Sturridge's mention of the word 'warning'. 'Thank you for your cooperation. PC Aldershot here will accompany you back to the station.'

As Sturridge walked away, Liam took a final glance at the nineteen stone effigies formed in a circle, wondering if, as Giselle had suggested, Tess Penrose's time of death would also be determined to have been on a Sunday.

And if she'd been killed as a warning to others.

Chapter Two

Another member of the CSI team, Tina Madeley, approached Liam as he waited for his direct supervisor, DI Maya Trent, to arrive.

Tina smiled shyly as she pulled off her mask, the net keeping her hair in place.

'Tina,' Liam said, matching her smile. 'We always seem to meet in the most unfortunate of circumstances.'

'You certainly bring trouble with you. How are you keeping?'

'All good,' Liam replied, matching her gaze. 'You?'

'Not too bad.'

Liam was never one for small talk but this was excruciating. He had history with Tina – a drunken kiss at a police Christmas party over a year ago which had seemingly been witnessed by half of headquarters. Something Maya liked to tease him about every time she saw them together.

Tina nodded at nothing in particular, the silence growing beyond awkward. 'Would you like to take my number, Liam?' she said eventually.

'Yes, yes, of course,' Liam said, a little too eagerly, handing her his phone.

Tina blushed, tapping in her number and giving the phone back as Maya arrived. 'Speak soon,' she said, hurrying away.

'Do you ever stop?' Maya said, a wry look on her face as they both watched Tina return to the rest of the team.

'Nice of you to join us, boss,' Liam said, doing his best to deflect the conversation. He filled her in on the discovery of the body and his conversation with the local farmhand, Kyle Sturridge, before she had a chance to quiz him further over Tina. 'Were you ever a raver?' he asked.

Maya rolled her eyes. Liam's teenage years had been spent in local pubs or at the beach on warm nights. The rave scene had definitely been over by then and he didn't remember hearing about gatherings in stone circles, but maybe he'd just been part of a different crowd. 'I can imagine you with white gloves and a whistle.'

'I'll pretend I didn't hear that, Detective Sergeant, so I don't have to report you to PSD,' Maya replied. 'Why are you leaving the crime scene?'

'I've got an address for the victim. Down the road in St Buryan.'

'And you were going to leave without me?'

'Well, if you will arrive late.' Liam opened the door of the car and nodded at the coffee in her hand. 'By the way, where's mine?'

This time, Maya came close to smiling. 'It's the subordinate officer's duty to buy the coffees, Liam, as you well know. I should be asking you why there wasn't one waiting for me.'

They drove the short distance to St Buryan. In the rear-view mirror, Liam caught sight of the white CSI tent being stretched over Tess Penrose's body and the Merry Maiden stone she was positioned against.

The village itself was little more than a hamlet. One church, a pub, a shop, and a scatter of houses, including the one where Tess had lived.

Liam parked outside a small terraced house on the edge of the village, squeezing between a rusting hatchback and a newer-looking SUV.

'You lead,' Maya said as they reached the front door.

Liam knocked, his warrant card already in hand. A few seconds later, the door creaked open. A slim, athletic woman stood in the doorway. She looked them both over, her brow furrowed. Her mouth twitched as if she was about to speak, but no words came.

'Mrs Penrose?' Liam said, softening his voice. 'I'm DS Liam Kilshaw. This is DI Maya Trent. You are Mrs Penrose?'

'Yes, Philippa Penrose,' she said, finding her voice. 'What's this about? Is it Tess? Is she okay?'

Liam hated death messages perhaps more than any other aspect of the job. It never got easier. No two reactions were the same. Some people froze, others lashed out. Mrs Penrose seemed caught somewhere between the two.

'Perhaps we should come in,' he said.

Mrs Penrose shook her head, a hollow sound escaping her lips, before she stepped back to let them into the house.

Maya entered first, Liam following. The interior was small, cluttered with ornaments and old furniture, but there was warmth to the place, a sense of homeliness. Liam caught a photo of Tess and her mother at the beach in a picture frame on the mantlepiece as he prepared what he was going to say.

'Just tell me,' Mrs Penrose said. 'Please.' Her body was shaking and Maya guided her to the sofa and sat beside her, casting a look at Liam.

He'd been rehearsing the words ever since he'd left the stone circle, but it never helped. No matter how many times he'd done it, they never came out the way he wanted. 'I'm so very sorry, Mrs Penrose. Tess's body was found earlier this morning at the Merry Maidens stone circle.'

'She's dead?' Mrs Penrose's body stiffened. Eyes wide, she stared at Liam in accusation and disbelief.

'I'm so sorry for your loss,' Liam said, painfully aware how hollow his words sounded.

Mrs Penrose's breathing became rapid. 'How?'

Maya placed her hand on Mrs Penrose's shoulder. She gave Liam a quick nod of encouragement. 'This is going to be very difficult to hear, Mrs Penrose, but our initial assumption is that Tess was murdered.'

'Murdered?' The word stretched out, as if it were foreign to her.

'As I said, her body was found at the Merry Maidens stone circle. There were clear signs of foul play,' Liam said, not needing, or wanting, to go into detail yet.

Mrs Penrose slumped back in her chair, her mouth hanging open, caught somewhere between a gasp and a silent scream.

'I'll make some tea,' Liam said, as Maya did her best to comfort the mother.

The kitchen was as cluttered as the rest of the house. Liam found the kettle, and brewed a pot of builder's tea, pouring it into three identical mugs decorated with the St Piran's flag.

Now he was out of sight of Mrs Penrose, he took some time to compose himself. He was used to seeing death, both in the police and military, but it was the aftershock he struggled with. Witnessing the raw emotion of people having to come to terms with their greatest fears. He guessed perhaps some of that was due to him losing his father as a child, but that too was something he didn't wish to dwell on.

He returned to the living room with the mugs on a tray. 'I brought you some sugar, just in case,' he said.

Mrs Penrose took the mug, hands trembling. Maya hovered beside her, as if ready to catch it if it dropped.

'I know this must be incredibly difficult,' Liam said, sure he was repeating himself, 'but we want to do everything we can to catch the person responsible. To do that, we need to move quickly. I need to ask you a few questions, if that's okay?'

Mrs Penrose said nothing for a long time before slowly sitting upright. She placed the mug on the small table, carefully resting it on a ceramic tile clearly used as a coaster.

'What would you like to know?' she said, her face hardening as she looked at Liam.

'When was the last time you saw your daughter?'

'Yesterday lunchtime. We had a Sunday roast. We always do.'

'And after that?'

'She went out. She's always out nowadays. She's in her final year of A-levels, at the college over in Penzance. Can't tell her anything. She likes to remind me she's eighteen, she can do what she likes. Though she's usually a little less sure of herself when she needs money.'

Liam nodded, uneasy about the way Mrs Penrose spoke in the present tense, as if still in denial about her daughter's death.

'What time did she leave?'

'Some of her friends came to pick her up. Around seven, I'd guess.'

'Do you have names for them?' Maya asked.

Mrs Penrose nodded. 'I can give you their numbers.' She hesitated, her face contorting as she fought back tears.

'Do you remember what she was wearing?' Liam asked.

'What sort of question is that? You've seen her, haven't you? What happened to her? Did someone take her? Was she . . .' Her voice cracked. 'Was she raped?' Tears spilt down her cheeks.

Liam looked to the floor, waiting for the crying to pass. He fought off the image of someone one day coming to his own door, telling him something had happened to George.

'She was wearing jeans. And a top. I told her she'd be cold. But when has a teenage girl ever cared about something like that?'

'Do you know where they were going?'

'I stopped asking a long time ago. But she at least told me she was staying over for the night. With a girl called Katie. Katie Brookmeyer.'

'Do you think Tess drank?' Liam asked. 'Or took drugs?'

Mrs Penrose shifted in her seat, her mouth contorting as if tasting something unpleasant. 'Are you trying to blame this on her?'

'Nothing like that,' Maya said. 'We're just trying to work out why Tess would have been at the stone circle. Maybe in the middle of the night. Do you know if her or any of her friends went to parties there?'

Mrs Penrose sat back again, eyes narrowing. She shook her head, but Liam wasn't sure if she believed it herself.

'They usually go out in Penzance. Or St Ives. She drinks, of course. She's eighteen. I'd hope she'd tell me if she took drugs. But I imagine they all do, don't they? She's stayed out a lot lately these past six months. It's hard for her to get back here late at night. I always offer to pick her up, but she's not interested.'

'Do you know if Tess was seeing anyone?' Liam asked.

'What?' Mrs Penrose said, caught off-guard.

'Was she in a relationship? A boyfriend? Girlfriend?'

'Tess didn't like to talk about that kind of thing. I only knew her friends because I made her introduce me to them. There's three of them. Four including Tess. Pretty girls. I'm sure they've all left their share of broken hearts behind them. But I don't know about any relationship.'

Mrs Penrose was clearly disappointed that Tess hadn't shared such details with her. It made Liam think about how little he knew about George's friendships, and how that might get worse as his son grew older.

'Thank you, Mrs Penrose,' Maya said. 'We won't keep you much longer. Can I ask about Tess's father? Does he live with you?'

Liam had already clocked the absence of a wedding ring.

'No, he does not,' Mrs Penrose said, the words sharp with resentment. 'That man is a philandering drunk. We got rid of him a long time ago. Not that it was easy.'

'What do you mean?' Maya asked.

Mrs Penrose turned her face to the side, revealing a small scar beneath her left eye.

'He liked to hit me. Especially after a drink. Men like that don't leave easily.'

'Where is he now?' Liam asked, wary of what might come next.

'People around here can be decent when it matters. We're a tight community. We got rid of him. I've barely seen him in five years. Last I heard, he was living out near Hayle. But I couldn't give you an address.'

Maya looked to Liam. 'Do you think he could've done this? To Tess?'

Mrs Penrose's hand went to the scar. She glared at Liam, as if the question itself was a betrayal. Her mouth opened, but for a moment she just stared, frozen, before saying, 'I don't know. As far as I'm aware she hasn't seen him since he left.'

Maya took the contact details for Tess's friends and Mrs Penrose's ex-husband as the family liaison officer arrived.

'Can I see her?' Mrs Penrose asked.

'There'll be a time for formal identification,' Maya said.

Mrs Penrose stood. 'Please can I see her now? You must have a photo of where she was found.'

'It's not something you'd want to see,' Maya said.

'Please, show me.'

Scratching the back of his neck, Liam thought of the images that had been taken. Tess's semi-naked body slumped against the Merry Maiden monolith, the ochre paint decorating her skin catching the sunlight, her face a mask of clay. He hoped Mrs Penrose would never get to see such an image.

'I'm sorry, Mrs Penrose, it's for the best,' Maya said, signalling to the FLO to take over, Liam feeling a guilty stab of relief as they left.

Chapter Three

The first thing Liam did when they got back to the car was call DC Jack Lawson and instruct him to locate Jerry Penrose, Tess's father. Liam knew most violent murders were committed by someone known to the victim, and an estranged, abusive, alcoholic father had to be a prime candidate.

They drove for a few minutes in silence, Liam lost in thought about the conversation with Mrs Penrose. Sometimes it was all but impossible to relate to how family members must feel on hearing such news. How lives could be ripped apart in a handful of sentences. He thought about how Mrs Penrose had answered the door to them seemingly without a care in the world, only for her life to be irrevocably changed.

He recalled her desire to see the crime-scene photograph of her daughter, and what her imagination must be going through. It was one thing so often forgotten about such horrific crimes: the fact that they extended far beyond the victim. Tess's death would resonate for years to come and would affect all those known to her for the rest of their lives. Not that he needed anything further, but that was motivation enough for Liam to do everything in his power to find those responsible.

The sea was in as they drove along the main road to Penzance, sunlight dappling the water. St Michael's Mount rose in the distance, the view never failing to stir awe in Liam, however many times he'd seen it.

'How are things with you, anyway?' Maya said. 'Good weekend?'

Their working relationship had grown over the past year. Maya had become more than a colleague. She was a confidant, someone he could trust, and sometimes, when pride allowed, he even found himself discussing personal matters.

'Just the usual. Running. Lifeboat station. I was on duty, but no callouts.'

'DI Hartley?' Maya asked, teasing.

Grace Hartley, Liam's ex, now headed up Major Crimes for the Devon side of Devon and Cornwall, based out of Exeter. She'd reappeared in Liam's life during a joint investigation with the Met last year and since her move to the south-west, they'd met up a few times. Nothing romantic had happened yet, and Liam still wasn't sure how he felt about her or the fact that she now lived much nearer to him.

'Not this weekend.'

'I prefer the schoolteacher, anyway,' Maya said, with a sideways glance.

'She's taken,' Liam said. 'So nothing's going to happen there.'

'And how do you feel about that?'

Liam grimaced. He appreciated Maya's interest, but it wasn't something he wanted to dwell on. It had been Millie's decision to end things, and over the last couple of months he'd started to realise the impact of that went deeper than he'd initially thought.

He didn't answer. And Maya didn't push, the rest of the drive passing in silence.

At the college reception, they showed their warrant cards as Maya asked to speak with Tess's friend, Katie Brookmeyer. The receptionist hesitated and Liam had to turn away to hide a smile as Maya fixed her with a look of pure steel and told her flatly that she didn't care if Katie was in a lesson, she needed to speak with her now.

Five minutes later, the girl arrived, sheepish and quiet. She was wearing jeans and a loose T-shirt, her gaze fixed to the ground, and to Liam's eyes looked far younger than eighteen.

Maya introduced them. 'We'd like to ask you some questions about your friend, Tess Penrose, if that's okay, Katie?'

Katie looked up. 'Why?'

'Would you like someone to sit in with you? You are eighteen, right?' Maya said, ignoring the question.

Katie looked up at Maya. 'I'm eighteen, yes. Is everything okay with Tess?'

The receptionist looked from Maya to Liam. 'Are you sure you don't want someone with you, Katie?'

'No. It's fine.'

The receptionist led them to a small office adjoining the main reception. She left the door open as Liam, Maya and Katie sat down around the table.

'When did you last see Tess?' Liam asked.

Katie looked at his face, but not before a quick glance at his bald scalp. Liam was used to it. At his age, being bald wasn't novel, but his complete lack of hair – not even stubble – tended to draw looks.

'She's not come to college today. I've been messaging her all day,' Katie said. 'She hasn't responded.'

No phone had been recovered from the scene, and as far as Liam was aware they still hadn't located the device.

'Is she okay?' Katie repeated.

'When did you last see her?'

'Last night. We were all out together.'

'All?' Maya asked.

'Me and Tess, Evie and Janice,' Katie said, confirming the names Mrs Penrose had given them.

'Where exactly did you go?'

'We were at a party. All evening. We met at mine first. I picked Tess up. We had a couple of drinks before heading out.'

'Where was the party?'

'Near Mousehole. Not far from where I live.'

'We'll need the exact address,' Liam said, noting that Mousehole was only a few miles from the stone circle.

Katie looked away. 'It was supposed to be a secret. His parents are away. I don't want him to get in trouble.'

Liam ran a hand over his head, fingers pausing at the ridge of a scar. 'We need the address, Katie, but let's start with what happened.'

'What do you mean, what happened?'

'Tess went to the party with you?'

'Yes.' Katie stared at him again, and for a moment Liam thought she was going to demand her parents be called, before she started crying.

'Is there something you need to tell us?' Maya asked gently.

'I knew I shouldn't have let her go with him,' Katie said, through her tears. 'Tess left the party with a boy.'

'From college?'

Katie shook her head.

'What's his name?' Maya asked.

'Anthony. Anthony Ellison. He works on a farm, out towards Newlyn.'

'Why didn't you want Tess to go with him?'

Katie's mouth twitched, her left eye squeezing shut as if she was glinting at the sun. 'He has a reputation.'

'What sort of a reputation?'

'He's a year older than us. He's a nice enough guy but you know . . . he sleeps around a bit.'

'Was he driving?' Liam asked.

Katie blew her nose and wiped her face with the back of her hand. 'He had this beat-up car. I tried to stop them. I think he'd been drinking, though he swore he hadn't. Did they get into an accident? Is Tess okay?' Katie was frantic, her words tumbling out.

Maya waited for her to settle before telling her what had happened, Liam studying the girl closely for her response.

It was like being back in Mrs Penrose's living room. The same disbelief, the same collapse as Katie's grief overtook her until she was sobbing uncontrollably.

The school receptionist burst in, demanding to know what was going on as Katie continued crying. It was nearly twenty minutes before they got anything coherent out of her. Tess gave them a rough description of Anthony Ellison, which Liam forwarded to Jack.

By the time they returned to the car, Jack had called back with an address, and a phone number for the man, which went straight to voicemail.

Liam double-checked the address with the notes he'd taken earlier that day, confirming his suspicion that Ellison worked at Bosvellan Farm. The same place as Kyle Sturridge, the man who'd found Tess's body.

Chapter Four

Liam called Jack who confirmed that Sturridge had left Penzance police station thirty minutes earlier, having completed the usual forensic tests.

'Did he say where he was heading?' Liam asked.

'Back to work. As far as I know.'

'Okay, send me his number. We're heading to the farm now. After that, we need all the six-formers at Penzance College interviewed.'

Sturridge had made no mention of his colleague, Anthony Ellison, when Liam had first interviewed him but there'd been no reason why he should have. Various scenarios played through Liam's head as Maya drove them to the farm. Ellison taking Tess to the stone circle and losing control, submitting to some primeval desire he didn't realise he had. Sturridge working together with his colleague, the pair of them using Tess for their own gratification. Sturridge waiting in ambush on the two young lovers, scaring Ellison off before attacking Tess.

There wasn't enough evidence at present for any of these scenarios to feel like a realistic possibility in Liam's mind. And nothing explained the ritual of the killing – the positioning of the body and the use of clay and ochre.

Although it was possible that the murder could have been spontaneous, everything they knew about it so far suggested it was anything but. It was too orchestrated and elaborate, and if Tess had died by suffocation or choking, as seemed likely, the killer would have needed time and space to carry out such a monstrous act.

Liam tried Anthony Ellison's phone again as Maya sped through the narrow lanes. His thoughts drifting to Mrs Penrose and Katie, the pain they'd endured as they received their death message, he hoped for a simple and quick resolution to the investigation.

'That's him,' said Maya, noting the battered SUV in the distance that was turning left into the farm.

Maya wasted no time, pulling up just as Sturridge stepped out of his vehicle, squinting into the early afternoon sun.

Sturridge scratched his beard as they approached. 'Something I forgot?'

'There have been some developments,' Liam said.

Sturridge didn't appear to be a flight risk, but Liam kept his wits about him, ready in case the man made a run for it.

'What developments?' Sturridge asked, looking genuinely perplexed.

'Anthony Ellison,' Maya said.

'Tony? What about him?'

'He's one of your colleagues?'

Sturridge shrugged. 'I guess you could call him that. More of a dogsbody, really. What's this got to do with Tony?'

'Tess. The victim you identified this morning. She was seen leaving a party with Tony last night.'

Sturridge's eyes darted from Maya to Liam, as if he didn't believe what he was being told. 'That's a bit weird,' he said, scratching his forehead, still squinting into the sun.

'You don't sound that surprised,' Liam said.

'I'm not surprised he left a party with some young girl. If his stories are to be believed, he does the same thing every week. But obviously, this is a lot different.'

'Let's go and speak to him, shall we?'

'That's the thing. As far as we're aware, he hasn't shown up for work today.'

They all turned at the sound of footsteps crunching on loose stones.

'Boss,' said Sturridge, nodding towards the sight of a man in work overalls and wellington boots walking towards them.

'Kyle? What's going on here?' said the man, dropping his arms to his sides. His body was tense, as if ready to pounce.

'This is the police I was telling you about,' Sturridge said. 'Sorry, I forgot your names.'

'DI Trent and DS Kilshaw,' Maya said. 'And you are?'

'Malcolm Whitstable. This is my farm. I just got off the phone with one of your colleagues. Lawson, I think. You're trying to find young Tony?' His voice had softened, but his stance remained aggressive.

'I understand he hasn't turned up for work today?' Liam said.

Whitstable shook his head. 'Not even a phone call. I rang his dad this morning when he didn't show. Said he'd been out all night again.'

'Again?'

'Like I told you, he's a bit of a reveller, our Tony,' said Sturridge.

'Does he often miss work like this?' Maya asked.

'To give him his due, he's a good worker and never misses work,' Whitstable said. 'I can smell the booze on him sometimes, especially on a Monday morning. I think on more than one occasion he's stayed out all night before getting into work, but he always shows up and puts in a good shift.'

'You mentioned he's never short of female attention,' Liam said to Sturridge.

'He's a good-looking lad. No one steady in his life, as far as I'm aware.'

'Think it'll be a few years before that happens,' Whitstable added with a chuckle. 'He has his pick of the litter.'

Liam didn't understand what appeared to be the pride in the responses from the two men, which didn't reflect glowingly on the missing lad. It was as if they'd forgotten that a young woman had been murdered a few miles from where they were standing.

'The stories he tells you – the ones you mentioned before – what sort of thing are we talking about?'

Sturridge half-smiled and turned to his boss before glancing at Maya. 'We have ladies present. I wouldn't like to say.'

Maya held his gaze. 'No need to be coy, Mr Sturridge. This is a murder investigation.'

Sturridge shrugged. 'He slept around. What can I say? He's a nineteen-year-old lad. I didn't much care to hear it, but he wouldn't shut up if he'd got lucky. He'd give us a full account until we were tired of hearing it.'

'Did Tony ever mention any violence between him and the girls he was with?' Liam asked.

The smirk vanished from Sturridge's face. His eyes twitched, as if the implication that Tony might be involved in Tess's death had only just dawned on him. 'You don't think Tony did this to that poor girl?'

'You tell us,' Maya said. 'You mentioned that he's very promiscuous.'

'Yeah, but there's no crime in that, now, is there? Come on,' Sturridge said, suddenly defensive.

'No, there isn't,' Liam said. 'But that's not what we're asking. We're asking if he ever mentioned anything violent happening between him and the girls he slept with.'

Sturridge scratched his beard, as if weighing up the question, his puzzlement slowly turning to anger. 'Of course he bloody didn't.

The most he'd do is tell us what he did to them, what they looked like. Why would he want to hurt them?'

Liam took a step towards the pair, reminding them of his presence. Although Sturridge was tall, Liam still towered over him. Sometimes men like Sturridge only responded to a physical challenge and he'd had enough of people not taking this seriously. 'Can you think where he might be? Anywhere he's been before? There's a chance he could be in trouble himself.'

Sturridge took a step back. 'If he's not here he's either at home or one of his locals. But he'd never skip work without good reason.'

Liam jotted down the names of the local pubs before insisting on a search of the farm.

'You said you spoke to Tony's father?' Liam asked Whitstable, as they looked through one of the barns.

'That's right. I can give you his number if you like,' said the farmer.

After they'd concluded the search, Liam turned to the two men. 'You'll let us know as soon as Tony turns up?'

They both nodded in unison, some of their earlier bravado having vanished, as Maya and Liam returned to their car.

'Lovely blokes,' Maya said as she drove them back towards the crime scene.

Sturridge had looked genuinely surprised when they'd suggested Tony could be behind the killing. Liam didn't think it had been an act, although he hadn't enjoyed the almost reverent way Sturridge had spoken about his younger colleague and his womanising ways.

Both men had softened their responses as they'd searched the farm, as if the reality of the situation was slowly dawning on them. Again, he was reminded how the consequences of a crime extended beyond the victim.

The CSI tent was still up at the Merry Maidens site. Although the body had been removed, a scattering of CSIs remained.

Maya questioned Giselle as Liam walked the circle, moving from stone to stone. He checked the folklore regarding the place on his phone as he made his way around the nineteen monoliths, double-checking his sources.

Although they were clear on the legend that the stones were said to represent the nineteen merry maidens caught dancing on the Sabbath who had been turned to stone for their alleged crimes, he discovered some additional information he hadn't previously known.

Liam ran his hand across the cold rock of the monolith directly opposite the one where Tess's body had been found. According to what he'd read, while the stones were hundreds of years old, some were believed to have been replaced or added in the intervening centuries. Some folklorists believed there had only been twelve stones originally. One particular theory caught his eye. It claimed there had been thirteen merry maidens in total, one forever missing, having somehow escaped her fate.

'Post-mortem's scheduled for tomorrow morning,' Maya said as he returned to the tent.

'I'm going to have a look at the adjoining fields,' Liam said. 'There are two more stones, apparently.'

'The Piper Stones,' said Giselle.

The stone circle was watched over from the south-west and north-east by two further monoliths. They were called the Piper Stones after the pipers who had supposedly played the music the maidens had danced to and had also been turned to stone as the sun rose.

Liam clambered over a hedgerow, a piece of wire piercing the skin of his left forearm as he made his way into the adjoining field.

The first Piper Stone stood alone in the field, angled towards him like it was watching. The sun caught it differently to the stones in the circle. He quickened his pace, considering why that might be.

He sprinted across the soft ground, his earlier run along the beach and through the town of St Ives feeling like a lifetime ago, as he reached the other monolith.

Liam let out a breath as he caught sight of yellow glinting on the stone's surface. He stepped nearer, and saw that the rock was dusted with the same ochre powder they had found on Tess's body.

Chapter Five

Liam couldn't find any trail of ochre from the Piper Stone to anywhere else in the field. He returned to the crime scene and informed Maya of what he'd discovered. Together with Giselle, they did another sweep of the stone circle, Giselle using her forensic torch to examine each stone in turn for signs of ochre or any other identifiable substance, before heading to the other field and the second Piper Stone.

Although no further traces of the limonite substance were found, it was decided that a full search of the surrounding area was warranted. Anthony Ellison was still unaccounted for, as was his vehicle – the beat-up SUV last seen leaving the party in Mousehole. Liam still wasn't sure if Ellison was a suspect or a potential victim, but finding him before nightfall was now a priority.

As they waited for the PolSA team to arrive on site, Liam and Maya coordinated efforts to locate Anthony Ellison. Liam arranged to meet the young man's father, Rory, who was currently away at a business meeting in Plymouth and wouldn't be returning to his home in Truro until later that evening. Just as the search team arrived, Maya was notified of a second possible address for Anthony in Penzance.

Jack arrived and liaised with the PolSAs as Maya and Liam headed the short distance to Penzance. A search helicopter was deployed into the early afternoon sky as they drove away, the dog team already out in the neighbouring fields.

The address they had for Anthony Ellison was a flatshare on the north side of town. A pasty-looking teenager in a black hoodie decorated with a cartoon cannabis leaf answered the door. He kept his eyes downcast, not looking up as they showed their warrant cards.

'Your name, sir?' Liam asked.

'Danny. Daniel Reeve.'

'Is Anthony Ellison here, Danny?'

'Tony?' The boy looked genuinely perplexed. 'Haven't seen him for a few days. Why?'

He looked up properly when Liam explained about Tess Penrose. 'Tess is dead?' he said, his face draining of colour.

'You knew her?' Maya asked.

'I was at the party last night. I've been sleeping it off all day.'

'Haven't you checked your phone?' Liam said.

The teenager shook his head. 'No juice. Haven't bothered to charge it.'

Liam could see the boy was suffering some form of hangover, but it was a little unusual for someone his age not to be surgically attached to their phone. 'Mind if we come in?'

Danny led them to a dingy living room. The curtains were shut, a large television screen connected to a games console the only illumination in the room. The boy collapsed into a battered black gaming chair, gesturing to a decrepit sofa. 'I still can't get my head around this. Tess has been murdered?'

'How well did you know her?' Maya asked.

'Hardly at all. She was a year below when I was at college. Last night was the first time I'd really spoken to her. I'd been chatting to her when Tony swooped in.'

'Swooped in?' Liam said.

Danny gave a sheepish grin. 'You know what I mean. He was talking to one of her friends, then came over to us. Suddenly Tess wasn't interested in me any more.'

'How did that make you feel?' Maya asked.

Danny shrugged. 'I'm used to it by now. Doesn't mean anything.'

'So, no jealousy?'

Danny frowned. 'No, of course not. I wasn't chatting Tess up. For clarity, I'm gay.'

'You said Tony swooped in. Is that how he is with girls? Bit of a charmer?' Liam asked.

'He's charming, sure – but not in the negative way you're suggesting.'

'We were talking to his bosses at the farm earlier. They said Tony had a reputation for being a bit of a ladies' man.'

Danny leant back, a look of distaste crossing his face. 'That's a bit old-fashioned, isn't it? I wouldn't call Tony a ladies' man. He's popular, but everything's consensual. He's respectful. He never leads anyone on.'

Liam nodded. 'Understood. Thing is, Danny, Tony hasn't been seen since the party last night. We checked with his dad and as far as we know he hasn't been home. Can you show us to his room?'

'I don't know what you've been told, but Tony doesn't live here. He's sofa-surfing at the moment. Gap year. Saving up for university. He stays with his dad when he can, but it's easier being here when he's working at the farm.'

'Are there other places he stays around Penzance?' Maya asked.

Danny plugged his phone into a loose socket. 'I'll give you names when this has power.'

'Where do you think he could be now?' Maya asked.

Danny wiped a layer of sweat from his forehead. 'Honestly, I'm still trying to process all this. It's so horrible. I was sitting with

Tess less than twenty-four hours ago,' he said, looking at his phone as if doing so could will it to life. 'There were a couple of girls he's been with recently. He could be with one of them. But I'm not his keeper.'

His phone buzzed to life, tens of messages pinging as Danny scrolled, his face pale. 'Jesus. It's true.'

'Anything from Tony?' Liam asked.

Danny handed his phone over. 'No, but these are the girls I think he was seeing. Do you think he's all right? Do you have any idea who did this to Tess?'

It seemed Danny hadn't even considered that Tony could be a suspect. 'You mentioned Tony's going to university?' Liam said.

'Yeah. We both are. I'm off to UCL. Tony's heading to Christ College, Oxford.'

Liam had to admit he was surprised. The rough portrait drawn by the farmhands didn't match Danny's description of Tony, which was a good reminder not to make assumptions.

'What will he be studying?' Maya asked.

'English. He's a big reader. Into folklore, mythology, all that. Actually . . .' Danny paused. 'Come to think of it, maybe that's why they were at the stone circle.'

'Go on,' Liam said.

'He's always going on about the stones, and how you could feel energy through them. Maybe that's why he took her there.'

'Could he have hurt Tess?' Maya asked.

Danny recoiled. 'No way. Tony's one of the kindest people I know. He would never hurt anyone.'

Liam had heard the same thing from friends and families of guilty people so many times in the past that it barely registered. 'You let us know as soon as you hear from him. Day or night. Understand?' he said, handing him a card with his details on it.

Danny nodded, and remained sitting as they left the place.

'Not quite what I was expecting,' Maya said as they returned to the car.

Liam searched through his phone as Maya drove back to the stone circle. 'I think I found that course,' he said, holding up his phone. 'English Literature. Christ College, Oxford. There's a mention of medieval literature and folklore on the syllabus.'

'I guess it's a potential explanation for why they were at the stone circle,' Maya said, as they arrived back at the scene, the helicopter still doing sweeps above them.

Jack updated them. Starting a search so late in the day was never ideal, and Liam wasn't surprised when the DC told him there was no news to report. Jack gave them a quick update on the interviews that had taken place that day at the college. Once they had all the information they needed, Liam and Maya set off in their separate cars for Truro, where they were due to meet Tony's father.

The house was a couple of miles outside the centre of Truro, one of a number of large, detached properties in a secluded area. Rory Ellison was waiting for them, still wearing the day's business attire, a tailored suit with a navy-blue tie pulled tight against the top button of a crisp white shirt.

'Have you found my boy?' he asked, studying both their warrant cards before letting them into the house.

'Not as yet, Mr Ellison,' Maya said.

'I take it he hasn't made contact with you?' Liam asked.

'As I told your colleague, I've been in meetings all day. But no, no messages from him. That in itself is not unusual. Please,' he said, leading them through to an open-plan kitchen and dining area, a large, rectangular antique table taking centre stage.

Liam and Maya sat next to each other on a long wooden church pew as Mr Ellison sat opposite, not bothering with any pleasantries.

Liam explained everything they knew so far, from the party the previous night to Tess's body being found that morning. 'Has Tony ever got himself into trouble before?' Liam asked.

Mr Ellison frowned. 'You can't possibly think my son has anything to do with this girl's death, do you?'

'For now, we're just trying to locate Tony. He was the last person to be seen with Tess, leaving the party last night in his SUV. We're still unable to locate the vehicle.'

'This is ludicrous. Tony would never do something like that,' said Mr Ellison, echoing Danny's earlier words.

'No one is suggesting anything at the moment,' Maya said. 'We're just trying to find Tony. When was the last time you heard from him?'

'A couple of weeks ago.'

'You're not close?' Liam said, thinking of his own son, reminding himself it had been over four days since he'd last seen George after taking him to cricket practice.

'He's a nineteen-year-old lad and I'm a very busy man. He usually pops back here every week or so to eat me out of house and home and to wash his clothes.'

'You know about his job on the farm, I take it?' Maya asked.

Mr Ellison nodded.

'You live here alone?' Liam asked.

Mr Ellison's shoulders slumped. 'My wife passed away eight years ago. Pancreatic cancer. I've been single ever since, bar the odd short relationship. So yes, I live here alone when Anthony isn't here.'

'That must have been tough for him. For both of you,' Liam said.

Liam's father had passed away when Liam had been a similar age as Tony would have been, so he understood the impact. From first appearances, it seemed Tony had a caring father who may have helped him through his grief. This contrasted with Liam's experience where his mother had turned to drink and drugs to dull her pain instead of putting her efforts into raising him.

'It was difficult, but we had each other. We still do. He's a sensible boy. He's going to Oxford in the autumn. It was his decision to take a year out. He claimed it was to save some money, but I think he just wanted some time for himself. He's very studious. I guess he wanted a year of fun.'

'Uni can be fun,' Liam said.

Mr Ellison smiled. 'I met my wife at university. Yes, of course it can be fun. But Tony knows there'll be pressure on him there. I agreed with his decision. Best to get it all out of his system.'

'Can you think of anywhere he could be?' Maya asked.

'I take it you've spoken to his friends and work?'

Liam nodded.

'I don't know,' Ellison said. 'He brought a girl back here once. Madison, I think her name was. I asked if he was serious, but he just smiled.'

Unlike the farmers earlier, Ellison didn't seem to take any pride in this revelation.

'When was this?' Liam asked, checking the contacts he'd taken from Danny's phone, which included someone called Maddy.

'Just before Christmas. Haven't seen her since. He just changes the subject when I ask about her.'

'Don't suppose you have a surname?'

'No, sorry.'

They spent the next few minutes checking through the contact list of friends and work colleagues they had already compiled, before Mr Ellison showed them upstairs.

'We need to take a DNA sample for Anthony,' Maya said. 'Does he have a toothbrush here, or hairbrush, maybe?'

Mr Ellison led them to Anthony's bedroom with its en suite. Liam had to stop himself from commenting that the bedroom was about the same size as his own flat in St Ives. It was otherwise a typical teenager's bedroom, similar to the set-up at Danny's house, though much tidier, with a computer monitor and games console taking up one side of the room.

The walls surrounding Tony's bed were covered in posters featuring bands, semi-naked women, and photos of people on skateboards. It was a wonder that Tony would be willing to give such a space up to sleep on a sofa in a cramped bedsit.

From the en suite, Liam bagged a toothbrush and a pair of nail clippers for DNA analysis. Maya caught his eye as he returned to the room, and Liam stepped over to join her.

On one of the side walls was a large, framed map of Cornwall, marked with sites of mythological interest.

Dozens of ancient locations were listed, but four had been singled out with small black star stickers.

One of them was the Merry Maidens.

Chapter Six

Mr Ellison had initially objected to the removal of the map from Tony's bedroom, but eventually relented when Maya suggested they could return with a warrant.

The following morning in the incident room, Liam, Maya and Jack sat facing the map. It showed over a hundred sites of mythological interest across Cornwall, including numerous stone circles. Four sites had asterisk stickers placed on them, each belonging to stone circles. The Merry Maidens, where Tess's body had been found. Tregeseal East stone circle near St Just. Boskednan, also known as the Nine Maidens of Boskednan. And the Hurlers, a triple circle formation on Bodmin Moor.

'Kill sites or sex sites?' Liam said, as the locations were displayed on the whiteboard.

The search for Tony was still ongoing at the Merry Maidens, but much of the surrounding area had been exhausted for now. 'Let's not jump to any conclusions,' Maya said. 'Jack, find out what you can about those other sites. It would be good to have the lowdown before we go. Let's speak to Madison first and see what she knows.'

Rory Ellison had informed them that Madison was Tony's ex, and her name had also been given to them by Tony's friend, Danny. She lived on the outskirts of St Ives in Lelant village, meaning that only a couple of hours after arriving at work, Liam had to drive back along the A30 towards his home.

The address was a two-bedroom converted flat, once part of an old public house. Maddy's parents were both present when Liam and Maya arrived at 10.30 a.m. Mr Charmers was in shorts and a T-shirt, dressed as if he were heading to the beach. His wife wore joggers and a sweatshirt.

To Liam's eye, Maddy looked like a replica of Katie and the other girls he'd seen at the college – pretty and petite, with long straight hair. Again, he was struck by how young she seemed, the way she hovered near her mother's side as they made tea, before all three sat together in the main living room.

'Just so everyone is clear,' Maya said, 'we spoke to Madison by phone last night. We're here in connection with the suspected murder of Tess Penrose and the whereabouts of Anthony Ellison, who we believe was the last person to see Tess alive. Did you know Tess, Maddy?'

Liam noted a slight shift in the teenager's eyes. 'No. Obviously, I heard what happened to her, but I'd never met her before,' Maddy said.

'Maddy's at university at the moment in Exeter. She's just back on study leave,' said Mr Charmers, a sturdy-looking man who wasn't hiding his displeasure at having the police in his house.

'And before that? Where did you study your A-levels?' Liam asked.

'Truro College.'

Despite her youth, Maddy held herself with more composure than Tess's college friends.

'You do know Tony Ellison, though, don't you, Maddy?' Liam asked.

Maddy blushed, the colour highlighting the freckles on her face.

'He was my boyfriend for a time, before I went to university. It was an on-off thing,' she said, avoiding eye contact with her parents.

'Did you ever meet Tony?' Maya asked Mr and Mrs Charmers.

They nodded. 'Seemed pleasant enough the couple of times we saw him,' Mr Charmers said, playing with the digital watch on his wrist.

'Though Maddy kept it to herself for quite a time, didn't you, Maddy?' Mrs Charmers added.

Maddy rolled her eyes. 'I hope you don't think Tony had anything to do with this. He would never . . .' She shook her head. 'He's a good person. Very thoughtful. There's no way he would hurt anyone.'

Although it was a familiar refrain in murder investigations, Liam was a little surprised by the constant affirmation of Tony's good character. Despite it being clear that he'd had a string of lovers, and the hurt that could sometimes cause, no one had a bad word to say about him.

Liam showed her a photo of the map taken from Tony's bedroom with the asterisks removed. 'Does this mean anything to you, Maddy?'

She blushed again. Liam wondered how often that particular tell had got her into trouble.

'I think it's Tony's. He likes all that stuff. He's going to be studying English at Oxford,' she said with a hint of pride. 'He's hoping to specialise in folklore at some point.'

Liam swiped across to another version of the map with the four asterisks. 'Do these sites mean anything to you?'

Maddy's face flushed deeper.

'Perhaps we can speak to Maddy on her own,' Maya suggested.

'I don't think that's appropriate,' Mr Charmers said, but Maddy raised a hand.

'It's fine, Dad.'

Both parents stood up, Mr Charmers scraping his chair across the floor.

'We'll be in the bedroom,' Mrs Charmers said, tapping her daughter on the shoulder.

Still red-faced, Maddy waited until the door shut behind them. 'I know two of those places,' she said, eyes cast down.

'Can you point to which ones?' Maya asked.

Maddy leant forward and touched the asterisks next to Boskednan and the Hurlers stone circles.

'How do you know those sites specifically?' Maya asked.

Maddy lifted her head, the flush draining slightly from her face as she composed herself. 'We had sex there. Tony liked . . . liked to do it outside. Particularly in weird places like that.'

'Stone circles?' Maya asked.

'Amongst other places. He was obsessed with that sort of thing. Folklore, mythology, the land itself. I don't know if it turned him on exactly, but he was very romantic and passionate about it. I've never met anyone like him.'

'And the other places?' Liam asked.

'That's where you found the girl's body, right?' Maddy said, pointing to the Merry Maidens. 'As for Tregeseal . . . I never went there with Tony.'

'You think he may have gone there with another girl?' Maya asked.

'Probably,' Maddy said, her voice rising slightly. 'He's a lovely boy in so many ways, but he's good-looking. He gets a lot of attention. He probably cheated, so I guess so. I always suspected it before I left for uni. Wouldn't surprise me if he slept with someone else there. To be honest, I'm surprised there are only four asterisks on that map.'

◆ ◆ ◆

'She said she was surprised there were only four asterisks,' Maya said to Liam, as they returned to the car.

'Yet she didn't seem that bothered. Certainly not overtly jealous.'

'She sounds like she came to terms with it pretty quickly. And she's at uni. Probably over him by now.'

They visited each site in turn, starting by returning to the Merry Maidens, where the search for Tony Ellison was winding down.

Nothing out of the ordinary awaited them at the other three locations. No ochre-dusted monuments or dead bodies, just desolate stone circles with a scattering of dog walkers and hikers.

By the time they reached the Hurlers, where a family was enjoying a picnic and a golden retriever made laps around the three stone circles, they were informed the search for Anthony Ellison at the Merry Maidens had officially ended.

'Strike you as odd that Tony already had an asterisk for the Merry Maidens?' Liam asked as they left the triple circles and headed back to the Bodmin station.

'It was somewhere he knew,' Maya said. 'Maybe it was just the nearest place to the party. By the sound of it, Maddy wasn't the only person he had sex with in such a place.'

They had already confirmed with Maddy that she hadn't had sex with Tony at the Merry Maidens, but it was now more apparent than ever that Tony had more than one love interest on the go.

Back at headquarters, Liam reviewed the interviews conducted with those who'd been at the party the night Tess was last seen. Two girls, both in the same year group as Tess, had come forward to say they had been involved with Tony in the past.

Liam instructed Jack to follow up with them, though neither had mentioned anything about meeting Tony at the stone circles.

The search reports came through piecemeal from the Merry Maidens site. It was confirmed that traces of ochre had only been found on the stone where Tess's body had been propped, and on the Piper Stone in the neighbouring field. A three-mile radius had been searched on foot. Helicopters had extended that reach even further but there was still no sign of Anthony Ellison or his SUV.

The longer time went by without Tony being found, the more the pendulum swayed from him being a likely victim to a potential suspect. Tony was the last person to be seen with Tess. He had a thing for outdoor sex, specifically at stone circles, and hadn't been seen since Tess was killed.

Liam tried to think of reasons why Tony couldn't be the killer, but came short. The only thing he could think of was the nature of Tess's death. The killer had taken great care to arrange the body in such a specific way. It suggested a high level of premeditation and Tony must have known he would be prime suspect.

If he was going to kill Tess in such a public way, why hadn't he tried to hide his involvement? He was going to Oxford in autumn, had his whole life ahead of him. Why would he risk blowing it all by leaving a party with Tess and killing her the same night in such an obvious way?

A text came through from his ex, Kim, checking if he could pick up George for cricket practice on Thursday. The text brought him back to his meeting with Rory Ellison, and he found himself wondering again how his own relationship with George would shift as his son moved further into adolescence.

They were still at the stage where George looked up to him, but Liam could already see signs of the boy pulling away. It was to be expected, and Liam was glad he was developing a sense of independence. But with Mark on the scene as a stepdad, Liam sometimes felt his role was obsolete and feared that might get worse as the years went by.

He took one last look through his notes and was about to shut down his computer when something on the drone footage of the Merry Maidens site caught his eye.

He found an older image of the site taken almost thirty years ago. He uploaded the photo on to the white screen and compared it to the aerial footage shot today.

The area surrounding the stone circle was vivid in Liam's mind now, as if he'd known it for years.

He zoomed in on both images to the eighth stone, counting clockwise from where Tess had been discovered. The stone itself was little different to the others; two-and-a-half feet high with a jagged top, it was tilted at an angle towards one of the Piper Stones. But something was amiss.

Liam recalled the legend he'd been taught as a child, that it was impossible to count the Merry Maidens circle without losing your place.

That was demonstrably incorrect, but if he was right about what he saw in the images, it seemed that in the last thirty years, the eighth stone had moved.

Chapter Seven

Liam's phone rang again as he double-checked the images, the call coming from Grace Hartley. Grace's move from the Met to Serious Crimes in Exeter had given him the opportunity to see more of his ex. Prior to that, they had last worked together during the Godrevy Island investigation the previous summer.

'To what do I owe this pleasure?' he said.

'I was just on my way into the city, and thought I'd alleviate my boredom by calling,' she said.

'City?' Liam said, smiling. 'You're talking about Exeter?'

'It might not be London, but it's still a city,' Grace said, pretending to sound offended.

'How are you finding the change?'

'Taking some getting used to. I could do with a juicy murder though. Like the one you're working on.'

Liam reached the end of the beach and stepped on to Porthmeor Hill. 'Here I was thinking you were calling about me.'

'Don't worry, DS Kilshaw, I wouldn't step on your toes. Not that your bosses would allow it, anyway.' Grace paused. 'Maya never really liked me, did she?'

Liam thought it an odd comment for Grace to make. It wasn't like her to be self-conscious. 'She's never said anything like that,' he said, trying to make her feel better, even though Maya had expressed reservations about her before.

'She doesn't need to. Her eyes tell me everything. Not that it matters. I'm not calling about her.'

'So what's the real reason?'

'I was wondering if you wanted to meet up over the weekend. I've got a few days off. It would be nice to see more of the county.'

Liam didn't answer straight away. He was a little surprised to find his thoughts turning to Millie, even when talking to Grace. They'd only dated for a few months, but he'd felt an intense connection with George's former schoolteacher, and he supposed part of him still held out hope they could get back together.

'That would be great,' he said, fearing he'd paused too long. 'I'll have to see how the investigation's going, but we could perhaps meet up on Saturday.'

'That's a date,' said Grace, hanging up before he had the chance to reply.

After printing up the screenshots of the eighth stone, he met Maya at Treliske hospital. She was waiting by the entrance and handed him a coffee. 'Drink this, if you dare.'

It was an inside joke. The hospital coffee from an independent stall, was usually the best they tasted all day. This time was no different. 'I can feel my blood waking up,' Liam said, as he took a sip.

They carried their drinks into the autopsy viewing room, settling behind the Perspex barrier. Dr Wetzel only allowed medical staff into the inner theatre, which suited Liam fine.

The hum of antiseptic ventilation broke the silence as Wetzel and his assistant arrived. Liam had attended too many post-mortems over the years. He feared the day it became normal, but that day felt distant as he watched Wetzel in action, standing over Tess Penrose's body, the sterile glare of the mortuary lighting revealing every detail.

Wetzel's assistant scribbled notes, adjusting her glasses, as Wetzel began his initial observations. 'Victim is posed deliberately,' he said, his voice clear and clinical through the intercom. He leant closer over the body, inspecting the ochre and clay smeared across Tess's hands, face and feet. 'Clay was removed from the face at the crime scene?'

'That's correct,' Maya said through the static of the intercom.

Wetzel gently tilted Tess's head, revealing hardened clay obstructing her nostrils and mouth. 'Airways almost completely blocked,' he said, taking careful swabs around the mouth and nostrils. 'Faint petechiae in the eyes. Signs indicate asphyxiation from clay and ochre particles, likely forced into the throat. No evidence of manual strangulation.'

He scraped residue from beneath Tess's fingernails. 'Absence of defensive wounds is notable. Victim was likely immobilised.'

'Drugged?' Maya asked, her eyes narrowing slightly.

'Lack of defensive injuries suggests paralysis, likely chemical, pending toxicology,' Wetzel said. 'It's clear she couldn't move voluntarily.'

Liam gripped his coffee, struggling to process Wetzel's words. As he continued, it appeared Tess had been forced to inhale the clay mixture, possibly through a device, while unable to move. He pictured her terror, the panic of suffocation without the ability to fight. He thought about Tony Ellison, and what would make him do such a thing.

Wetzel continued, everything documented visually and verbally, his assistant snapping photographs as he worked, noting where the clay had dried into a crust, cracking to reveal pale skin beneath, and where the ochre had seeped into Tess's hair and skin.

'Here,' Wetzel murmured, gesturing to his assistant. 'Puncture mark, likely where she was injected.'

'How long would she have been conscious?' Liam asked, his voice tight.

Wetzel paused. 'Minutes, potentially longer. Paralysis means complete muscular incapacitation, but it's possible she'd have been aware throughout.'

After the Y-incision, Wetzel began the internal examination, focusing on the airway and lungs. He extracted tissue, examining it under the light. 'Lungs show clear signs of clay and ochre particles deeply embedded, confirming asphyxiation through inhalation and obstruction.'

He moved to the digestive system, inspecting stomach contents. 'Recent ingestion of food, digestion minimal. Time of ingestion consistent with a short window prior to death, perhaps two or three hours.'

Liam tried to stay professional, but the thought of Tess's slow suffering haunted him. Wetzel continued, probing muscle tissue. 'Muscles unmarked, no bruising or tearing consistent with struggle. Paralysis definite, no natural muscle contraction evident. The agent was chemical, likely intravenous or intramuscular.'

'You're certain about paralysis?' Maya pressed.

'Pending toxicology, yes,' Wetzel confirmed. 'Victim would have been fully aware but physically helpless. She inhaled the clay mixture involuntarily over several minutes, unable to cough or move.'

The post-mortem stayed with both Liam and Maya as they drove to the Merry Maidens stone circle. Liam couldn't help himself picturing Tess's ordeal over and over.

He thought of his own trauma from his time in the SBS where he'd come close to drowning, but it felt like nothing in comparison. He'd had a chance; Tess hadn't. She would have most likely been helpless in seconds, unable to move as the killer had begun their sick process. What had gone through her mind as she'd felt the clay mixture slip into her lungs was all but impossible to conceive.

Liam coughed, his chest tightening at the thought. Although he hadn't endured it himself, Liam knew former colleagues from his time in the SBS who had endured waterboarding during conflict. He'd seen hardened men who'd witnessed countless atrocities break down at the memory of their torture.

What Tess had endured must have been similar, but Liam imagined it would have been so much worse. She would have suffered all the panic and pain without having been able to move or fight back. Her sanity must have been stretched to its limits, and most likely beyond.

The sight of the Merry Maidens appeared in the windscreen and Liam knew he would never be able to pass the site again without thinking of Tess and her ordeal.

They left their car in silence. The absence of the search teams and CSI tent did little to dampen the tragic atmosphere of the place.

Liam showed Maya the drone footage and the comparison shot taken thirty years ago as they walked towards the circle. 'This is the stone,' he said, counting clockwise to the eighth stone from the one where Tess's body had been discovered.

'It's subtle,' Maya said, 'but there's definitely a difference in the positioning. How the hell did you spot that?'

'I'd like to take credit, but it was the luck of seeing both photographs at the same time.'

They walked around each stone in turn as Liam had done previously. There was something hypnotic about following the path, a type of rhythm to the circle that was all encompassing. Once more, Liam thought of the playful legend that the stones could never be accurately counted. He could imagine getting lost in the repetition of the journey around the circle and imagined it was easy to forget where you were.

They checked each stone against the old photos. Neither had an expert eye, but they both agreed that only the eighth stone appeared out of place.

They'd arranged to meet a local archaeologist, Raymond Preston, at the site. He'd just texted Maya to say he was running twenty minutes late. That gave them time to check in with Jack for a quick briefing. Nearly everyone at the house party had now been questioned, but there were still a couple of women thought to have had brief relationships with Anthony Ellison they'd yet to speak with.

In the end, it was another half-hour before Raymond Preston arrived. A tall, lanky figure dressed in tweed, he strode purposefully across the field, his hand raised in greeting, a leather satchel draped over his shoulder.

'DI Maya Trent,' Maya said, as Preston stood before them with his hand held out.

'Raymond Preston,' the archaeologist said, shaking her hand before turning to Liam.

'DS Liam Kilshaw,' Liam said, noting the man's weak grip as they shook hands. 'You know this site well?' Liam asked as they began pacing the circle again.

'The Merry Maidens? It's like a second home. I wrote a book that contains more than one chapter on the place.'

Preston hadn't stopped smiling since he arrived on the scene. Maya hadn't explicitly told him why they were there, although he'd been told about Tess's murder. As they moved from stone to stone, Preston ran his hands across the surfaces, taking a fresh delight in each one, as though he were on a pilgrimage.

'Terrible news about that poor girl,' he said as they reached the headstone, which still had police tape cordoned around it. He sounded sincere but it didn't take long for his attention to wander.

'I understand ochre was found on her body. May I?' He looked towards the tape.

Liam pulled it away, the area having now been fully cleared by the CSIs for access. 'There was yellow ochre on her body,' he said. 'And on the stone. Limonite. You can see it here.'

Preston retrieved a small torch and shone it on the stone. 'Limonite is thought to be very symbolic,' he said. 'As with all these things, it's up for debate. But my research suggests it's been used over the centuries in representations of spring, summer, sun worship, new life . . . And perhaps more relevant in this situation, sacrifice.'

A gust of wind moved through the field. Liam felt the chill ripple across his skin. 'Sacrifice?' he repeated, thinking of his last major investigation, where multiple bodies had been discovered across the coastlines, each wrapped in hessian. Some of the talk back then had been about potential sacrifices to the mythical sea serpent Bucca Dhu, though the reality had been even more disturbing.

'Sacrifice runs throughout mythology and folklore,' Preston said, walking slowly around the headstone, as if completing a ritual. 'Legends vary, and naturally the sources are unreliable. But there are tales of human sacrifice, usually involving women, where the victims were dusted in ochre, limonite to be specific, to catch the sun's rays.'

'Anything ever happen at this particular site?' Maya asked.

'I imagine many things occurred. As I'm sure you're aware, legend says it was the sun that turned the maidens, and the two pipers, to stone. So I suppose there's a connection there.'

They continued around the circle until they reached the eighth stone. Neither officer said anything as Preston swept his torch over the monolith before moving on. It wasn't until they had completed the full circuit that Liam explained what he'd seen in the photographs.

Still smiling, Preston studied the comparison photos. 'Well, I never,' he said. 'You've a better eye than me, DS Kilshaw.'

He trotted back to the eighth stone, dropping to his knees with visible excitement.

'Could it be natural?' Maya asked. 'Land movement? That sort of thing?'

'If it had shifted the way you'd expect over time, maybe. But look at the gradient in the earth. If the soil had moved, the stone would have tilted counter-clockwise as I'm facing it. But from the old photo and what I can see now, it's shifted the other way. I'd say it's a good quarter of a metre off. This really is an amazing spot,' he said, still beaming at Liam.

'It's thought that not all the stones are original anyway, right?' Liam asked.

'Correct. Almost definitely true. The legend says there were twelve maidens who died, and a thirteenth who survived to tell the tale. That I can neither confirm nor deny. But in my book you'll see that at least four of these stones were added in the past two hundred years. This one, however . . .' He tapped the eighth stone. 'This is one of the originals. At least, as far as we can tell.'

'What do you think happened?' Liam asked, Preston's second mention of his book not going missed.

Preston's smile and enthusiasm were infectious. 'I'm not sure but I'd love to find out. The only explanation I can think of is that someone excavated the ground surrounding this stone and this affected the positioning. Careless work and, I'd dare say, illegal. I've known this place for over forty years and at no point has permission ever been granted to move the stones.'

Maya called DCI Hargreaves and explained the situation. Liam listened on speakerphone as the archaeologist, Preston, walked the perimeter of the stones once more, the smile never leaving his face.

Liam still found DCI Hargreaves difficult to read. At times, he'd considered him something of a pushover for someone so high up in the force. But that impression had shifted, particularly during the Godrevy investigation, where he'd shown real fortitude in managing the inter-departmental relationship with the Met.

'What exactly is it you're asking?' Hargreaves said.

'I think we have to excavate the site,' Maya replied.

Liam pictured the DCI with his eyes closed, sighing at the request. 'Can you imagine the turmoil that would cause?'

'We have a dead body, sir. Placed in the stone circle. And a stone that's clearly been disturbed. I don't think we have any other option.'

Hargreaves went quiet for thirty seconds before replying with another sigh. 'I suppose you're right. But let's limit it to this one particular stone, shall we? I can already imagine the backlash we're going to receive.'

'Thank you, sir,' Maya said, ending the call.

They spent the next hour at the site making calls. It was decided Liam would remain and wait for the specialist teams while Maya returned to headquarters.

Preston asked to stay, and Liam opted to wait at a nearby café, where he bought the archaeologist lunch.

Usually, he would have found the man's enthusiasm wearing, but there was something about his smile and innocent charm that Liam couldn't help but warm to.

They discussed the Merry Maidens legend in more detail before Liam brought up the other sites marked on Anthony Ellison's map of Cornwall.

Preston's face lit up again as their sandwiches arrived, before dimming slightly.

'Sorry, in all this excitement I forget that a girl died. Was murdered. Have you been to these three sites?'

‘We visited them yesterday. Searched for signs of ochre. I’ve got the photographs here.’ He showed Preston the comparison images. ‘As far as we can tell, there’s been no movement in any of those stones. It would be good to get an expert eye on it,’ Liam added, taking a bite of his sandwich.

‘I’d be very happy to take a look. All three sites feature in my book.’

‘I need to get a copy of this book. Is it available online?’

Preston lowered his sandwich and rummaged through his bag, still smiling. ‘I didn’t want to be presumptuous, but I brought along a copy just in case.’

Liam flicked through the small booklet as they ate. Preston discussed the stories and legends tied to the other three sites with a level of enthusiasm Liam had rarely encountered.

‘Is there any significance linking the four places, beyond them being ancient stone circles?’ Liam asked, not wishing to mention the asterisks on Tony’s map just yet.

‘Much of what we know, or think we know, about these places is still shrouded in mystery. Take Stonehenge, for example. All the legends and stories, and yet we still don’t really know why the stones were placed or how. We have theories, of course. But to answer your question, there’s nothing specific linking those four circles that I know of, aside from the fact that they date back to roughly the same time in history. If you don’t mind me asking, what’s the significance of those four sites?’

Preston was no longer smiling, though even his neutral expression held a trace of humour to it, the corners of his lips slightly upturned, his eyes wide and warm.

‘We’re investigating a possible link at the moment,’ Liam said. ‘Was your book popular when it came out?’

‘Oh, straight into the *Sunday Times* bestseller list,’ Preston said with a laugh. ‘No, I’m afraid this sort of thing only appeals to a select few. I did a print run of a thousand copies, but my optimism got the better of me. I still have more than a couple of boxes at home.'

Liam began listing names tied to the case, starting with Tess and Anthony Ellison, studying Preston's expression each time a name was mentioned.

'I'm afraid I don't know any of them, though I've run a few classes in the past at various schools and I held a couple of free courses at the town hall in Penzance.'

'What sort of crowd did you get?'

'Retirees mainly, when I wasn't at the schools.' He snapped his fingers, something occurring to him. 'The girl you found, the victim. Tess, was it? What school did you say she went to?'

'I'm not sure about her secondary school, but she was studying A-levels at Penzance College.'

'I see. I haven't been there.'

'But you've taught at schools in Cornwall?'

'All over, yes. Assemblies, class chat, that sort of thing.'

'You're still doing this?' Liam asked.

'Yes, it's ongoing. One or two a year. Last year I did a sixth-form college in Redruth and another in Truro.'

Liam checked his notes, confirming that Anthony Ellison had attended Truro College. He checked the dates with Preston, who said he'd given the talk when Ellison would have been in Year Thirteen.

'Do you remember him?' Liam asked, showing him a picture of the missing man.

'I'm afraid not. I'm not great with faces at the best of times. But that particular encounter was a long time ago.'

After lunch, Liam called Jack, instructing him to check with Truro College about Preston's course, to find out if they kept any sort of attendance record, before driving back to the Merry Maidens site, where the specialist excavation teams had arrived, Maya having secured emergency permission from Historic England to move the stone. After chatting to the team, he stood with Preston on the edge of the field as the diggers began their work.

He was immediately transported back to December, the last time he'd seen the team in action, when they'd been digging graves at a private property in Sennen, where several bodies, some still unidentified, had been unearthed.

Preston watched on, rapt, every now and then going completely still as the team began to remove the eighth stone.

'I do hope they're careful,' he said as the digger lifted the stone into the air.

Liam was surprised to see the foundations extended nearly as deep as the height of the stone itself. The team began brushing back the soil, working steadily until one of them stopped and signalled Liam over.

'Please wait here, Mr Preston,' Liam said, walking towards the excavation perimeter.

'We've found something,' one of the team said.

Liam stepped to the edge of the hole. Six feet down, one of the specialists crouched beside an object wrapped in cloth.

Liam was reminded again of the body he'd discovered sealed in a hessian bag by the shoreline in Sennen. He pushed the image aside and nodded for his colleague to proceed.

He'd suspected they might find a body beneath the stone.

But as the cloth was pulled back, Liam saw not one skeleton, but two.

Chapter Eight

DCI Hargreaves arrived two hours after the discovery of the remains. The CSIs were already on site, carefully working through the area.

It was late afternoon. The sky was grey, unbroken cloud blocking the sun. Liam pulled his collar up against the damp chill as Hargreaves stepped out of his car, his figure dark against the muted green as he made his way across the wet grass.

Maya had already called ahead to warn Liam about Hargreaves' arrival. She was heading things up from headquarters for now, but Hargreaves had insisted on visiting the site.

Preston was still by the cordon, arms folded, eyes fixed on the excavation site. He hadn't moved much since the dig began, his usual smile finally erased by the gravity of the discovery.

Liam met Hargreaves halfway. The field felt different now – the absence of the eighth stone left a visible gap in the circle. The missing monolith lay on its side further off, temporarily discarded as CSIs continued their meticulous work around the hole.

'Two sets of remains?' Hargreaves asked, his voice low as they approached the excavation.

Liam nodded. 'Wrapped together. The cloth's still intact in places.' The air near the hole was thick with the pungent, peaty smell of disturbed earth which caught in Liam's throat.

Hargreaves looked away, folding his arms, his gaze tracing the curve of the remaining stones. 'A hell of a place to hide bodies.'

'It was a lucky find, sir,' Liam said. 'But I think we may have to look under the others.'

'The other stones?' Hargreaves couldn't hide his incredulousness.

'For all we know, there could be remains hidden under each one.'

Hargreaves shook his head. 'You had clear evidence this stone had been tampered with. There's nothing to suggest the others have.'

'Nothing physical, no. But something is obviously going on here, sir. First Tess Penrose and now this.'

Hargreaves turned, squinting as sunlight leaked through the clouds. 'Do you have any idea what that would mean, Liam? Start pulling these stones out of the ground and you'll have every historian, conservationist and weekend druid filing complaints. And that's before the press gets wind.'

'I'm not suggesting we rip up the whole of Cornwall, sir, but we can't leave those stones unchecked.'

'Not to mention the cost,' Hargreaves said, as if he hadn't heard Liam. 'Let's try a softer approach first. Ground-penetrating radar, soil disturbance scans . . . I don't know, there must be some sort of tech they can bring without turning this whole place into an archaeological dig.'

'I'll get on to it, sir,' Liam said, as Hargreaves walked over to the specialist teams, clearly keen not to think about the current situation any more.

It was late afternoon before the skeletal remains were lifted from the earth and transferred for examination. Hargreaves remained at the site, standing apart, his phone permanently to his ear.

Liam liaised with the team back at headquarters, and was thankful when Jack arranged for a specialist to attend the site the following day. It was something positive to tell Hargreaves and meant for now they wouldn't have to dig up any of the other stones.

Preston also continued to linger by the perimeter tape, watching everything that was happening, even taking notes in a journal. Liam still wasn't sure what to think about the man. His eccentricity was infectious but there were hints he was a little obsessed with the circles.

Liam walked over. 'Another book?' he said, nodding towards the notebook.

Preston's smile faltered before returning. 'Who knows? Need to sell all the others first.'

'Thanks for your help today, Raymond. I'll take a look at your book tonight.'

Preston nodded. His fingers tightened on the strap of his satchel as his eyes drifted towards the broken circle. 'When will they return the stone?'

'I'll have to check. Once the area has been fully analysed, I expect.'

'Analysed?' The archaeologist looked genuinely alarmed. 'You're not going to touch the other stones, are you?'

Liam frowned, wondering if Preston's concerns extended beyond the sanctity of the stones to what might lie beneath them. He decided it made sense to keep the archaeologist close to hand. 'Hopefully we can ascertain what's underneath without further excavation, but that's at least three bodies connected to this site now. If you're free, I'd be happy to have you on board as a consultant.'

Preston couldn't hide his delight. 'I'll help as much as I can.'

The remains were secured in the back of the waiting forensics van. As it pulled away, Liam headed for his own car. He was supposed to be volunteering with the lifeboat crew this evening but had another stop first in Hayle; they'd finally managed to track down Tess's father, Jerry.

◆ ◆ ◆

The Hayle estuary tide was high as he drove along the main road, moored boats bobbing on the grey water. He turned off, navigating the winding back roads into the Copperhouse area, pulling up outside one of the terraced houses on a small estate.

It had been a relief when Jerry Penrose made contact with headquarters earlier that day. From what Liam understood, Mrs Penrose had spoken to her estranged husband and explained what had happened with Tess. The conversation with the station had been short and to the point. Mr Penrose had confirmed he'd be home that afternoon, but Liam knocked on the door of his house for over ten minutes with no response.

'You looking for Jerry?'

Liam turned to see one of Penrose's neighbours stepping out of his front door. 'That's right,' he said.

'Saw him leave about an hour ago. Face like thunder.'

'And you are, sir?' Liam asked, flashing his warrant card.

'Lester Williams. Long-suffering neighbour.'

'Any idea where he's gone?'

'I've got a great idea. The pub.'

Liam thanked the man and drove the short distance to the Copperhouse pub. The pub was one of two bars that were close together on the main road opposite the river. It had a certain old-world charm, especially in contrast to the faceless chains that seemed to be sprouting up everywhere.

'I'm looking for Jerry Penrose,' he said to the sole barman, a young guy with tattooed arms and distended earlobes threaded with looped discs.

The barman scanned the room. 'Garden,' he said, with a nod.

Liam's irritation faded the moment he stepped outside and spotted Jerry Penrose at a table in the far corner of the beer garden. He was hunched over, smoking a roll-up, a half-full pint of cider resting in front of him.

'Mr Penrose? DS Kilshaw. I was due to meet you at your house.'

'I was thirsty,' Penrose said, taking a drag of his cigarette.

Liam had been thinking of Mrs Penrose's description of her ex-husband as an abuser. There were no official criminal charges against him, but Liam had uncovered several reports from social services. That and the scar she had showed them was enough for Liam to understand what he was dealing with. 'Mind if I sit?'

'Free country.'

Penrose's face was lined, his skin leathery and deeply tanned, as if he spent all his time outside.

'You've been informed about your daughter, Mr Penrose?'

Penrose took a gulp of his cider but didn't respond.

'I need to know your whereabouts over the weekend.'

'Fishing.'

'You'll need to elaborate.'

Penrose stared at Liam. 'I was out trying to catch fish,' he said, elongating each word.

Liam let the petulance go. He imagined Penrose's evasiveness was typical of him, but he was probably grieving in his own particular fashion. 'Where were you fishing?'

'Out to sea. Deep sea. Left Friday, back Sunday night.'

'Anyone who can verify that?'

'Boat's captain. Davy Mason.'

'You have a number?'

Penrose checked his phone and held it out.

Liam noted the number. 'What time were you back Sunday?'

'Around four.'

'And after that?'

'Got drunk.'

'Here?'

'To begin with.'

Liam took down a list of pubs Penrose claimed to have visited. He told Liam he returned home around eleven and had been sleeping it off since. Liam would verify the details later, but he wasn't ready to let the man off the hook just yet.

'When was the last time you saw Tess?'

Penrose finished his drink. 'You buying the next one?'

'Not right now. Your daughter's been murdered, Mr Penrose. I'm trying to find out who killed her.'

'You think I did it?'

'Did you?'

'Of course I bloody didn't. I might be a lot of things, but I'm no murderer.'

Liam thought of the scar beneath Mrs Penrose's eye but stopped short of asking where he drew the line. 'So, when did you last see Tess?'

'I don't know. Couple of years ago.'

'You didn't speak at all in that time?'

'Her mum poisoned her against me. What can I say?' He traced the rim of the empty glass with a fingertip.

'That must've been difficult.'

'It is what it is.'

Liam snatched the beer glass from the man. Self-pity was one thing, but Penrose was being obtuse. His daughter was dead, and they had two more sets of remains to identify. Liam had no idea what would happen next and he didn't want to waste his time on a bitter drunk. 'Can you think of anyone who might want to hurt Tess?'

Penrose frowned, as if the question hadn't crossed his mind. 'Is it true what they're saying? That she was covered in clay? At the stones?'

It was the first real concern Liam had seen from the man.

'I'm afraid that's true.'

Penrose shook his head. 'Why would someone do that? Why would they do that to anyone? Why would they do it to Tess?'

Liam softened his tone. 'Can you think of anyone who might hold a grudge against Tess, or your family?'

'There's plenty don't like me. But hate me enough for that? I don't think so.'

Liam stood and handed him his card. 'If anything comes to mind, get in touch.'

He returned through the bar and ordered a pint of cider for the man before leaving.

◆ ◆ ◆

The tide was retreating by the time Liam reached St Ives harbour twenty minutes later, the familiar curve of the bay shrouded in mist and low cloud. The water lay flat and grey, creeping on to the shore, the air heavy with salt and seaweed as gulls drifted overhead.

Liam had called Davy Wilson on the way over. He'd confirmed that Jerry Penrose had been with him on a fishing expedition over the weekend. It didn't rule Penrose out, and he'd need to confirm the rest of his alibis, which included an extended drinking session on Sunday evening. But due to the elaborateness of the murder, it seemed doubtful that Mr Penrose would have had the time to arrange everything, at least without outside help.

The lifeboat's coxswain, Phil Skewes, was outside the crew room, mug in hand, shoulders hunched against the damp. He didn't speak at first, just raised the mug in a curt greeting. 'Nice of you to make it,' he said eventually.

'What can I say, Phil? Had an overwhelming urge to see your cheerful face.'

Phil gave a short grunt. The coxswain, a transfer from Looe last summer during a period of upheaval, was a steady presence in the team, though the same could have been said for his predecessor, before things had unravelled.

Liam poured himself tea from the urn, catching sight of Godrevy lighthouse, a faint shape out on the horizon, just as Maya called.

'Forensic anthropologist booked for tomorrow,' she said.

'How are you, Liam? Did you enjoy your day in the field with the two skeletons, Liam?' Liam said.

'You poor lamb. How are you?' Maya said.

Liam updated her on his meeting with Jerry Penrose.

'You think we need to get him in?'

'Not for now. I need to check a few things tomorrow. He's an arsehole but I don't think he's involved.'

He said goodbye and pocketed the phone, looking out across the bay. The wind had picked up slightly, swirling the mist clinging to the headland.

'Shout from Hayle,' Phil said from the doorway behind him. 'Kayak adrift near Godrevy. Empty. Coastguard wants eyes on it. You good?'

Liam nodded, already heading for the changing room. Five minutes later, the *Annie Wilkinson* hit the water, the launch cradle rattling above them as they cleared the ramp.

Phil took the helm as Liam stood behind him, bracing against the bite of the wind. The engine throbbed underfoot, the vibration travelling up through the deck plates. As they rounded the headland, a squall swept in from the north, spitting cold spray. Salt stung Liam's face as he gripped the rail, fixing his eyes on the choppy grey water ahead.

Despite the work he'd put into recovery, being out in the open water always played on his fears and PTSD from the botched SBS operation. If he closed his eyes, he was back in the icy water, re-experiencing the terror of the pressure on his chest as he tried to breach the surface. That memory bled into the more recent trauma of the Godrevy investigation, another time the sea had nearly killed him, and thoughts of what Tess Penrose had endured in her final moments.

Although land was still visible, a familiar tightness gripped his chest. He focused on his breathing, slow and steady, battling the rising panic as Phil cut the engines as they approached the abandoned kayak lodged in the rocks just off Gwithian Beach.

It was pale blue, half-submerged, no paddle in sight. The hope was that it had slipped off a car roof rack or swept out on the tide rather than the alternative that the person paddling it had fallen out at sea. The crew quickly secured the object, Phil logging the time and position with the coastguard.

They began a slow arc westward, running a search grid from the edge of the bay back towards Hayle. The mist thickened again, Liam battling his thoughts of claustrophobia as the visibility grew worse.

The search lasted fifty minutes before a call came through confirming a kayaker in Portreath had reported losing the craft earlier that afternoon.

Phil swore under his breath at the wasted time and turned the *Annie Wilkinson* back towards St Ives.

At the lifeboat house, Liam stripped off his sodden oilskins in the changing room, the sweat chilling on his back in the damp air. He noticed a missed call from Jack as he reached for his jacket. It was half-past nine, but he called back immediately, Jack answering on the first ring. The young officer was hard-working to a fault. 'Tell me you're not still at the office, Jack?'

'Just got home, guv. I called earlier to say that I talked to those schools and colleges. According to Truro College, Raymond Preston gave a talk there early last year. They kept a register of those who attended. And Anthony Ellison was definitely on the list.'

Chapter Nine

He had to hand it to them. Someone had a good eye.

He hadn't dared return to the Merry Maidens site, but the discovery of the bones was now widespread.

He hoped it would prove a distraction, would focus all their attention on the stone circle so he could look elsewhere, but he feared where it would lead them.

It had taken him a long time to appreciate and understand the book. It was part of something much larger, an explanation in part for everything that went before.

There was so much information, so many misguided fools with their own interpretations, but only a select few truly understood.

And she, more than anyone, had understood the real truth.

Reality and fantasy, he now understood, were separated by a very thin veil. The book had taught him that much. Slowly, he'd come to recognise the allegories in the tale, the hidden messages she'd left for him.

The instructions.

He'd gone through the list once already that year. A dry run, which had seen him mark his targets, the sites of importance he'd interpreted both from her book and other works.

He had to see them for himself. Had to feel the power of each place, some stronger than others.

It would be a culmination, that much he understood. He had to create something in her honour, and only then would he be ready for the final, ultimate sacrifice – one that would see everything closed once more.

For now, it was time to check the second list. The impressive list of maidens. And to make his next selection.

Chapter Ten

The pre-dawn chill still clung to Liam as he walked into headquarters the following morning, the warmth inside the building doing little to dispel the lingering dampness from his earlier run at Porthmeor.

He bypassed the main CID floor, pouring himself a coffee from the kitchen area. As he drank the fresh brew, which was mercifully still hot, Liam's mind replayed the scene at the Merry Maidens yesterday. The eighth stone lifted away, disturbing the earth, to reveal the cloth bundle containing the skeletons.

He recalled the look of shock on Raymond Preston's face, the archaeologist still needing to return the call he'd made last night after discovering that Preston had once given a talk to Anthony Ellison.

'There you are.'

Liam turned, mug in hand, to see Maya leaning against the doorway of the incident room, nursing her own coffee.

'Any news from your archaeologist friend?' she asked.

'No response yet.' Liam wasn't sure if Preston was an asset to their investigation or a hindrance. His eccentricity was just the right side of wearing, but he was annoyed that the man hadn't returned his call. He may have already explained that he couldn't recall Anthony Ellison being present at one of his talks but, in retrospect, he had tried to dismiss the question out of hand. 'I'll track him down if he doesn't get back to me soon.'

Maya nodded, her gaze distant for a second before they joined Jack and Hargreaves in the incident room for the morning briefing. The crime board now displayed images of Tess Penrose alongside the pair of skeletal remains. Below the victims were photos of Anthony Ellison and Jerry Penrose as potential suspects, and surrounding them were the names of people they'd interviewed, including Danny Reeve and Raymond Preston.

The briefing went over what they already knew, and formulated their plans. The immediate goal was to locate Raymond Preston for further questioning and to continue interviewing those close to Anthony Ellison.

Afterwards, Liam drove with Maya to visit Jenna Keppel, the second of the two young women Danny Reeve had told them about who'd been in some form of relationship with Tony.

Pain reached Liam's chest, a tightening similar to reflux, as he thought once more about what Tess had endured during the night. That she had effectively suffocated from the clay was bad enough but the paralysis made it so much worse. He understood too well the panic of not being able to breathe, but could barely imagine what she would have gone through as the clay had seeped into her lungs.

He was glad when they arrived at the address and he was able to get some fresh air.

He rubbed the dome of his head as he walked to the front door, the skin glistening with sweat.

'You okay?' Maya asked, as he knocked on the door.

She was one of the few people in the world to know what he had gone through with the SBS and latterly in the seas of Cornwall, and would have known that what had happened to Tess specifically could have triggered something in him.

'Fine,' he said, dragging his thoughts away from the post-mortem as the door was answered.

Jenna was the eldest of the women connected to Tony they'd spoken to so far, but she looked younger than her twenty-two years. Her dark hair was pulled back severely, her eyes slightly puffy as she looked over their warrant cards, unsmiling, stepping aside without comment so Liam and Maya could enter.

Inside, the small house had the same transient feel as Danny Reeve's flat. Bookcases lined the walls, and mismatched dishes filled the sink in the cramped kitchenette.

'Thanks for speaking with us, Jenna,' Liam began. 'My colleague explained why I'm here?'

'The girl at the stone circle? I didn't know her.'

'Understood. Her name was Tess Penrose but the reason we are here is Anthony Ellison. We believe he was the last person seen with her.'

Jenna crossed her arms. 'I haven't seen Tony in ages. Is he okay?'

'You dated?' Maya asked.

Jenna gave a wry half-shrug. 'If you can call it that. We saw each other for a bit, end of last year.'

'What was he like?'

A reluctant smile formed on Jenna's lips. 'He wasn't like other lads.'

'In what way?'

'He was . . . intense. Not weird-weird, just into weird stuff, you know?'

'Such as?'

'Folky stuff. Old Cornish history things. He dragged me to all sorts of places. Standing stones, hilltops I'd never heard of.'

'Would he take you there to be alone?' Liam asked.

Jenna raised an eyebrow, a hint of a grin on her face, then glanced away. 'Sometimes,' she admitted, her voice barely a whisper.

Liam showed her the image of the marked map on his phone. 'Any of these places familiar?'

She hesitated, her finger tracing the rim of a chipped mug on the counter. 'There.' She pointed. 'Logan Rock. Windy as hell, but he loved it. Said it felt . . . exposed, in the right way. And Carn Euny, that underground tunnel thing? The fogou. Hated that one.'

Liam noted the names, neither of which were marked with Tony's asterisks. 'Just to be clear, Jenna . . . You had sex at these locations?' Maya asked.

'Yes.'

'Did he ever talk about what these places meant to him?'

'All the time. That's his map, isn't it? Seen it before. He said it was personal, not just about geography. Said it was about the . . . energy. Never really got it myself.'

'Not to get too personal, Jenna, but was the sex different when Tony took you to those places? Different from when you were here, for instance,' Maya asked.

Jenna nodded slowly, her eyes drifting upwards. 'I guess you could say that. For him, not me. He really got off on that stuff. It was fun, I guess, a bit out of the ordinary. Listen, is he missing or something?'

Maya ignored the question. 'Why did you split up?'

Jenna shrugged again. 'He's passionate, but it was never going to be serious, was it?'

Liam decided to get to the point. 'Do you think he could have had anything to do with Tess Penrose's death?'

Jenna squirmed. 'No, of course not. Tony wouldn't hurt anyone.'

'No one has a bad word to say about him,' Maya said, back in the car.

Denial from friends and family was pretty standard in these types of situations, but Liam agreed that the consistency and vehemence was noticeable. He thought of the two skeletons unearthed yesterday as they drove back towards Penzance and wondered if and how they might be linked to Tony.

They drove to Treliske hospital, where they met Dr Aris Thorne in the pathology department.

Liam hadn't met the forensic anthropologist before. In her mid-forties, her dark hair was tied back in a tight bun. 'Please,' she said, gesturing them inside the room, which aside from the operating table with the two skeletons contained little more than a table, chairs, and a blank whiteboard. She placed a thin file on a side table but didn't open it straight away.

'I've conducted the preliminary osteological assessment of the remains recovered from the Merry Maidens site,' she began. 'Worked through the night, so you'll have to accept my apologies if I sound a little tired. As requested, I prioritised establishing the biological profile.

'As I'm sure you are aware, the remains are of two individuals. Based on pelvic morphology and specific cranial features, we have one male and one female.'

'Their ages?' Maya asked.

'Skeletal and dental development indicators, primarily epiphyseal fusion status and third molar development, suggest both individuals were mid-age adults. Early to late thirties at time of death.'

'And time since death?' Liam asked.

'That's always more estimation than hard fact. But considering the burial context, the condition of the bone, and the associated material degradation, a post-mortem interval of approximately five years seems probable. Let's say four and a half to five and a half years to be safe.'

'Cause of death?'

'From the bones alone, there is no identifiable perimortem trauma. No cut marks indicating sharp force, no fractures suggesting significant blunt force impact, no projectile damage. The skeletons are, in that respect, unremarkable.'

Maya asked for a comparison between the manner in which the two had died, and what had happened to Tess.

'Choking and suffocation leave no diagnostic markers on the skeleton. It cannot be confirmed . . . But neither can it be ruled out based on my examination.'

'There was cloth recovered with the remains?' Liam asked.

'Fragmentary, heavily degraded by soil conditions. It's with the forensic trace evidence team now for full analysis. However, initial visual inspection under magnification revealed some localised particulate staining.'

'What sort of staining?'

'A faint yellowish powder adhering to some fibres,' Dr Thorne clarified. 'I have read the file on the body you found. It might be consistent with an ochre substance, perhaps limonite-based. But I must stress, that is purely observational at this stage. The lab analysis is required for any definitive identification.'

'Is there anything else you can tell us about the remains, Dr Thorne?' Maya asked.

Dr Thorne gave them a weary smile. 'My preliminary report covers everything definitive. The full analysis will take more time, particularly regarding any trace evidence. I'll prioritise the ochre comparison but I'm afraid I can't tell you any more than that at this stage.'

They took a quick break at the hospital's coffee shop.

'If they died, say, five years ago, Tony would have been, what, fourteen then?' Maya said.

Liam nodded. He'd dealt with major crimes committed by minors in the past, but he couldn't see how a fourteen-year-old could have killed two adults and buried them in a stone circle undetected. 'What if we are looking for a killer who targets couples?'

'You think Tony's going to turn up dead, too?'

'If these killings are linked then it's plausible.'

Liam dialled Preston's number back in the car, putting it on speaker, the archaeologist answering on the fourth ring.

'DS Kilshaw,' Preston said, the enthusiastic voice Liam had heard yesterday sounding flat. Preston sounded as if he was outdoors. Wind whistled past the microphone, causing static down the line, and when Preston spoke he sounded distant, as if he was in another country.

'Raymond, I've been trying to reach you since last night. We have some follow-up questions about the stone circle.'

'Apologies. I'm afraid yesterday took it out of me somewhat. I wasn't prepared for that discovery of the bones.' Preston sounded as if he was shouting, his voice dropping in and out.

'That's partly why I'm calling. We've learnt the remains have been in the ground for approximately five years.'

'I see.'

'We also spoke with Truro College,' Liam continued, watching Maya's face as she listened. 'They confirmed that Anthony Ellison would have been present when you gave your talk last year.'

A longer pause, only the roar of the wind suggesting Preston was still there. 'I give many talks, Detective Sergeant.' Preston's voice had hardened despite the background noise. 'At schools, historical societies, community centres. I couldn't possibly remember every face. If he was there, he was there, but I don't recall him.'

'Where are you now, Raymond?'

'Out. Working.' Preston's breathing had quickened. 'Look, I need to go. Signal's poor here.'

'We're heading to Carn Euny today,' Liam said.

When Preston spoke again, his voice had regained some of its usual measured tone. 'Carn Euny? Yes, fascinating site. One of the best-preserved ancient villages in Cornwall. The fogou there is particularly interesting.'

'Any suggestions on what we should be looking for?'

'The usual archaeological features. Nothing specific comes to mind.' Preston's words were becoming lost in the wind. 'I really must go. I'll call you later if I think of anything relevant.'

The line went dead before Liam could respond.

'That didn't sound like the eager archaeologist from yesterday,' said Maya, as they pulled away.

'No, definitely on edge about something.'

'The Truro College connection?'

'Maybe.' Liam thought about the book Preston had given him, which he hadn't started reading yet. 'I think we should have Jack look deeper into Raymond Preston's background.'

'Already texting him,' Maya said. 'I'm also having him track Preston's phone location.'

As they headed towards the site Jenna had shared with them, the drizzle intensified into proper rain, drumming on the roof of the car.

Liam drove, the car slicing through puddles forming on the narrow country roads. The countryside closed in around them, hedgerows pressing close on either side, the occasional farm gate offering brief glimpses of sodden fields stretching towards the horizon.

Rain hammered against the windscreen as they drove through a particularly heavy downpour. The grey sky pressed down on the landscape. 'What do you know about fogous?' Liam asked.

'Me? Everything,' Maya said, as she typed into her phone. 'Underground passages built into Iron Age settlements. Theories range from food storage to defensive refuges to ritual spaces. No one knows for certain.'

'I wonder why Tony Ellison was so enamoured with this place?'

‘The mystery, maybe. The connection to ancient practices. Jenna said he talked about the “energy” of these places but it sounds to me that he’s just a horny young lad who likes having sex in weird places.’

They rounded a bend and the small car park for Carn Euny came into view, deserted except for a weathered information sign and a footpath marker pointing up the hillside. The ancient settlement itself wasn’t visible, hidden beyond the rise.

Liam pulled into the muddy parking area and cut the engine. For a moment, they sat in silence, listening to the soft patter of rain on the roof before donning their wet-weather gear. Liam had long ago stopped marvelling at how easily the Cornish weather shifted. Yesterday had been a glorious dry spring day, and now it was like they were back in autumn.

They left the car, the ancient settlement of Carn Euny emerging from the mist as they climbed the hill, stone foundations tracing the ghostly outlines of dwellings abandoned nearly two millennia ago.

‘The fogou should be over there,’ Liam said, pointing towards a depression in the centre of the settlement.

As they approached, the entrance revealed itself: a low, dark mouth in the earth, framed by massive granite slabs, leading downwards and inwards. A modern metal gate secured the entrance, but it was unlocked, creaking open as Maya pushed against it.

‘Not my choice of a romantic location,’ she remarked, shining her torch into the darkness.

Liam breathed in through his nose as he stared into the narrow passage, experiencing the same constriction he’d felt on the lifeboat as he thought about the low ceiling and leaning sides of the tunnel.

‘You all right?’ Maya asked, noticing his hesitation.

'Fine. I'm just not really built for such small spaces,' he said, clambering through the opening before he could talk himself out of it.

The entrance required Liam to bend almost double, the ceiling dropping sharply after the first few metres. The beam of their torches caught on rough stone walls, revealing a passageway that extended perhaps twenty metres before opening into a slightly larger chamber. The air inside felt different, cooler and heavy.

'Watch your step,' Maya warned, illuminating the uneven floor. 'And your head.'

They moved slowly through the passage, torchlight revealing smoothed stones set into the walls and ceiling.

They continued forwards, the passage widening gradually until they could stand upright again in the central chamber. It was a roughly circular space, perhaps three metres across, with a stone-lined roof that arched overhead. A narrow shaft above allowed a small amount of natural light to filter down, casting weak illumination on the chamber floor.

'There's another passage.' Maya pointed to a smaller opening on the far side, little more than a crawlspace.

'Wait,' Liam said, directing his torch beam along the wall nearest to them. 'There's something here.'

Faint markings were visible on several of the stones, crude symbols scratched into the surface. Some appeared ancient, weathered by centuries, but others looked fresher, the scratches revealing lighter stone beneath.

'Some kind of graffiti?' Maya suggested, moving closer to examine them.

As they circled the chamber, Liam noticed several niches built into the walls, small recesses that might have once held offerings or artifacts. One such recess, set at about waist height, contained what appeared to be a small pile of dust.

'Maya,' he called, his voice echoing in the confined space. 'Look at this.'

She joined him, directing her torch at the recess. The beam illuminated a small heap of fine powder, distinctly yellow against the dark stone.

'Is that ochre?'

Liam pulled on a pair of latex gloves and carefully collected a sample into an evidence bag. The yellow substance was unmistakable, the same limonite-based mineral they'd found on Tess's body and at the Piper Stone.

Chapter Eleven

Liam arrived at headquarters a little after six the following morning. He'd cut his morning run short, the dark clouds over St Ives threatening a deluge that had eventually materialised on his drive into work. After Liam and Maya's discovery at Carn Euny, a full search had been undertaken of the fogou and the surrounding area, resulting in Liam not going to bed until the early hours of the morning.

Maya had called as he drove in to inform him that the pathologist, Dr Wetzel, had requested a meeting at headquarters to go over the toxicology reports.

Liam found Wetzel waiting in the briefing room. He was wearing a three-piece suit, his hair neatly combed. It was strange seeing him out of the mortuary, but he still retained the same humourless demeanour. 'DS Kilshaw,' he said. 'Will your colleague be long in joining us?'

'Shouldn't be. Can I get you a drink?' Liam asked, keen to get out of the room until Maya arrived.

'No, I'm fine, thank you.'

Liam was just about to excuse himself when the door opened. 'Apologies,' Maya said, taking a seat, her hair damp from the rain now lashing at the windows.

Wetzel took an iPad from his bag. 'I thought, given the context, it was better we did this face to face,' he said, switching the tablet on and handing them both a printed report.

'We've identified the agent found in Tess Penrose's bloodstream. As thought, it is a paralytic. Structurally similar to succinylcholine, but it's not a pharmaceutical batch. Whoever made this either synthesised it themselves or got it from someone with access to restricted compounds. It would have acted very fast. Full paralysis within two minutes.'

'She couldn't move at all?' Maya asked.

'No. Complete muscular shutdown. But, as we thought, her brain activity would've remained intact. This wasn't sedation. She would have seen, heard, and felt everything.'

Liam closed the folder. 'Does this affect how she died?'

'It's like I originally suggested. The diaphragm's a muscle like anything else. No movement means no ventilation. But it wouldn't have resulted in instant suffocation. She still had passive oxygen exchange for a time. If the clay hadn't fully blocked her airways, she might have lingered in that state for ten, maybe fifteen, minutes.'

'So she didn't choke as soon as it was applied,' Liam said.

'Correct. The mixture hardened gradually. As it set inside the nasal and oral cavities, it formed a seal. She couldn't clear it. Couldn't cough, couldn't gag. Once the blockage reached her trachea, it became terminal.'

'Jesus,' Maya muttered.

'Death by progressive asphyxiation,' Wetzel added. 'But not before full consciousness faded. That's what you're looking at.'

Liam sensed his own breathing intensifying as Wetzel spoke. His hand instinctively went to his chest as he glanced towards the shut door. 'You think she would have been aware the entire time?' he said, his voice distant.

'Almost certainly.'

Liam rushed downstairs after the meeting and stood beneath the awning as rain lashed against the building. He needed to be outside – away from the cloying walls of headquarters – as he thought about what had happened to Tess.

He took in the air, fighting his own memories of being trapped and unable to breathe, before reluctantly returning inside.

His mood remained sullen as he returned to CID. It was all but impossible to come to terms with what had happened to Tess. At some point, it would have to be explained to the parents, and that was a burden he didn't wish to give to anyone.

'Morning,' said Jack, stifling a yawn as he caught Liam's mood. 'Lab's been working through the night on that ochre substance you found at Carn Euny.'

'The limonite? Anything useful?' Liam said.

'It's definitely the same substance found on Tess's body and at the Piper Stone. Identical mineral composition, apparently.'

Liam looked through the report, ignoring the technical language before focusing on the conclusions. He glanced up at the crime wall where Jack had pinned a large replica of Tony's map, a clean version showing the full Cornwall peninsula with each site carefully marked. The four stone circles Tony had highlighted with asterisks were flagged – the Merry Maidens, Tregeseal, Boskednan, and the Hurlers – as had the sites mentioned by Jenna – Logan Rock and Carn Euny – where they'd found the ochre residue in the fogou.

Beside the map, the crime board had expanded overnight. Photos of Tess Penrose now shared space with placeholder silhouettes labelled *Male and Female Remains*, faceless representatives of the skeletons they'd unearthed beneath the eighth stone.

The potential suspect section was light. Small images of everyone they'd talked to so far had been uploaded, as well as a more prominent image of Tony Ellison.

'What about the organic material Dr Thorne mentioned?' Maya asked, moving closer to examine the board.

'Plant material mixed with the ochre. Lab's still working on identifying the exact species.' Jack rubbed his eyes. 'They think it was deliberately added, not environmental contamination.'

Liam nodded, his attention fixed on the placeholders for the unknown victims and, not for the first time, he wondered at the links between the remains, Tess Penrose, and the still missing Tony Ellison.

Ellison was the obvious prime suspect, and the more discoveries they made – like the limonite found in Carn Euny, where Ellison had taken some of his previous sexual partners – the more the evidence pointed his way.

The door to the incident room swung open as Liam was examining the map. DCI Hargreaves stepped in, his expression grim beneath the fluorescent lights.

He moved to the crime board, hands clasped behind his back as he studied the photographs and placeholder silhouettes. 'Right, let's recap where we are. We have one confirmed murder. Tess Penrose, eighteen years old, found at the Merry Maidens stone circle three days ago. Cause of death: enforced suffocation. Body marked with ochre dust.'

He gestured to the placeholder images. 'We have two sets of skeletal remains, estimated to have been buried five years ago, discovered beneath one of the stones at the same site. Male and female, both young adults.

'And a missing person, Anthony Ellison, nineteen years old, last seen with the murder victim. Oh, and before I forget, we have this.' He tapped the large map. 'A list of stone circles and remote sites across Cornwall, which could be linked. Am I missing anything?'

Liam had to stop himself from rolling his eyes at his boss's tone.

Maya cleared her throat. 'Sir, the ochre found at Carn Euny yesterday matches what was found on Tess's body and at the Piper Stone . . .'

'I'm aware, DI Trent,' Hargreaves cut in. 'And that's my concern. This investigation is growing out of hand. We can't chase shadows across every stone circle in Cornwall.'

'With respect, sir,' Liam said, 'we have evidence suggesting a connection between these sites.'

'And what would you have us do, DS Kilshaw?' Hargreaves asked. 'Dig up every ancient monument in the county? Search all twenty-plus sites marked on Ellison's map? There is no body in Carn Euny?'

The question hung in the air. Although the search had yet to be complete, it didn't appear any body was located at Carn Euny. Liam glanced at the map, wondering what pressure his boss was under from those above to warrant speaking this way.

'The public outcry would be immense,' Hargreaves continued, softer now. 'Not to mention the cost, the resources, the damage to sites of historical significance. We need to narrow our focus, not expand it.'

Liam shifted his weight. He'd pushed for the excavation at the Merry Maidens, despite the objections. And because he'd done so, they had two more victims to account for. 'We're doing a scan on the soil at the Merry Maidens today. Hopefully that will stop any further excavation. Unless we find something, of course,' he said.

Hargreaves looked away from the crime board. Sighing, he said, 'If we expand the search, we will have to bring in support from Devon.'

Maya's head snapped up, her eyes narrowing as she caught Liam's gaze. Liam knew exactly what she was thinking. Devon meant Grace Hartley. As Grace had suggested on her call, Maya had never fully warmed to her, and no one wanted to have to share the investigation with Devon, which would feel like a kind of defeat. 'I don't think that's necessary just yet, sir,' she said.

'Let's hope not,' Hargreaves said, leaving the room.

Liam, Maya, and Jack remained in silence. The recent cuts to CID meant they were all stretched but Liam was sure no one wanted to have to enlist Devon's help unless necessary.

Maya assigned duties to Jack as Liam went to the kitchen to pour himself some coffee. He thought back to his early morning call with Grace, wondering if she'd already known about the possibility of Devon being called in to help.

Liam found Philippa Penrose in conversation with a man as he arrived at her house later that morning. He wasted no time parking up and walking over in time to introduce himself.

Mrs Penrose went silent as he approached, glancing from the man to Liam.

'DS Kilshaw,' she said after a moment. 'I wasn't expecting you.'

'Mrs Penrose, sorry to arrive unannounced.' Liam turned to the man. He had a slim, athletic build and was dressed all in black, a gold crucifix around his neck.

'Callum Frayne,' the man said, offering his hand.

'DS Kilshaw.'

'Reverend Frayne,' said Mrs Penrose. 'Callum is a close family friend.'

'Reverend?'

'The Church of the Followed Path. No affiliation with any traditional religions.'

Frayne said 'traditional' with something approaching a sneer.

'Christian-based?' Liam asked.

'In a way. I'm a former Church of England vicar. I still follow the teachings of Jesus Christ, but I saw my own light. I realised there was more religion could offer beyond strict dogma. I wanted to set up something more spiritual, something more entwined with the land.'

Liam was suspicious of religion at the best of times, let alone breakaway sects.

'Where are you based?'

Frayne smiled and gave him a card. 'It's nothing much, but then it doesn't have to be, does it?' he said, taking Philippa's hand. 'I'm here for you whenever you need, Philippa.'

Mrs Penrose bowed her head. 'Thank you, Callum.'

Liam nodded to the reverend as he walked away, returning with Mrs Penrose into the house. If anything, it was tidier than the last time they'd been, and he wondered if she'd been putting her energy into domestic chores to take her mind off her current tragic reality.

'Can I make you a tea?' she asked.

'That would be lovely,' said Liam, following her into the kitchen.

There was no need to go into any detail about the pathology report just yet. He'd come to see how Mrs Penrose was faring, and whether time had given her any new insight into who could have done such a terrible thing to her daughter.

'Where's your family liaison officer?' he asked as she handed him a tea.

'I told her to go home for the night. I just . . . I needed to be alone. I hope that's okay.'

'I totally understand. Whatever works best for you, Mrs Penrose.'

'I think you can call me Philippa now, don't you?' she said, as they sat down in the living room.

'Liam.'

She smiled. 'So why are you here, Liam?'

Liam told her about his meeting with Tess's father.

'Yes, I'd heard. He called me late last night. Incoherent, as usual. I think he mumbled something about getting back together. I told him where to go.'

Liam sipped his tea, glancing around the room at the pictures of Tess. 'I know it's difficult to consider, but do you think there's any chance Jerry could have done this?'

Philippa placed her cup down, a slight tremble to her hand.

'Jerry? I don't think so, do you? I've nothing good to say about the man, but this . . . For one, I don't think he could have organised such a thing. And I don't really believe he would've hurt Tess, even out of spite.'

Liam agreed about Jerry lacking the organisational skills. 'Reverend Frayne must be a great comfort to you?'

Philippa picked up her cup again. 'He has been, for a long time now. He was the one who suggested I go to the police when Jerry was . . . you know.'

Liam nodded. 'He mentioned his approach is more spiritual.'

'That's just his way of looking at things. I think he always hated the stuffiness of normal churches, the ceremony and the paraphernalia that came with it.'

Liam thought of the man's outfit, reminiscent of a vicar's wardrobe except for the dog collar, but didn't comment. 'You still go to his services?'

'Sometimes. They're not as regular as usual church services. He likes holding gatherings in different places. He owns farmland and has a big yurt there. Sounds dreadful, I know, but he often holds them during sunsets and it can be beautiful. He really has been a great comfort to me.'

The FLO arrived and looked sheepish at Liam being there during her absence. Liam brushed aside her apology and informed her about Reverend Frayne, taking her aside to explain the results of the post-mortem.

'I haven't gone into any detail yet, but sooner or later she'll need to know what happened to her daughter.'

'I'll try to prepare her as best I can,' said the FLO.

'See if you can find out more about this church-type thing, and anything else about the husband.'

'Of course, but my first concern is—'

'The family of the victim. I understand that,' said Liam, matching the FLO's smile before saying his goodbyes.

Chapter Twelve

Liam called Jack as he headed towards the address on the card Reverend Frayne had given him.

'What can you tell me about him?' he asked, a sudden flurry of rain stopping as abruptly as it had started.

Jack repeated what the reverend and Philippa had told him. 'Looks like there may have been some uneasiness when he left the church. I'll do some digging, but I've got an article here suggesting a falling out with the archbishop.'

'Okay. Let me know what you find,' Liam said as the rain resumed pelting the windscreen.

The smell of damp grass greeted him as he reached Reverend Frayne's farm a few minutes later. In the distance, a large white yurt occupied an adjoining field. In the grey daylight, the scene reminded Liam more of a CSI tent than a place of worship.

'DS Kilshaw. I was expecting you – though not so soon.'

Liam turned from the view of the yurt to see Frayne leaving his farmhouse.

'I was in the area, so thought, when in Rome . . .'

'Please,' said Frayne, 'let me show you. I hope you don't mind getting your feet a bit muddy.'

They walked across the field to the yurt, Liam stepping carefully to avoid fresh puddles. A damp, cloying smell greeted him as they stepped inside, reminding him momentarily of Carn Euny.

'Not much to look at now, I realise,' Frayne said, 'but picture people, lights, music. You must come when we next hold a service.'

'Mrs Penrose mentioned you've been a great support to her during the separation . . . And during this last day or so.'

Frayne shook his head. 'That poor woman has suffered more than anyone should ever have to suffer. And now Tess. I still can't really believe it. No one can.'

'Did Tess go to your services?'

'Sometimes. Though I think younger members often come because there's nothing else to do around here. They seem to have a good time. We try to make sure they do.'

Liam walked through the tent. Seven rows of chairs faced a makeshift altar made from a large rectangular table. 'How did you hear about what was happening with Mrs Penrose? With her husband, I mean?'

'I'm a licensed counsellor as well as a reverend. Philippa attended a regular group meeting I hold for the wider area for victims of domestic violence.'

Frayne was engaging and chatty, on the right side of familiar. It sounded like he was doing good work in the community, but Liam had no option other than to ask the necessary questions. 'Mrs Penrose says you hold services in other places?'

Frayne paused. 'Ah, I see. That is true. Especially during the warmer months, we try to increase our scope. Beach and coastal services are always popular. Though I imagine you're more interested in our stone circle services.'

Liam hid his surprise. He'd wanted to ask about Frayne's connection to nature but hadn't realised he conducted services at stone circles.

'How often have you done that?'

'Just the once. Bodmin Moor. The Hurlers. Do you know the place?'

Liam had been to the Hurlers after seeing it on Tony's map. That Frayne had once held a ceremony there was something he hadn't been prepared for. 'A beautiful place.'

'Here,' said Frayne, showing him pictures on his phone.

The stones Liam had walked through were lit with decorative lights in the photographs. The gathering was of far more people than Liam had expected, easily into the hundreds.

'Got accused of paganism for that one.'

Liam allowed himself to smile. The photos had been taken at night, and Liam had only caught a fleeting glimpse. Frayne had been open about his association to the stone circle. Maybe a little too open.

'Do you ever use ochre in your services?' Liam asked, an image of Tess kneeling, her hair tainted with the yellow substance, appearing in his mind.

Frayne paused again. 'Ochre? Well, yes, I guess we do on occasion. That particular ceremony at the Hurlers took place on the summer solstice, hence some of the accusations of paganism. We were using ochre to demonstrate our connection to the earth, and the sun. Rebirth and promise.'

'Any particular colours used?'

'Since you ask yes, there was. What other colour could you use for the solstice?'

'Yellow?' Liam said.

Frayne smiled. 'That's right. Yellow.'

Frayne said it as if it was nothing. But the fact that he used the same colour of ochre that had been found on Tess was enough for Liam to think the man warranted further investigation.

Liam took a sample of the ochre Frayne had used during his solstice ceremony – the reverend seeming more than happy to cooperate – before he went to meet Maya at the Merry Maidens.

The stones stood silent in a light drizzle as Liam and Maya watched a white van arrive in the car park. The door opened, and a tall woman with cropped silver hair stepped out, followed by an equipment case she dragged behind her.

'Dr Helen Summers,' she said, as Liam and Maya left the car. 'Cornwall Archaeological Trust.'

Maya introduced them as they made the short journey to the stone circle, the eighth stone still removed from position. Dr Summers opened her case, revealing a complex apparatus that resembled a lawnmower with a digital display. She explained the process. 'We'll scan the ground around each stone using radar to check for any signs of past disturbance. Voids, shifted soil, anything that might suggest a burial or excavation.'

'How long we looking at?' asked Liam.

Dr Summers smiled as if just noticing his presence. Liam began to wonder if this distracted quality was something shared by all archaeologists. 'Three to five hours,' she said, adjusting the settings on a handheld control unit. 'Depending on soil conditions. The rain actually helps – better conductivity.'

They followed her to the perimeter of the circle where she began assembling the equipment with practised efficiency. 'I'll start with the location where you found the remains.'

Liam glanced over to the mound, thinking how it didn't feel like only three days since Tess's body had been discovered.

The specialist began her methodical work, pushing the scanner in straight lines across the surface surrounding each stone. The display flickered with subsurface images which she explained were layers of soil, rocks, roots, and the occasional void space.

Liam and Maya trailed behind, Liam wondering what would happen if Dr Summers found something of significance. He was reminded again of the burial site at the farm in Sennen; an image of the stone circle being dismantled appearing in his head, each stone being torn from the ground to reveal nineteen graves.

'We're basically looking for disturbances in the soil profile,' Dr Summers explained as they arrived at the headstone where Tess's body had been found. 'Excavations leave a signature, even after years. Different density, composition breaks, intrusive materials.'

'You'll be able to tell if there is a body beneath?'

She grinned without looking up, Liam getting the distinct feeling he was being patronised. 'Organic remains create distinct anomalies. So do burial wrappings, clothing, personal effects. It's certainly a distinct possibility that we'll find something on a site of this age.'

Rain continued to fall, fine and persistent, beading on Liam's jacket. The sound of a vehicle arriving drew his attention, and he left Maya with the specialist and made his way across the field.

By the time he was halfway, Raymond Preston was approaching from the car park, clutching his leather satchel. The ever-present smile was there but strained, his eyes darting between Liam and the GPR equipment.

'DS Kilshaw,' he called, crossing the field with hurried steps. 'I thought you'd be at Carn Euny but I was told you were here instead.'

Preston looked slightly flustered, his tweed jacket buttoned incorrectly, hair dishevelled from the wind. Despite this, his eyes gleamed with undisguised fascination as he watched Dr Summers work.

'Ground-penetrating radar,' he said. 'Fascinating technology.'

After the abrupt way Preston had ended their last call, Liam was surprised to see the archaeologist and was surprised further to see his renewed enthusiasm.

'Any luck identifying the remains?' he asked, gazing at the empty space where the eighth stone had been.

'Not yet. The lab's still working on it,' Liam replied, watching Preston's reaction carefully. 'We're checking for any similar disturbances under the other stones.'

'A wise precaution,' Preston agreed, as if he was an active member of the investigation.

Maya joined them, her expression neutral. She was a formidable character at the best of the times, and her stern glare had an immediate effect on Preston, the archaeologist blinking rapidly, shifting his weight from one foot to the other.

'Any luck remembering Anthony Ellison from your talk, Mr Preston?' Maya said, not wasting any time.

Preston stammered. 'As I mentioned to your colleague, I speak to hundreds of students each year. I couldn't possibly remember every face.'

'He was accepted to Oxford to study English, and is hoping to specialise in folklore,' Liam pressed gently. 'He seems like the kind of student who might have stood out, asked questions, shown particular interest in your field.'

'I'm sorry.' Preston shook his head, genuine regret in his voice. 'The name means nothing to me. Though I'm flattered to think I might have influenced his academic interests. Have you had a chance to read my book yet? There's a whole chapter on burial rituals associated with stone circles. It might be relevant to your investigation.'

'I'm afraid not. With the investigation and everything.'

Preston nodded. 'Of course, of course. Please let me know if I can help in any way.' He turned back to watch Dr Summers, who had completed nearly half the circle. 'Fascinating stuff.'

Preston remained, hovering at a respectful distance as Dr Summers completed her circuit, the GPR unit whirring as she pushed it over the damp ground.

Liam and Maya spent the time making calls, and liaising with Jack, who was coordinating everything from headquarters.

Finally, with the last stone surveyed, Dr Summers straightened her back and stretched, wincing slightly before disconnecting the display unit from the scanner. Liam and Maya approached as she studied the digital readouts.

'Anything?' Maya asked, squinting at the screen.

Dr Summers shook her head, her silver hair catching a ray of weak sunlight. 'Not sure if it's good or bad news for you, but there's nothing anomalous under any of the other stones. No disturbances, no voids, no irregular density patterns.' She scrolled through several saved images. 'Just the expected geology. Bedrock, soil layers, the occasional natural pocket of air or water.'

She looked almost disappointed as she zoomed in on one scan, showing them a cross-section of earth beneath the stone opposite where Tess had been found. 'This is typical of what I'm seeing across the site. Undisturbed soil profile, consistent compaction, no signs of excavation.'

'You're certain?' Liam asked.

'As certain as the technology allows,' Dr Summers replied. 'GPR isn't infallible, but it's very good at detecting the kind of disturbance we saw at the eighth stone. That site shows clear evidence of excavation and refill with different soil composition. None of the others show anything similar.'

Maya exhaled. 'We don't need to excavate more of the circle?'

'Not based on my findings, no,' the specialist confirmed, beginning to disassemble her equipment. 'Whatever happened at the eighth stone appears to be isolated within this circle.'

Liam glanced towards Preston, who stood gazing at the stones, hands clasped behind his back. The archaeologist's expression was unreadable, but Liam thought there was tension in his posture that hadn't been there before.

'Thank you, Dr Summers,' Maya said, walking her back to the car park.

As the van pulled away, Maya turned to Liam. 'That's a relief, I suppose.'

'What now?' Liam said. Although there was much to do, the investigation felt momentarily on hold. The remains from the eighth stone were still unidentified, and until they had names, it was all but impossible to have a plausible link to Tess Penrose.

'Tony Ellison's work colleagues again? Then his dad?'

Preston had drifted towards the eighth stone's empty space, and was staring down at the fallen stone with an expression Liam couldn't quite read.

'Mr Preston,' Liam called. 'We'll be in touch if we need anything further.'

The archaeologist nodded, his attention fixed on the disturbed ground. Liam was about to quiz him on it when Jack called.

'Boss, got a hit on the plate for Tony Ellison. A walker's reported a vehicle abandoned at the Carfury Quarry. Uniform on their way now.'

Chapter Thirteen

Liam and Maya pulled into a gravelled lay-by next to Carfury Quarry, where Anthony Ellison's SUV had been found, the vehicle half-concealed by trailing vines.

The quarry felt almost alien under the darkening skies. The rough stone faces were pitted with patches of gorse and heather, weeds poking through the scattered debris and abandoned industrial equipment. A shallow pool glistened near the far wall, water lilies gathering at its edges.

Liam parked up next to the patrol car, Maya introducing them to the local officer, the wind whistling around the quarry floor.

'How long since this place was last active?' Maya asked.

'Been shut for over fifteen years, ma'am,' the officer said, his Cornish accent almost impenetrable. He pointed over towards where Tony Ellison's old SUV had been discovered, its wheels sunk into the soft ground.

They walked over, Liam wondering if somewhere beyond the quarry another body was waiting for them.

'Not exactly the actions of someone on the run,' Maya said, peering through the driver's side window. 'No key. Looks like he just parked up.'

Liam couldn't see any obvious signs of damage to the vehicle, inside or out. 'I agree. If he's trying to hide from us, he could have done a better job. I guess he could have abandoned this for a second vehicle. Or he could be somewhere in there,' he said, pointing to the dense woodland surrounding the quarry.

The forensics van arrived twenty minutes later. Two CSIs stepped out, both already in partial kit, one carrying the scene log, the other unloading gear from the back.

Liam stood with Maya just beyond the vehicle, watching as the team began its work. The car was photographed from every angle, dusted for prints, and fibre traps run along the door seals. Nothing was found inside beyond a single blanket and an empty bottle of water.

'Why abandon it here?' asked Maya, almost to herself.

Liam moved away from the immediate scene, his boots crunching over loose stone and moss. The quarry opened out ahead, steep on one side, shallower where it curved towards the treeline. Pools of standing water glinted in the rock. Maya followed him along a narrow path that skirted the upper edge. Dense woodland pressed in on all sides. 'We could bring in PolSA again?' Liam said, looking once more to the woodland.

'You really think he's hiding in there? If he was going to do that, surely he would hide the vehicle better?'

Liam agreed the placing of the vehicle made little sense. For all they knew, Tony was miles away now. Everything pointed to Tess's death being premeditated, so it wasn't a stretch to imagine Tony having a second vehicle here ready for a planned escape, if he was indeed the killer, as Liam suspected.

He took out his phone and checked Tony's map. Boskednan stone circle, one of the marked sites they'd visited, was only a mile away. 'Seems like too much of a coincidence to ignore,' he said to Maya. 'Shall we take another look?'

'Let's get there before night falls,' Maya said.

Liam called Jack. 'We need ANPR from this area. Ten-mile radius. Let's see if we can get some ID on who was driving.'

'On it,' Jack said. 'Any specific timeframe you want me to focus on?'

'Start six hours before Tess went missing and move forward. Look for the SUV, but flag anything else that repeats or seems out of place. Bypass roads, farm tracks, don't just check the obvious points,' he said, the sound of Jack typing coming through the phone.

Liam ended the call. He took a final look at Tony's beat-up SUV, trying to make sense of why it had been left here, and wondered what they would find at the stone circle.

The CSI team had set up portable floodlights, and now harsh white beams cut through the dusk, creating long shadows that stretched across the excavated stone. Finding the vehicle should have felt like a step forward, but for now it had only created more uncertainty.

It was a short journey to the stone circle, Maya winding her way through the backroads until they arrived at the nearest accessible place for the car.

'Two police officers found brutally murdered in wilderness of the Boskednan stone circle,' Maya said, as they left the car and walked into the falling darkness.

They switched on their torches to illuminate the narrow pathway. Side by side, their boots squelched over patches of moss and soft turf, their beams cutting the night air. Liam took his time as he covered the rough terrain, still nursing the remnants of an injury he'd suffered during a similar night-time chase in the Sennen investigation.

The circle came into view slowly. Liam had read about so many of the sites, they'd begun to blur into one. Boskednan was also known as the Nine Maidens of Madron – more dancing maidens turned to stone, like their counterparts at the Merry Maidens site.

The circle stood on a rise of open moorland, half-lost in the rough scrub and knee-high heather. Some of the stones rose waist-high, others barely poked through the soil, as if sinking or struggling to emerge. A few leant at precarious angles, reminding Liam of the eighth stone at the Merry Maidens, their bases wreathed in bracken and moss.

There were more gaps than stones. Liam counted ten stones, or twelve if he included the stumps, which begged the question of why they were known as the Nine Maidens. The ground underfoot was soft in places, worn to mud by sheep and weather, pitted with rabbit holes.

They stopped just outside the jagged ring, the remoteness and solitude oppressive. 'Shall we split up?' Liam said, with a laugh.

'You've been watching too much *Scooby Doo*,' Maya replied, as they moved from stone to stone, their torches held out in front of them like weapons.

'This is when the boogeyman jumps out on us,' Liam said, trying to lighten the situation as Maya stopped, her torch shining towards a stone in the distance.

The wind picked up, sending a rustle through the tall grass as they followed the path of the beam. Liam wondered if Tony's vehicle had been left by the quarry on purpose as he moved closer to what Maya had seen: a blurred shape, low to the ground, partially hidden by the grass.

'Jesus,' said Maya, as they arrived at the stone.

It was a mini replica of what they had found at the Merry Maidens.

Another young woman, fallen on to her side. She was partially clothed, her arms folded ritualistically in front of her, hands and feet painted in the same drying mix of ochre and clay, as if mid-transformation into stone.

Her face was another mask of clay, dusted with limonite and fixed in stillness under the torchlight.

Chapter Fourteen

By 2 a.m., the Boskednan stone circle was illuminated, floodlights casting pale light across the moor. Even with the full CSI team in place, the land still felt desolate. Liam and Maya stood just beyond the taped-off area while the body and surrounding ground were examined by the CSIs.

'Feels like we're being manipulated,' Liam said, thinking about the discovery of Anthony Ellison's vehicle less than a mile away. It seemed plausible it had been left in the quarry deliberately, to lead them here. The planning would have taken time, suggesting the killer wanted them to find the body.

He rechecked the map on his phone. Two of the asterisked sites were now active crime scenes. The pattern between the two murders was unmistakable. This new victim may have fallen on to her side but she was arranged in the same prayer-like fashion as Tess Penrose. Given that her face was compacted with clay, Liam had no doubt that the post-mortem would reveal she'd died in the same macabre way. He shuddered at the thought of another drawn-out death and the sadistic pleasure the killer would have taken from watching her suffer.

Beyond the body falling to its side, there appeared to be little sign of disruption in the localised area. The immediate view from CSI was that the victim had likely been killed beforehand.

Liam pictured the killer – his mind's eye conjuring a vision of Tony Ellison, still the number-one suspect – carrying the body across the moor and placing it deliberately among the stones. The lane they had taken to the circle wasn't the only access point, but however the killer had reached the stones, it wouldn't have been an easy journey.

It would have been something of a risk, even in the fading light, and raised the possibility of a witness being found. It was also conceivable that Tony had parked up in the quarry, or left the vehicle there for a quick getaway.

Hargreaves had arranged for the PolSA to attend the scene, and had requested a helicopter to search the local area, but they were still waiting for it to arrive.

With CSI handling the rest and nothing more to gain from standing around in the dark, they drove back to headquarters. The building was quiet, a single light glowing in CID where Jack was hunched over his laptop.

'Just got the photos from CSI,' he said as they arrived.

Neither Liam nor Maya commented. Liam moved to the kitchenette and started a fresh pot of coffee. 'Do you live here, Jack?' he asked as the machine hissed.

Jack smiled, his eyes still on the screen. 'Feels like it, sometimes.' The detective constable had been nothing short of a marvel since he'd joined the team. Everyone was hard working in the department, but Jack's work ethic threatened to put them all to shame.

Maya placed a red pin on the map next to the Boskednan site, matching the one already marking the Merry Maidens. Blue pins highlighted Tony's starred sites. There were now two remaining. The Hurlers in Bodmin Moor, and Tregeseal to the west.

Liam handed round the coffees. 'We should get patrol cars to the two remaining sites,' he said, nodding to the board.

Jack sipped his drink, tapping away at the keyboard. 'Here you go,' he said, as images from Boskednan appeared on the white screen.

The photos captured the way the killer had posed her perfectly. Like Tess, her hands were clasped, head bowed, the clay thick around her wrists and ankles, covering her face completely.

More images appeared, the CSIs slowly removing the clay from the victim's face until her features were visible.

'I'll run it through the new facial recognition software and see what happens,' said Jack, as Liam watched more images appear on the screen.

Everything pointed to Tony Ellison now and Liam was all but sure when they uncovered the identity of the second body that there would be a connection to Tony.

'Bloody hell,' said Jack, pressing some buttons. The white screen went blank, before a new photo appeared. It was a mugshot dated three months earlier. 'Carys Rowden. Eighteen. Cautioned for drunk and disorderly in Newquay. I think this is her.'

He split the screen – mugshot on one side, crime-scene photo on the other.

Liam pinched the bridge of his nose. Despite the residue of clay on the victim's face, the match was clear. 'Address?'

'Helston. No missing persons alert.'

'Same college as Tess?' Maya asked.

'Nothing in her file. Just the caution and current address. I'll keep digging.'

Liam took a final look at the two photos, already preparing himself for another death message as he wondered if and how Carys Rowden knew Tony Ellison.

It was after 4 a.m. when they reached the address in Helston. The street was cloaked in darkness save for one downstairs light glowing in a small semi-detached house. 'That's the one,' Maya said.

They knocked gently on the door, catching a glimpse of movement behind the curtains. A young woman answered. She appeared to be in her early twenties, and so similar in appearance to Carys that Liam wondered if they'd made a mistake with the identification. She took one look at their warrant cards and burst into tears.

'Bethany, what is it?' came a voice from inside. A woman in her fifties stepped into view, her arm immediately going around the girl. 'Who are you?'

'I'm DI Maya Trent. This is DS Liam Kilshaw. Are you Mrs Rowden?' The woman nodded slowly as Bethany trembled in her arms. 'It's Carys, isn't it? Something's happened. Just tell me.'

'I'm so sorry, Mrs Rowden,' Maya said. 'There's no easy way to say this. We believe we've found Carys's body.'

Mrs Rowden stood in silence, shaking her head. 'No. You're mistaken. It can't be,' she said, before collapsing to her knees beside her daughter.

Liam waited patiently for the family to console one another. In the living room, Bethany and her mother held each other on the sofa as Maya sat opposite, Liam making tea.

'Where's Mr Rowden?' Maya asked quietly.

'He's out looking for them,' Bethany said, her voice hoarse.

'Them?'

'Carys and her boyfriend. She was supposed to be back by half eleven.'

'Carys was out with her boyfriend tonight?'

'That's why we were up,' Bethany said. 'They went out together earlier. Mum told her to be back on time. She said she would. It's not the first time she's stayed out, but . . .'

'She's done it before,' Mrs Rowden added. 'But that boy, he's a bad influence.'

Liam handed out the teas, wondering if what had happened had really sunk in yet.

'Did you contact any of her friends when she didn't come back?' Maya asked.

'No. We knew who she was with. As I said, it wasn't the first time she's been late but it doesn't stop you worrying, does it?'

'The boy's name?' Liam asked, half-expecting for it to be Anthony Ellison.

Mrs Rowden went to speak but choked with tears, Bethany answering instead. 'Kian. Kian Burrell. He's twenty-two. Was he not there, when you found . . .'

Liam shook his head, Maya calling through the details of Kian Burrell to Jack.

Mr Rowden returned a short while later, and broke down as his wife explained what had happened to Carys. Maya tried her best to console both grieving parents as Liam spoke to Bethany alone in the hallway.

'How long had Carys been seeing Kian?'

'About six months.' She kept sneaking glances into the other room at the sound of her father crying. Her eyes were hollow, her skin blotched and red. 'She was infatuated. God knows why.'

Kian's address was a single-bed property on the outskirts of town. Uniform police had attended the place but there was no sign of him or his car.

'Do you know anywhere they might have gone?' Liam asked. 'Somewhere they could be alone, perhaps?'

Bethany looked down at her feet. 'I don't really want to think about that, but they used to go off in his car. She said they'd go to car parks, lay-bys, places they wouldn't be disturbed, if you know what I mean.'

'Could they have gone as far as Boskednan?'

She shrugged. 'There's nothing to do around here. I guess it's possible. But I don't know for sure.'

Liam showed her a picture of Tony Ellison. 'Do you know this man?'

Bethany squinted at the photo but shook her head.

'This is Tony Ellison.'

She shrugged. 'He's the one you think did all this?'

'Do you think Carys knew him?'

'Not that I'm aware of. She certainly didn't mention him.'

'If you think of anything else, please call me,' Liam said, handing her his card, once more noting the haunting similarity between the two sisters.

They waited for the FLO to arrive before leaving. Maya instructed Liam to go home for a few hours. Despite the recent developments, he understood why. The case was accelerating, and there would be long nights ahead, but although he'd been awake nearly twenty-four hours, his mind was still moving in a hundred directions, trying to make sense of what had happened, and searching for ideas as to what might happen next.

Exhaustion crept over him when he finally reached his flat. He didn't bother undressing. He set a timer for two hours, before collapsing on the bed.

Sleep must have come immediately, as it felt like the alarm went off the second he lay down. He rubbed his eyes at the sunlight leaking through the bedroom window, feeling more tired than ever.

He checked in with headquarters before he showered and changed. He thought about Carys Rowden and her boyfriend, Kian, who was still missing.

Maya's phone went to voicemail, so he decided to head straight to the office after grabbing Raymond Preston's book from the kitchen counter.

Adrenaline flushed his system as he sped towards Bodmin, but it was only serving to mask his fatigue. He called Maya again as he drove, but she didn't pick up.

Things were so stretched at the moment that he couldn't blame her for taking some extra time to rest, though the investigation was threatening to unravel.

They now had two victims posed in almost identical ways, a buried couple no one had yet identified, and two missing men, one who was all but certainly the killer.

As he drove, he glanced at Preston's book on the passenger seat. Cornwall was rich in stories, myths and legends. The Sennen investigation had raised possibilities of ritual sacrifice – Liam smiled at the memory of the mythical sea serpent, Bucca Dhu. And here they were, only months later, investigating murders at historical stone circles.

April clouds hung low as he arrived at headquarters in Bodmin. Liam noticed a familiar car in the car park but thought nothing of it until he reached CID, where Hargreaves was seemingly conducting a morning briefing without him.

'Nice of you to join us, DS Kilshaw,' his boss said, barely looking over.

Liam shot a glance at Maya, surprised to see her there after her not taking his call.

He was even more surprised to see three new faces in the room, one of which belonged to Grace Hartley.

Chapter Fifteen

At time likes this, he took great comfort in the book.

The planning he'd put in over the last few months had been extensive but he was still a prisoner to fortune. Some things were beyond his control, and as things progressed, he understood that would become more evident.

The police turning up at Carn Euny had been a surprise. He'd watched from a distance as they'd entered the fogou, relieved they hadn't arrived earlier when he'd been inside – the chamber a place of great peace and power for him which he now couldn't return to.

He hadn't expected the vehicle to be discovered.

Maybe it had been a mistake to ditch it, but it wasn't as if he could have kept it anywhere near him without drawing attention.

He'd risked a lot by leaving the vehicle so near the circle, and if his timing had been wrong there was a good chance he would have been caught. But the book had told him that wouldn't be the case. He didn't think he was infallible as such, but his work was important and if he was true to his cause, he would succeed.

Still it wasn't easy. The boy was an added complication. As he'd watched them, rutting like animals in the back of the car that had yet to be discovered, he'd come close to walking away.

Carys had sullied herself. He wasn't sure if she was worthy of the eternity he'd planned for her.

He'd made her watch as he'd dispatched the irrelevance she'd been with, putting her transgression down to the broken heart she was no doubt carrying with her. 'It's okay, Carys,' he'd whispered into her ear as he'd carried her away. 'Soon you can forget all this happened.'

But she'd forgotten too soon.

He'd barely had a chance to complete the ritual when Carys had succumbed to the mixture. It had sent him into a panic, and for the first time since this had started he'd doubted himself. He hadn't been sure if the transformation had been complete. One moment she was lucid, if unable to move, the next she was gone. He'd missed that magic process, was denied the opportunity to look into her eyes as she'd progressed into eternity.

And that scared him.

It wouldn't work if the circle was broken and he searched through the text for clues that he'd done the right thing.

Had she left any more hidden messages for him?

He knew well enough that much of what he was doing was subject to his own interpretation but everything had seemed so clear before.

The words had sung to him, telling him what needed to be done for his own salvation and he had to trust what he had done was right.

The next one would be harder. He didn't think the police knew of his list, but they were upping security everywhere.

He would have to be even more careful with the next maiden.

Chapter Sixteen

Hargreaves gave a brief introduction, though everyone already knew each other. The constabularies were officially merged, and there had been several cross-regional investigations in the past.

Even so, Liam couldn't help but feel slighted. Hargreaves had brought up the possibility of utilising Devon CID, but had seemingly made a unilateral decision to go ahead without first consulting the rest of the team.

'We appreciate your assistance on this,' Hargreaves said, as if answering Liam's unspoken accusation. 'As you can see from the crime board, things are developing.'

Was that another slight? Liam winced at the comment and the latent suggestion that Hargreaves' own team couldn't handle things. He glanced across at Maya, but her eyes were fixed forwards as Hargreaves repeated the current situation – with the recent update about the discovery of Anthony Ellison's vehicle and Carys's body at the stone circle the night before.

'You think the vehicle was left there on purpose? To prompt you to visit the stone circle?' Grace asked.

Maya smiled. Liam noted it didn't reach her eyes. 'We'd already visited all the asterisked sites including Boskednan. But yes, we think the vehicle may well have been dumped at the quarry to lead us to the circle.'

'Anthony Ellison is our prime suspect?' asked DC Oliver Quinlan, one of Grace's colleagues from Devon.

Maya shrugged. 'For now, yes. Although the fact that Carys's boyfriend, Kian, is missing, complicates things. If the killer is targeting couples, there is a chance Tony Ellison may also be a victim.'

Maya posted images of Tess and Carys side by side in the prayer pose they'd been arranged into, a hush coming over the team as they looked at faceless corpses with their masks of clay.

Carys's post-mortem wasn't scheduled until the following day, but the presumption had to be that she'd also been injected with the paralytic and Liam understood everyone was considering what that meant.

Although Grace held the same rank as Maya, it was Maya who continued as SIO, assigning duties to the now double-size team. Jerry Penrose, Reverend Frayne and Tony Ellison's work colleagues were to be interviewed again, as were Carys's family and friends, among others.

Liam was tasked with speaking to one of Carys's friends, Debbie Hawthorne, a shop worker from Penzance.

'You could've told me that before I drove all the way up here,' he said to Maya under his breath after the meeting ended.

'Then you never would've got the chance to see your girlfriend again,' Maya replied with a sly grin before walking off towards Hargreaves' office.

'Hello, stranger,' Grace said, stepping in as soon as Maya moved off, as if she'd been lying in wait.

Despite his unease about Devon's involvement, Liam was glad to see her. She looked well, a light blouse beneath a sharp suit, her long hair in a ponytail, a familiar brightness in her eyes he'd always been attracted to.

'I thought you were meant to be on leave this weekend,' he said.

'I hope you're not implying I muscled my way into your case, DS Kilshaw.'

Liam shrugged, remaining deadpan. 'I said we could meet up. You didn't need to crash the investigation to make it happen.'

Grace arched an eyebrow. 'Don't get ahead of yourself. I'm still your superior.'

'Don't I know it,' Liam said. 'Still, if there's time, I'd be up for that drink.'

Grace's face softened. 'If time allows,' she said.

◆ ◆ ◆

Liam arrived in Penzance an hour later. He parked just off Chapel Street, the morning traffic starting to thicken. The surf shop where Debbie worked was on the corner, a pale-blue-fronted unit with bleached signage and racks of hoodies and board shorts visible through the window. He pushed the door open, a bell chiming above his head.

The place was empty except for a young woman standing behind the till. Early twenties, dressed in a faded fleece and jeans. She looked up as he entered, her eyes bloodshot.

'Debbie Hawthorne?' he asked.

She nodded, her eyes watering again as she took in the warrant card.

'Do you know why I am here?' Liam asked gently.

Debbie's face crumpled. She turned away, pressing the heels of her hands to her eyes, but the tears came anyway. Her shoulders shook, her voice caught in her throat.

'I only found out this morning. Carys's mum called me. I couldn't believe it. I still don't.'

The bell above the door rang again. A customer stepped into the shop, glancing between the racks, oblivious to what they'd walked in on.

Liam turned, held up his warrant card with a firm shake of the head. 'Sorry. We're closed.'

Once the door had shut behind the customer, Liam turned back to Debbie.

'I'm surprised you came in today,' he said. 'You could've taken the day. No one would've blamed you.'

She gave a hollow laugh, wiping at her face with the sleeve of her fleece. 'I didn't have a choice. It's just me on rota today. And I didn't want to be at home. Some of Carys's stuff is still there. She has her own toothbrush for when she stays over.' She sniffed hard, trying to pull herself back together. 'I thought being here might help. Keep me distracted.'

'Can you lock the door for me, Debbie? Just while we talk.'

She nodded and moved stiffly, flicking the lock and turning the sign to 'Closed'. Liam followed her through a narrow staff-only door at the back of the shop into a small kitchenette. It smelt faintly of coffee and sea salt. Debbie opened a cupboard and filled a glass from the tap.

'Is it all right if I sit?' she asked.

'Of course.'

She lowered herself on to the edge of a stool, the glass trembling slightly in her hand.

'Tell me about Carys,' Liam said.

Debbie stared at the water for a second. 'We grew up on the same street. Same school, same classes. She was loud and funny and always into stuff before anyone else. I've known her my whole life.' Her voice cracked again.

Liam watched her, wondering why she was in the shop all alone. 'Do you know Kian?'

Debbie's mouth tightened. She didn't answer straight away, just stared down at the rim of the glass, her fingers tracing a small chip along the edge.

'Yeah,' she said eventually. 'Sort of.'

'You didn't like him?'

She shrugged – a small, dismissive movement. 'He was . . . controlling. Jealous, I think. Carys changed when she was with him. Didn't see much of anyone. Not like before.' Debbie looked up, her tired eyes meeting Liam's for the first time. 'We used to talk every day. Then it was once a week. Then only when she needed something.'

Debbie let out a slow breath as if she was on the verge of tears again.

'But I get it,' she said. 'That was just Carys. She always got swept up in things.' She looked away once more, and when she spoke her voice was lower. 'Didn't mean he was good for her.'

'Do you know where they used to go?' Liam asked. 'If they had somewhere private? Where they could be alone?'

Debbie shifted on the stool. 'Mostly his place. He's got this grotty little bedsit out near the bypass. But sometimes . . .'

Liam waited. 'Sometimes?'

Debbie sighed. 'They'd take the car – his horrible little purple car – and drive out somewhere quiet. She didn't really go into too much detail but you know . . .'

'Anywhere specific?'

'There's a spot. By the circle walk. Bit off the track, kind of tucked in behind some trees, I think.' She blushed. 'I went there once. With another boy.'

Liam stood. 'Thank you, Debbie. You should think about getting someone to cover your shift. You shouldn't be here on your own after something like this.'

Debbie gave a half-shrug, but didn't argue.

Liam showed her photographs of Tess Penrose and Anthony Ellison on his phone before leaving. 'Do you recognise either of them?'

She took the phone, staring at the screen as if looking right through it. 'From the news. The girl's the one they found first, right? And the boy's still missing?'

'Did Carys know Tony Ellison?'

Debbie shook her head, insistent. 'No. Not that I ever heard.'

'You sure?'

She hesitated. 'I'm sure.'

Liam held her gaze for a second longer, the pause dragging just enough to make him doubt her. He slipped a card from his pocket and placed it on the counter.

'If you remember anything else, anything at all, give me a call.'

Liam rang Jack as he reached the car, setting the phone to speaker as he pulled the door shut against the wind.

'Debbie said they used to drive out somewhere quiet,' he said. 'Somewhere near the Cober Valley walk in Helston.'

He could already hear Jack tapping away. 'That covers a fair stretch. Runs alongside the old railway line, wooded in parts, few pull-ins along the back lanes. There's one spot that might be worth a look just past Coverack Bridges, where the viaduct crosses the valley. Old lay-by behind the quarry workings. Bit overgrown, but looks like it's still accessible. Could have been used before the granite operations shut down.'

'Start there,' Liam said. 'Mark the others, too. Anything with cover, limited footfall and road access.'

'On it. I'll send you the grid and anything else that matches.'

Liam drove south, the morning pressing grey against the windscreen. The road curved through the outskirts of Helston, Liam's thoughts returning to how unjust it felt that Debbie should be working alone that day after such a loss.

He shook the thought away, his mind turning to Grace. She'd caught him off guard that morning and it had been good to see her. He hadn't expected to feel that, not after how strained things had become during the Godrevy case where her Met team's involvement had almost derailed everything. Hopefully things would be different this time. Grace was here to help and not to take over, and it was undeniable that they needed all the help they could get at present.

The copy of Preston's book was still on the passenger seat, its wrinkled edges the result of having been carried around more than read. Liam glanced at the cover as he turned off the main road, the track narrowing and the trees closing in. He still hadn't managed more than a few pages. The idea that a plausible explanation might be sitting there, tucked between chapters on ley lines and burial rites, was almost laughable but sometimes revelations came from the most unlikely sources.

Liam moved on to a single-track lane, wheels crunching over gravel and fallen twigs. The trees pressed close, heavy with rain, branches scraping the roof of the car. He followed the route Jack had marked, eyes scanning for any sign of the purple hatchback Kian Burrell had last been seen in.

A few cars were scattered along the verge, the area not as deserted as he'd expected. He passed a van half-sunk into the hedgerow, a family hatchback with steamed windows, a blue Peugeot with a broken wing mirror – but none of them matched the description Debbie had given him of Kian's car.

The track dipped slightly, the lane narrowing to the point where he was struggling to manoeuvre the car. As he rounded a corner, he spotted a small side path, half-hidden by branches. He pulled over, blocking the road, and made his way through the tangle of overgrowth. It only took him a few steps.

Half hidden beyond the bend, tucked just beyond a rise in the verge, he caught sight of a vehicle. A purple hatchback, the paint dulled by dirt, rear bumper scuffed, passenger window streaked with grime.

At first glance, there didn't seem to be any signs of a struggle. Like Anthony Ellison's vehicle, the car was locked. The windows were fogged and streaked, but through the grime Liam could make out the interior. Empty takeaway cartons on the passenger seat, crushed cans in the footwell, a hoodie balled up on the dashboard. Hardly the most romantic hangout, he thought as he called it in.

'We're going to have to tow it,' he said to Jack. 'It won't be an easy job.'

Liam stepped around to the rear of the hatchback and rapped his knuckles against the boot. It was the only part he couldn't see inside. He knocked again before returning to his car and retrieving the pry tools from the kit in the boot, Jack still on the call.

'What's going on here?' came a voice. A family SUV was parked up beside Liam's car, the driver's window down and a man looking at Liam like he'd just deliberately closed the road out of spite.

'Sorry, sir, police business,' Liam said, flashing his warrant card. 'Could be a while. I'd suggest backing up and trying another route.'

'Another route?' said the man, incredulous.

Liam ignored him and returned to Kian's car. 'Jack, I have reason to believe Kian may be in danger. I'm going to open the boot,' he said, for procedure's sake.

He wedged the flat end of the pry bar beneath the latch and gave it a careful nudge. The lock was stiff so he adjusted his grip, braced his foot against the bumper, and leant in with more force. The metal groaned but didn't budge. Taking a deep breath he tried again, the latch creaking and breaking, the boot popping open.

The smell was instant. Thick and cloying, its source unmistakable. Liam recoiled a step, one hand over his mouth.

The body was curled into the space like a discarded piece of furniture. Knees drawn up, arms tucked in tight. Kian Burrell's face was covered like the others, his features obliterated by a mask of clay.

Only this time, a red powder clung to the hardened clay, not the yellow they'd found on the two female victims.

Kian wasn't arranged like Tess and Carys. There was no formal prayer position for him. He'd been dumped in the boot of the car as if forgotten.

It suggested to Liam that Kian hadn't been the original target. It seemed more likely that he was a distraction. That the killer had murdered him so they could get access to Carys.

If that was true, the killer was even more ruthless than they'd imagined, and there was a significant danger there were more killings to come.

Chapter Seventeen

Liam cordoned off the road, taking shelter from the rain as he waited for the CSIs to arrive. He pulled Preston's book from the passenger seat, finally opening it properly for the first time. The pages were dense with historical references and folklore, but as he flicked through the chapter on stone circle legends, familiar details began to surface.

As Preston had alluded to previously, the myth of the Merry Maidens and people being turned to stone wasn't unique to that particular circle. Page after page described similar tales across Cornwall. The Nine Maidens of Boskednan – nine women petrified for dancing on the Sabbath, their fiddler frozen in a solitary stone nearby – needed no introduction, especially with the memory of Carys's tilted body never far from Liam's thoughts.

But there were other sites he already knew about. The Hurlers – the triple stone circles on Bodmin Moor – where men were turned to stone for playing the Cornish game of hurling on a Sunday, their musicians becoming the Pipers Stones. In addition, there were the Tregeseal Dancing Stones and Trippet Stones, all with the same theme of divine punishment for breaking sacred time.

And unless something turned in the investigation, it seemed inevitable that more bodies would be found at these sites.

Liam had closed the boot holding Kian's body, not wishing to contaminate the scene any further. The image of the young man crammed into the interior was fresh in his mind, the ochre found on his body a dirty red, not the limonite found on Tess and Carys. It suggested the killer appeared to be making a distinction between the sexes, and Liam searched for an explanation in Preston's book.

The legends said both men and women were turned to stone for breaking the Sabbath, so why had the killer arranged the female victims in the circles doused in limonite, while Kian had been dumped in the boot doused in red?

He searched through Preston's book for meaning, but couldn't see any distinction between the fates of males and females in the legends.

Preston had mentioned before about yellow being connected to new life, as well as sacrifice, and Liam wondered if there was something more sinister to the use of the dirty red ochre instead.

They'd been working on the logical conclusion that Tony Ellison was behind all of this. But Kian and Carys's deaths coming so soon after the discovery of the couple buried at the Merry Maidens gave Liam pause to reconsider.

If the killer was murdering couples, then it was feasible that Tony could be a victim too. Maybe his body was rotting in a discarded vehicle somewhere like Kian's. Though Liam's initial feeling was that Kian was almost an afterthought for the killer – a distraction from their ultimate goal of killing Carys – which would mean Tony still had to be considered as the prime suspect.

His phone buzzed with a text from Jack. CSI was fifteen minutes out. Liam turned back to Preston's book, searching for any reference to red ochre, any explanation for why males might be distinguished from females in these ancient punishments, but nothing obvious presented itself.

He dialled Preston's number, which went to voicemail after three rings.

'Raymond, it's DS Kilshaw. I need to speak with you urgently about your book. Specifically, about the different types of ochre mentioned and what they might mean in these legends. Please call me back as soon as possible.'

Two cars parked up behind him – a CSI van, and Maya's car. Maya stepped out, pulling on a raincoat.

'Can't leave you alone for a second, can we?' she said as Liam walked over to the car, Preston's book in his hand.

'Victim's in the boot. Similar MO, but he's dusted with red ochre instead of yellow.'

They waited for the CSIs to set up and open the boot once more. 'You know, Kilshaw, for someone who supposedly solves murders, you have a remarkable talent for finding the bodies first. At this rate, people are going to start getting suspicious,' Maya said, as they put on their CSI overcovers.

'Maybe I'm just that good at my job,' Liam said, deadpan.

'Stranger things have been known to be true, I suppose.' Maya glanced at the book in his hand. 'Finally getting round to reading it?'

'Just finished the chapter on stone circle legends. Still no explanation for the difference in yellow and red, beyond what we now know. I've left a message for Preston. If there is a particular pattern the killer is using, maybe he can point us in the right direction.'

'Let's hope so.'

The CSI team moved with practised efficiency, documenting the new crime scene.

Liam and Maya watched them from a distance. 'So, Grace just happened to show up for work the same weekend you're both supposed to have time off together?' Maya said. 'That's rather convenient.'

Maya was the only one of the team Liam trusted enough to have told about his previous relationship with Grace, though he imagined it was now common knowledge. 'Don't start. You know Hargreaves called them in.'

Maya smiled, making it clear her teasing wasn't over. 'Oh, I know. Just saying, she's looking particularly organised this morning. Very . . . focused. Might want to watch your back.'

'Watch my back? If anything, you should be worried. She's the same rank as you now, and she's got that whole Devon efficiency thing going. You'd have competition if a promotion ever came up.'

Maya laughed outright. 'Please. She can't even work out how to use our coffee machine. I'm safe. Besides, unlike her, I actually know how to handle you.'

'Handle me?' Liam raised an eyebrow.

'Someone has to,' Maya said, patting his shoulder.

By the time CSI had finished, dusk was settling. Kian's body had been loaded into the forensics van, the purple hatchback secured for transport to the police compound.

One of the CSI technicians approached Liam and Maya, peeling off her gloves as she walked. 'Preliminary observations,' she said, consulting her tablet. 'Cause of death is most likely suffocation, like the others. He's been there a good twelve hours or so.'

'And the paralytic?' Maya asked.

'There's at least one injection mark but no defensive wounds, so it's possible. My guess is he died the same way as the others but of course that is all subject to post-mortem findings.'

Liam took a deep breath, refusing to dwell on what Kian may have experienced. He could already feel his chest tightening.

His phone buzzed, a number on the screen he didn't recognise.

'Kilshaw.'

'Hello, DS Kilshaw. It's Debbie. From the shop. Earlier today.'

'Hi, Debbie. Is everything alright?'

'I've been thinking all day. About what you asked. About Carys and those places they used to go.' Her voice was tight, and she hesitated before continuing. 'There's something I didn't tell you.'

'What didn't you tell me, Debbie?'

Liam heard her breath quickening on the other end of the line. 'I lied to you when you asked if Carys knew that boy. The one who's missing.'

'Anthony Ellison?' Liam said, receiving a look from Maya.

'Yes.' The word came out barely above a whisper. 'Carys did know him. They . . . they slept together. It was supposed to be a secret. She was still with Kian at the time. She swore me to secrecy.'

Liam exchanged a look with Maya, who had moved closer to listen. 'Why didn't you tell me this earlier?'

'I panicked. I didn't want to get involved. And Carys made me promise not to tell anyone about it. She was terrified Kian would find out.'

'When did this happen?'

'A few weeks ago. Just once, she said. But she felt awful about it. Kept talking about how she needed to end things with Kian, but I think she was scared of him.'

Liam was about to ask another question when Debbie's voice cracked.

'There's something else,' she said.

The line went silent, and for a second Liam thought she'd hung up until he heard her laboured breathing, as if she was on the verge of tears. 'What is it, Debbie?'

Liam heard the sobs, Debbie battling through her distress until she managed to speak.

'I slept with him too.'

Chapter Eighteen

The biting wind off Mount's Bay did little to improve Liam's mood as he parked at Penzance police station, where he'd arranged to meet Debbie. The sky was a bruised purple, threatening more rain. It pushed down on the town as if trying to engulf it, and Liam was glad when he reached the station and the familiar scent of old coffee and damp hit him.

Ted Fletcher looked up from the front desk as Liam walked through reception, a knowing glint in his eye. 'Well, well, if it isn't DS Kilshaw gracing us with his presence,' he said, his voice carrying its usual hint of amusement. 'Thought you'd be tucked up warm in Bodmin on a day like this. Your DI Trent beat you here, by the way. Waiting for you upstairs. Seemed keen. The girl is here too – Debbie Hawthorne.'

'Always a pleasure,' Liam said, heading upstairs after Ted had beeped him through.

The interview room at Penzance lacked the worn-in familiarity of headquarters. It felt regressive being in the place where Liam had started his police career. Liam had suggested meeting Debbie here. It was closer for her and, as Maya pointed out, closer for him. He entered the interview room to see Maya already in conversation with Debbie. 'You remember my colleague,' she said.

Perched on the edge of a standard-issue plastic chair, Debbie Hawthorne looked up at him. She clutched a paper cup of water in both hands, her knuckles white. Liam noted the tremor in her hands, and the way her eyes avoided his and Maya's.

It had been another long night. After Debbie's call, he'd gone back to headquarters, eventually getting home around midnight. Sleep had been a long time coming. He'd gone over Kian Burrell's death, the red ochre, and the new link between Tony Ellison and the second victim, as well as to Debbie. He'd tried Preston's phone again before leaving his flat, the archaeologist yet to return his call.

Now, facing Debbie in the interview room, the unease surrounding Anthony Ellison solidified. If what Debbie had told him yesterday was true, Ellison had slept with both the victims, which more than implicated him as the prime suspect. It also meant that Debbie was in potential danger – not to mention the same perhaps being true of a growing number of young women countywide.

Maya leant forward a fraction, her voice calm but firm the way it always was when she began an interview. 'Debbie, thank you again for coming in. We appreciate this is difficult. We just need to go over some of what you told DS Kilshaw last night, fill in a few more details. Let's start with Carys Rowden and Anthony Ellison. You mentioned Carys knew him?'

Debbie nodded, her gaze still fixed on the paper cup.

Liam looked towards Maya. 'You said on the phone Carys had slept with Tony Ellison. Can you tell us about that? How did they meet?'

Debbie twisted the cup in her hands. 'It was three or four months ago, not long after Christmas. We'd gone out in Penzance. Just us girls. Carys had a bit too much to drink, you know how it is.' She gave a small, nervous shrug. 'We were in that club near the harbour, the one that's always packed. This lad, Tony, he just came over. Started talking to Carys. He was . . . charming, I guess. Carys was laughing a lot. She seemed really taken with him, proper smitten. Even then, I thought she should slow down, take it easy.'

She paused again, taking a sip of water. 'As the night went on, Carys got more into it. They were dancing for ages. Then I saw them kissing over by the bar. I told her to take it steady, but she just waved me off.' Debbie looked down. 'Tony wasn't drinking. When it was time to go, he said he'd drive Carys home. I got a taxi with one of the other girls.'

'So Tony drove Carys home that night? Did you speak to Carys the next day, Debbie?' Maya asked.

Debbie nodded, her eyes flicking up to meet Maya's for a moment before dropping back down. 'Yeah. She called me. She was . . . a mess. Proper upset.' She picked at a loose thread. 'Said it was a mistake, that she shouldn't have gone with him. Just a one-night thing. She sounded really down on herself. She was supposed to be seeing Kian, and I think she was worried he would find out.'

'What was she worried about? That he would split up with her?'

'She said he'd go mad if he knew. She kept saying, "He can't know, Debs. He just can't know."'

'Did Carys see Tony Ellison again after that night?' Liam asked.

Debbie shook her head. 'No. She swore she wouldn't. She said it was a stupid mistake. She just wanted to forget it, pretend it never happened and I'm pretty sure Kian never found out.'

Maya shifted, her pen making a small scratch on the notepad. 'Debbie,' she began, her voice maintaining a calm and even tone, 'you told DS Kilshaw last night that you also . . . had an encounter with Tony Ellison. Can you tell us how that came about, given what you knew about Carys's experience?'

Debbie looked up, a flush rising on her cheeks. She took another breath, this one deeper. 'He just turned up at the surf shop one afternoon. I recognised him immediately. It was maybe a week or two after . . . after Carys. I was on my own. He was just . . . nice. He remembered me from that night out. I was flattered, I suppose.' She dropped her gaze. 'Carys was back with Kian, trying to make things normal. It just sort of happened.'

Debbie's face was a deep red now, her eyes fixed on the crumpled cup she was systematically destroying between her fingers. Liam and Maya waited for some time in silence. Liam kept his expression neutral. Pushing too hard might make the young woman clam up. 'How many times did you meet with Tony after that day in the shop?' he asked.

Debbie bit her lip. 'Four times. We met up four times.' Her voice was close to a whisper. 'Then he just called it off. Said it wasn't working for him, or something like that.' She shrugged – a small, defeated movement. 'I was a bit upset but I knew what it was. For him, it was just sex, wasn't it? Not like it meant anything more.'

Liam watched Debbie's fingers work the last of the cup into shreds. Her statement was painting a fuller picture of Tony Ellison, closer to the portrayal initially given by Sturridge and Whitstable at the farm.

It suggested Ellison was acutely aware of his appeal to women, and was willing to use it to the full, whatever the consequences.

However, it was markedly different to the way Danny Reeve had spoken about his friend. Liam thought the truth about Tony Ellison might fall somewhere between the two.

Maya leant in again. 'Debbie, apart from yourself and Carys, do you know of any other girls Tony was seeing or had seen?'

Debbie shook her head, the flush yet to leave her cheeks. 'He's popular. Girls like him. But no, I don't know any names. He wasn't one to talk about things like that – not with me, anyway.'

'Has he tried to contact you at all, Debbie? Since Tess Penrose died?' Liam asked.

Debbie's eyes widened. 'What? No. Of course not. Why would he?' she said before something seemed to dawn on her. 'Oh god,' she whispered, her voice faint. 'You think Tony . . . you think he killed them?' Her gaze darted between Liam and Maya, raw fear now replacing the embarrassment. 'Am I in danger?'

'Right now, Debbie, we don't have enough information to say for sure,' Liam said, keeping his voice calm. 'But it's sensible to be cautious. Be aware of your surroundings. If you see anything or anyone that makes you feel uneasy, you call us straight away. Is there somewhere else you could stay for a few days? Family? Friends?'

Debbie nodded, seeming to shrink a little further into the hard plastic chair. She drew a shaky hand across her eyes. 'My dad,' she said, her voice still thin but with a new resolve. 'He's got a flat over in Camborne. I can go and stay with him for a bit.'

After Debbie left, escorted by a uniformed officer who would take her to her father's flat, Liam and Maya paid Danny Reeve another visit. Reeve's vision of Tony Ellison appeared to be at odds with what they were discovering, and Liam agreed it would be good to get another take from him after recent events.

They took their separate cars to Danny's flat share. The wipers on Liam's car pushed sheets of rain across the windscreen as he headed out of Penzance. The grey sea to his left churned under the wind. He thought of Ellison as he drove, and wondered how many other women he'd slept with, and how many of them were in danger.

He pulled up a few doors down from Danny Reeve's house, Maya parking behind him. The rain was relentless now, soaking them as they ran to the house and knocked on the door.

Footsteps shuffled inside, the door creaking open a few inches. Danny Reeve peered out, his face pale, his hair tousled. He was wearing a faded dressing gown, pulled tight at the waist. He blinked at them as if surprised to see anyone, his lethargic movements suggesting to Liam that he might be stoned. Recognition slowly flickered in his eyes, then quickly turned to apprehension.

He pulled the dressing gown tighter. 'What's going on? Is it . . . Has something happened to Tony?'

Liam met Danny's worried gaze. He looked like he hadn't slept much since their last visit. 'Can we come in, Danny?' Liam asked, his voice low against the drumming rain. 'It's about Tony, yes. There have been some developments, but he's still missing. We were hoping you might be able to help us again.'

Danny hesitated for a moment, his eyes darting past them to the rainswept street before he stepped back, pulling the door wider. 'Yeah, course. Come in.'

The air in the living room was stale, thick with the smell of unwashed clothes and old takeaways. A half-eaten pizza sat on a low table, and on the large television screen, a brightly coloured video game was paused mid-action. It looked like little had moved since they were last here and Liam wondered to himself if Danny ever left the place.

Danny gestured vaguely towards the battered sofa where Liam had sat previously, before slumping into the same worn gaming chair he'd occupied during their first conversation. Maya took the other end of the sofa.

They sat that way for a while, the silence broken only by the relentless drumming of rain against the window. Liam waited a moment, letting Danny settle. 'You heard about Carys Rowden, Danny?' he asked, his voice even.

Danny nodded, his gaze fixed on the paused game on the screen. 'Yeah. Saw it on the news. Terrible.' He swallowed hard.

'From what we've been told, Tony had a one-night stand with Carys not long before she died.'

Danny shifted in the gaming chair, the worn material creaking under his slight weight. His eyes, which had been fixed on the frozen image on the television, flicked towards Liam, then away again fast. 'A one-night stand?' he repeated, running a hand through his already messy hair. 'What . . . what does that mean?'

Liam held Danny's gaze. 'It means Tony was involved with Tess Penrose, who was murdered. And now we know he was involved with Carys Rowden, who was also murdered. That makes two young women Tony had known – had slept with – both found dead in near identical circumstances.'

Danny's face, already pale, seemed to lose all remaining colour. He stared at Liam, then at Maya, as if searching for a way out. The hand that had been running through his hair now gripped the armrest of the gaming chair. 'No,' he said, his voice cracking. 'No, that's not right. I told you, Tony would never hurt anyone. He's not like that.'

'Carys Rowden had a boyfriend, Danny. Kian Burrell. He was found murdered too,' Maya said. 'Did Tony ever mention Kian to you?'

'Kian? No. Never heard of him. Who's Kian?'

'We just told you. Kian Burrell was Carys Rowden's boyfriend, Danny. His body was found yesterday. It hasn't been released to the news yet,' Liam said.

Danny pushed himself upright in the gaming chair, his knuckles white from where he'd gripped the armrests. 'What the hell is going on?' he said, his voice rising. 'Tess, Carys, and now her boyfriend? And Tony's still missing? This is insane.'

Liam kept his tone level, trying to cut through Danny's rising panic. 'We know Tony is popular with girls, Danny. We've spoken to a few people now. Did he talk about them much? Did he see them as conquests, notches on his bedpost?'

Danny's head snapped towards Liam. 'Conquests? What are you on about? He's a nineteen-year-old lad, for Christ's sake. He liked girls, girls liked him. Where's the crime in that?'

Liam held up a hand. 'We're just trying to get to the bottom of this. We think Tony might be in danger and getting a better understanding of what motivated him will only help us.'

'Well, he never referred to them as conquests. At least not to me.'

Maya nodded. 'Understood, Danny. What more can you tell us about his interest in folklore and the stone circles? Do you know where that interest came from?'

Danny seemed to deflate a little at the change of subject. He slumped back into the gaming chair, running both hands through his hair this time. He stared at the TV screen, as if the answer might be hidden there.

'His mum, I think,' he said at last, his voice quiet again. 'Tony said she was proper into all that stuff. Cornish legends, old stones, the lot. Said she was some sort of literary professor, or something like that. I don't know, maybe it's to do with that. Obviously, he was hugely affected when she died. Could be that was when it started.'

Liam understood Danny was talking about Tony's interest in mythology, but Liam had to wonder if his mother's death would prove to be the catalyst for Tony's eventual killing spree.

Chapter Nineteen

They quizzed Danny some more about Tony's mother before leaving, but the boy was so high he'd stopped making sense. Liam called Jack on his way back to St Ives and asked him to look further into Tony's mother before calling Rory Ellison. Tony's father confirmed his late wife's deep immersion in Cornish legends and historic sites, and that Tony's own interest had stemmed directly from her books and stories as a child.

A text from Jack flashed up as Liam arrived in St Ives – a digital flyer about a vigil due to take place on the beach opposite St Michael's Mount in the next hour. A service being held by Reverend Frayne's congregation.

Liam was due to meet Grace later for a drink, but this wasn't something he could ignore. He took the road south, noting the nearby car parks in Marazion were already filling with vehicles.

The vigil was in celebration of Tess Penrose and the other recent victims, and had clearly caught the imagination of the locals. Liam drove on and parked in the gravel lot of a small hotel, not wanting to draw attention to himself.

By the time he reached the beach, people had started gathering. It was still light, but they held candles and lit torches. The crowd must have numbered over a hundred. Liam tried to remain inconspicuous, but with his height and bald scalp, he blended in poorly.

He caught sight of Reverend Frayne, dressed in brightly coloured robes, standing beside Phillipa Penrose, who wore a yellow summer dress. Liam tried to reconcile what he was seeing. Frayne had mentioned the use of ochre in his services and the colour yellow, but Tess and the other victims had been dusted with limonite when their bodies were positioned. It made him uncomfortable to see her mother dressed in that colour. Perhaps Phillipa was trying to reclaim some power from whoever had taken her daughter. If so, she could only be applauded, but Liam still felt uneasy about the whole situation.

The crowd began to move, Frayne and Phillipa at the front, leading everyone towards St Michael's Mount. Liam joined the rear of the procession, following the flickering glow of the flames.

He sidestepped a washed-up jellyfish as a woman handed him a candle with a welcoming smile. The group began singing, a traditional Christian hymn he recognised but didn't know the words to.

A feeling of peace came over him as he walked in silence. The sound of the hymns, the eerie glow of the torches and the salt air . . . He hadn't expected it to be moving, but it was.

Frayne stopped at the stone causeway that stretched across the bay to the Mount. The path was still visible, but with the tide turning, it wouldn't remain dry for long. Liam smiled to himself, remembering past summers watching tourists caught by the tide, wading awkwardly through the rising waters to safety.

The singing died down as Frayne addressed the crowd. 'We are here to celebrate the life of Tess Penrose, taken too soon from us,' he said.

Behind him, St Michael's Mount rose into the clouds. The sky was darkening now, the flames casting a warm glow across the crowd and the silhouette of the island.

As Frayne continued talking, a man turned towards Liam.

'What are you doing here?' he asked, the words confrontational, and causing a number of people to look his way.

It was Jerry Penrose, Tess's father. The last time they'd met, Jerry had been drunk and slurring his words. He wasn't carrying a candle now, and Liam saw in his face the drawn look of someone who hadn't slept in days.

'I'm just here to pay my respects,' Liam said, keeping his voice low.

The singing resumed before Jerry could respond. Liam was glad of the interruption. Though Jerry's alibis had checked out, Liam couldn't help but view him with suspicion, especially as he'd chosen to lurk at the back rather than stand at the front with his estranged wife.

As the tide crept in, Frayne stepped forward to announce a final ceremony. 'We cannot let this evil defeat us,' he said.

The congregation formed into lines, as if it were a routine they had rehearsed.

Liam took the moment to slip away, moving towards the darker edges of the rocks. From there he watched the congregation step forward one by one, each bowing their head. At first, he thought they were receiving a blessing, or perhaps communion. But as they returned to the group, he caught glimpses of their foreheads, which had been marked with something.

He crept back towards the edge of the group, the torchlight forming broken patterns in the darkening sky. Close enough to confirm what he'd suspected. Each forehead had been marked with a streak of paint, which on closer inspection almost had to be yellow ochre.

◆ ◆ ◆

If Frayne was involved in the killings, he was certainly being brazen about it. Liam supposed the dousing of limonite could be a double bluff, but it would be a stupid way to draw attention to himself.

Either way, Liam made a note to do further research into Frayne's organisation as he headed back towards St Ives to meet Grace. He understood why they may have chosen to douse each other with the limonite, and Phillipa Penrose had been one of their number on the beach, so he didn't think there was anything sinister about the ceremony he'd witnessed. But if nothing else it demonstrated that multiple people in the congregation had access to limonite, and he wanted the material used during the vigil to be tested against that found at the crime scenes.

The bar Grace had chosen was on the top floor of a hotel near the Tate, its wide windows offering a panoramic, if rain-streaked, view of St Ives Bay. She was sitting at a small table in the corner, a half-empty wine glass in front of her. The place was quiet, only a few other drinkers scattered around, the low lighting and the sound of the wind outside creating a subdued atmosphere.

She looked up as he approached, a small smile forming on her lips. 'Better late than never.'

Liam sat down and took a slow sip of the beer the waitress had placed before him. 'Apologies, some of us just never stop working. You'd understand that if you were a member of the Cornwall team.'

He told her about what Danny Reeve had told him about Tony's mother, the literary professor who was into folklore, and what happened at the vigil.

'They were dousing each other with limonite?'

'As far as I could make out.'

'I suppose that's one way to retain power.' Grace picked up her wine glass, slowly swirling the red liquid before taking a small sip. 'You hadn't picked up on the mother before?'

There was no accusation in the comment. At least, none that Liam could discern. 'We knew she was an English academic, which was probably where Tony's interest in the subject came from.

According to Danny, much of her work was on folklore, including an interest in mythical sites.'

'Such as stone circles?'

'Yep.'

'What are you thinking? Her death hit him so hard that it turned into some kind of obsession?'

'Wouldn't be the first time, would it?'

Grace smiled and Liam felt his shoulders slump. 'Too much shop talk?' he asked.

'Maybe a little. Shall we take a couple of hours off?'

Grace was right but Liam couldn't completely banish thoughts of the investigation. He always did this, let the job seep into every corner of his life. 'Deal,' he said, taking another sip of his beer. 'No more shop talk, I promise.'

Just as the words left his mouth, his phone buzzed.

Liam glanced at the screen, an unknown number. 'Sorry, I should probably take this. Be right back, promise.' Grace gave a small smirk as Liam pushed his chair back and stood up.

He walked out of the main bar area, finding a quieter spot on a small, covered balcony overlooking the harbour. The wind whipped around him, carrying the sharp scent of salt and the distant cries of gulls. 'Kilshaw.'

'DS Kilshaw? It's Raymond Preston. I hope I'm not interrupting anything.'

'Raymond,' Liam said, his voice raised a little against the wind. 'You're a hard man to get hold of.'

He heard Preston's apologetic chuckle on the other end. 'My sincere apologies. It's been a rather busy day – fieldwork, you know how it is.'

Liam pictured the archaeologist, tweed-clad and enthusiastic, despite the weather. 'Actually, I've been meaning to tell you. I've started reading your book,' he said.

A distinct note of pleasure entered Preston's voice. 'Have you indeed? Excellent. I do hope you're finding it informative.'

'It is,' Liam said, the image of Kian Burrell's body, curled tightly in the boot of his car, flashing unwelcome in his mind. 'I've been trying to uncover some more information about the ochre we have found at the sites. You mentioned before about limonite representing rebirth, spring and summer – that sort of thing. I couldn't see any mention of it in the book.'

'Ah, the ochres – yes, fascinating subject,' Preston said, his voice warming to the topic. 'The symbolism can be quite specific, though interpretations vary, of course, across cultures and time. Generally speaking, yellow ochre, or limonite as it's often derived, is frequently associated with the sun, with the earth itself, as I think I mentioned to you before. It can represent life, creation, the sacred feminine. You see it used in contexts of fertility rites, or to mark spaces or figures connected to earth goddesses, that sort of thing.'

Liam pictured Tess and Carys, their faceless bodies coated with yellow, and the night's vigil. 'What about in remembrance?'

'Yes, that as well, I guess. Death is often seen as a beginning in many cultures.'

Liam frowned, letting that implication settle in his mind. 'And red ochre?'

'Red is a very potent symbol. Most obviously, it connects to blood, to life force, but also to death and burial. It's often found in funerary contexts, perhaps to restore vitality to the deceased in the afterlife, or as a protective element. It can also signify power, masculine energy, sometimes used for warriors or in rituals pertaining to male deities or significant male figures.'

Preston's explanation slotted into the way they'd been thinking. Yellow for the female victims, Tess and Carys – the 'maidens', perhaps. Red for Kian Burrell, the male. 'That's very helpful, Raymond, thank you. One last thing, if you don't mind.

Have you ever come across an academic by the name of Dr Althea Marlowe? I believe she also had a keen interest in Cornish folklore. She was a literary professor at Exeter University.'

There was a sharp intake of breath on the other end of the line. 'Dr Marlowe?' Preston's voice sounded distant. 'Yes, of course. Why do you ask?'

'What can you tell me?' Liam said, not ready to divulge any details about her being Tony's mother.

'Her work was seminal, groundbreaking in many ways. Particularly her theories on the psycho-geography of the ancient sites, the ritualistic alignments. Many considered her views unorthodox, of course – even radical – but her understanding of the deeper narratives embedded in the landscape were quite unparalleled. I've cited her extensively. A brilliant mind. Tragically lost too soon. What possible connection could she have to all of this?'

Liam gripped the phone tighter. 'That's what we're trying to determine, Mr Preston. Dr Marlowe was Anthony Ellison's mother.'

The line went quiet. The only sound was the wind howling around the balcony and the distant crash of waves. After a long moment, Preston finally spoke, his voice devoid of its usual energy. 'I see.'

Liam was growing suspicious. Preston had given talks at Truro College when Tony Ellison had been a student there. A student whose mother was a seminal figure in Preston's own field of study, a student who shared that same deep interest, and yet he claimed not to remember Anthony Ellison.

'Did you know Tony was her son, Raymond? A young man, keen on folklore, son of an academic you admired. It seems like he might have made an impression.'

The pause was longer this time. 'As I said, Sergeant, many students pass through those talks. I meet a great number of enthusiasts. No, the name Anthony Ellison still doesn't ring any specific bells beyond what I now know of him, I'm afraid.'

Preston's voice, though polite, carried a note of finality. Liam knew he wouldn't get any more from him on that point now. 'Right. Well, thank you for your time again, Raymond.'

He stepped back into the warmth of the bar. Grace looked up from her phone, a fresh glass of wine and another beer now on the table. 'Everything alright?'

Liam nodded, taking his seat. 'No more shop talk, remember.'

It felt good to be in Grace's company. They finished their drinks in a more relaxed silence this time, the case pushed to the back of his mind for a moment.

'Another?' Liam asked, when their glasses were empty.

Grace shook her head. 'Better not. I'm driving.'

Liam hesitated, the words forming before he'd fully considered them. 'You could always stay?'

Chapter Twenty

He placed his hand over the book and whispered a prayer before marking it with the limonite.

She would probably have chided him for such a thing, but it was all he had of her now and as such was the holiest thing he knew.

Plans were going awry. The maidens were being cautious. He'd always known that after the first, things would be difficult, but he hadn't anticipated this. He was struggling to find anyone alone.

His mind wandered to the other evening and the dismal sight of Carys and that non-entity in the back of the car. He shuddered at the memory, still unsure if he'd made a mistake with her.

She'd looked so beautiful at the circle, head bowed in contrition, but she hadn't had proper time to repent. He wondered if that was to do with the boy she'd been with, if the way he'd sullied her had affected her somehow, had allowed the clay to harden before she'd fully learnt to endure.

He moved from address to address, biding his time. He had contingencies. The maidens didn't necessarily have to come from the list, and sooner or later that wouldn't be possible anyway. But for now, there was a symmetry in moving through the list and he'd spotted a perfect opportunity.

Innocence meant something different in this day and age. There hadn't been much innocence left in Carys, but he'd seen it that first time at the Merry Maidens. Tess had been special, and there had been such exquisite joy in watching her turn. He'd been telling Carys all about it when she'd succumbed, which had been a great shame.

But now, catching sight of the young woman down the road, he thought that may have been part of the plan.

Chapter Twenty-One

The sharp crack of the cricket ball meeting the bat carried across the playing field. Liam sat alone on a low wooden bench just beyond the boundary rope, huddled against the cold for the early season match, his gaze fixed on George at the crease. His son held the bat with a determined stance, eyes narrowed on the bowler.

Further along the boundary, near the small pavilion, he saw Kim, George's mother, talking to her partner, Mark. They were laughing at something, Mark's arm resting easy on Kim's shoulder. A familiar pang, dull and distant, went through Liam.

Grace had ended up staying the night and things were all of a sudden much more complicated. He watched Kim and Mark, a picture of settled domesticity, and wondered if inviting Grace back, even for one night, had been a mistake.

Since Kim, his longest relationships had been with Grace, that first time years ago, and then more recently with Millie. There had been a string of others – mostly one-night stands or short-term flings that burnt out quickly. He thought of Tony Ellison, the young man at the centre of everything, moving between women with an ease that now felt uncomfortably familiar. Was he really that different from a nineteen-year-old lad when it came to women?

He'd had breakfast with Grace that morning at a little café by the wharf. For a while, it had felt easy, like the old times when they were just starting out. But they had both been restless, Liam's thoughts drifting from thoughts of Grace and Millie to the investigation and where it would take him next.

A shout pulled him from his reverie. He looked up to see that George was out, caught by the wicketkeeper. His son trudged back towards the boundary, head down.

'Unlucky, mate. Good effort,' Liam called, as George strode past without looking at him.

Liam stood as Kim and Mark approached, the usual awkward pleasantries exchanged as George walked over, having taken his pads off.

Mark clapped George on the back, offering words of encouragement that Liam felt he should have said.

Liam held no resentment towards Mark. He'd stepped in when Liam had failed in his duties, and was a big part of the reason why George was so well adjusted. Any envy he felt was due to the reminder of his own failures. It was George who was the important one and for that he was glad Mark was in their lives.

The conversation was brief and soon Liam was saying his goodbyes. He gave George a hug, a familiar melancholy creeping over him as he walked back to his car alone.

He banished the feeling by focusing on the investigation, his thoughts turning to the other women Tony had slept with, who would not even know they were in danger.

Back in his flat he made a cup of tea, the warmth doing little to combat the chill that had settled in his bones from the cricket field. Raymond Preston's book lay on the small table beside his armchair. He picked it up, forcing himself to focus. There had to be something in its pages, some detail about ritual, about the significance of the sites, that he'd missed.

He turned the pages, the academic text dense, but the week's accumulated tiredness pressed down, making the words blur. His eyelids grew heavy, the book slipping from his grasp as a wave of exhaustion finally claimed him.

He woke with a start, the room still dark, his neck stiff from sleeping slumped in the chair. His phone screen glowed: 5.03 a.m. Monday morning. The exhaustion still clung to him, but he was already growing restless to be back at work. He pushed himself up, the floorboards cold underfoot, and pulled on his running gear. The pre-dawn air outside would be biting, but he needed the burn in his lungs to help him focus.

◆ ◆ ◆

After his run, he met with Maya at a coffee shop in Truro city centre. She sat at a table near the front, a black coffee waiting for him. They'd arranged a meeting with Rory Ellison in thirty minutes.

'How was your weekend?' Maya asked, a familiar look on her face. One that suggested she knew he'd been up to no good.

'Sleep, mainly,' Liam said, fighting the urge to tell Maya about his night out with Grace and her staying the night. He wanted to share with someone his doubts and concerns, but it didn't feel fair on Grace at that point, and his own thoughts on the subject were still jumbled.

Maya held his gaze for a few seconds, Liam understanding why so many interviewees crumbled in her presence. 'What about you?'

Although Maya took a strong interest in Liam's personal life, she didn't tend to share much detail about her own. The most Liam knew was that she had an on-and-off girlfriend called Jane, about whom she rarely offered updates.

'Catching up on my sleep, too,' she said, sipping her coffee.

Liam waited, knowing she'd yet to stop grilling him. It was something he saw in her interview techniques, a relentlessness that often got the most tight-lipped talking.

‘What’s it like having Grace back on the team?’ she asked.

Liam noted a slight raise of her eyebrows, an upturn in her mouth. He wondered if she somehow knew about him sleeping with Grace again, and once more it was all he could do not to blurt it out.

‘What’s it like for you?’ he said, trying to turn the tables. ‘Must be difficult having another DI on staff.’

Maya shrugged the comment off as she had the last time. ‘There’s only one DI on our team, as you well know,’ she said with a smile. ‘Now drink up, I don’t want to be late.’

They took the short walk along King Street to the Truro offices of Rory Ellison’s firm. The man was waiting for them in reception. He was wearing an immaculately tailored three-piece navy suit, but Liam spotted red lines in his eyes and rash marks on his neck where he’d shaved too quickly. The last time they’d spoken to him had been by phone when his son’s vehicle had been discovered abandoned.

‘I’ve got us a conference room so we can speak. I’ve got twenty minutes at most,’ Rory said by way of greeting. ‘Can I get either of you a drink?’

Liam and Maya shook their heads.

‘Just black coffee for me,’ Rory said to the receptionist before walking off down the corridor. Liam noted a slight tremor in the man’s hand as he opened the conference room door, and wondered if he was hungover.

‘What are you doing to find my son?’ Rory asked, sitting down at a large oval table.

‘We’re doing everything we can,’ Liam replied, knowing how redundant the words must sound and the blind panic he would be feeling if it was George who’d gone missing.

The receptionist arrived with a tray of drinks. ‘I brought a couple of extra cups, just in case,’ she said, placing a pot of coffee on the table. Rory gave her a short, curt smile before she left, closing the door behind her.

'Sure I can't tempt you?' Rory said, pouring for himself.

Liam still had the taste of coffee in his mouth. 'Go on, then,' he said, helping himself to a cup.

Maya explained the reason they were there and gave an update on recent events, though Rory likely already knew. She told him about Carys's body being found at the stone circle and the subsequent discovery of her boyfriend, Kian, in the boot of his car.

Rory held the coffee cup in front of him, steam billowing in the air-conditioned room. 'I heard about that young man. What does it all mean? There was no sign of Tony by his car?' He winced as he sipped his coffee, gripping the mug tightly to control his trembling hand.

'That's what we're trying to ascertain,' Maya said. 'One thing we have discovered – although only anecdotally at the moment – is that the second victim, Carys, previously had sexual relations with your son.'

Rory placed his coffee down, eyes widening as he looked from Maya to Liam. He shook his head slowly, clearly drawing his own conclusions as to what he was being told. 'You can't be serious. Tony would never do something like this. It must be a coincidence.'

'Of course, it could be,' Liam said, playing along. 'From what we understand, Tony is particularly sexually active.'

'What the hell does that mean?'

'It means we know of at least four women he's slept with in the last six months, two of whom are now dead,' Maya said, her face unreadable.

'He's nineteen years old. I don't think that's a particularly high number.'

'Maybe, maybe not,' Maya said, 'but the two deaths are a statistic I'm particularly interested in at the moment. You need to help us, Mr

Ellison. The sooner we find Tony, the sooner we can rule him out as a potential suspect.'

Neither of them added the main reason they wanted to find Tony – the fear that if they didn't do so soon, then there would be another dead body to add to the list of victims.

'Of course, that's what I want. I'm at my wit's end. I can barely sleep. I've phoned all his friends, our family – as you suggested – but no one's seen or heard from him. Have you managed to track his phone yet?' Rory asked, trying to regain control.

Liam shook his head. 'The last time Tony's phone was active was the night of the party in Penzance when he left with Tess. There's definitely no sign he returned to your house at any point?'

'Of course not. I'd tell you if he had.'

Liam pictured the Piper Stone at the Merry Maidens site and the yellow ochre found on the monolith. It was all too easy to see another young woman against the plinth, caught forever in the prayer pose.

Maya steered the conversation to the other reason they were there. 'We understand Tony's mum was a university lecturer,' she said.

Rory glanced at the expensive watch on his wrist. 'That's right,' he said, his voice lowering. 'Medieval literature.'

'She was interested in mythology and folklore?' Liam asked.

'She loved all that stuff,' Rory said with a smile. 'I guess that's where Tony got his interest. He's always been into fantasy. When Althea died, I think he buried himself in books to escape reality. It was a difficult time for both of us, as you can imagine. In fact, it doesn't really get any easier.'

'Did your wife ever discuss or write about stone circles or sites of mythological interest in Cornwall?' Maya asked.

'I don't know what you're getting at, but you can check her published works. I'm sure she would've covered that topic. I'm much more of a practical man than she was or Tony is. I never quite understood such things. I'm about facts and figures – more numbers than words.' He glanced at his watch again. 'I'm sorry, but I have an important meeting now.'

He stood, his coffee cup still half-full.

'One thing before you go,' Liam said, remaining seated. 'Have you ever come across a man called Raymond Preston? He has similar interests to your wife's.'

Rory shook his head. 'I'm afraid not. I'm sure you'll get a list of her colleagues from her old faculty, but I don't recall meeting anyone named Preston. Now if you'll excuse me, I really must go.'

Chapter Twenty-Two

Liam and Maya returned to headquarters, where Grace was working in the incident room with her two colleagues.

As Maya ran through a morning briefing, the main focus of which was securing the stone circle sites and checking the safety of Tony's previous love interests, Liam and Grace did their best to ignore each other. Although he felt like it would soon become obvious to everyone what had happened between them, Liam still wasn't sure how he felt about the encounter.

In many ways, it had felt right. The continuation of a relationship that had prematurely ended when he had moved back to Cornwall and Grace had stayed in London.

It could be that Grace wanted nothing more than something physical, and he was getting ahead of himself. But Liam thought it was probably more than that. And he wasn't sure if that was what he wanted. Whether his mind was still on Millie, or because he simply didn't feel that way any more, he wasn't sure.

He didn't get time to speak to her before driving home that evening. She and her team had been assigned further interview duties, Maya keen to exhaust every contact known to Tony Ellison, particularly in developing the list of known sexual partners, which seemed to be growing by the day.

That evening, Liam downloaded a couple of Althea Marlowe's books. The first was, to his eyes, a dry textbook on medieval literature. He skimmed the chapters related to Cornwall but found little relevant to stone circles. It was the second book that piqued his interest, however. In some ways, it reminded him of the smaller volume he'd read by Raymond Preston, though the language was more academic, at times bordering on impenetrable.

One of the major chapters focused on stone circles, specifically the Merry Maidens and the Hurlers on Bodmin Moor – the triple stone circles linking to a legend where men playing games on the Sabbath were turned to stone – which he and Maya had already visited.

Although Liam didn't fully understand some of the allusions, he felt the passion in Althea's writing. It was clear she was fascinated by the idea of miscreants being petrified, and she linked it to various religious doctrines, suggesting that the stones may have been erected as a form of control, a deterrent to prevent people from defying the rituals and beliefs of the time.

A further chapter caught his eye. Though less in-depth, it described the use of body paint and colouring, specifically ochre. As Preston had suggested, yellow limonite was associated with spring and blossoming, often used in seasonal ceremonies worshipping the sun, while the brown and red ochre had a deeper, darker purpose. Often used in burial, sometimes to ward off evil spirits.

Liam closed the book, surprised to see it was after midnight. As he tried to sleep, he wondered whether, even from the grave, Althea Marlowe somehow had a part to play in these recent killings.

◆ ◆ ◆

Liam slept soundly through the night, though when he woke, he vividly recalled dreams of pagan festivals with women doused in yellow ochre turning to stone. In one ceremony, Anthony Ellison dusted the victims with ochre; in another, it was Raymond Preston.

He poured a glass of water and changed into his running gear.

It was a beautiful spring morning, no sign of the recent inclement weather as he set off towards the seafront. He was halfway down the hill when he caught sight of a familiar car he hadn't seen in months.

Millie saw him as she was about to get into her car. She raised her hand as he slowed down and walked over, wiping a bead of sweat from his scalp. 'I couldn't find a parking spot outside my house,' Millie explained, as if needing to justify why she was parked just off the main road, a few streets away from her home – a road Liam purposely avoided during his morning runs.

'You teachers work harder than I do,' Liam said, glancing at his watch.

'It's nearing the end of term. SATs coming up, as I'm sure you know. How are things with you?'

'Same old,' Liam replied, suddenly conscious about his appearance in his running gear.

'You're looking well,' Millie said, as if sensing his discomfort.

Liam inwardly squirmed. It wasn't like him to be lost for words, but seeing Millie unexpectedly had thrown him. It reminded him of the awkward teenager he'd once been, self-conscious about his lack of hair and unable to speak to girls despite their obvious interest. 'Everything's going well.'

'George looking forward to starting secondary school?'

'Yeah, you know how it is. He's already at that stage where it's hard to get much out of him, but I think he's excited, if a little apprehensive.'

Millie smiled, nodding slowly as Liam desperately sought something intelligent or witty to say.

'Well, it's great to see you again,' Millie said after a few seconds, breaking the awkward silence.

Liam recalled seeing her holding hands with a stranger on the wharf at the end of last year and wondered if that man was still on the scene. 'It's good to see you again too,' he said. 'Need to get my miles in,' he added as she got into the car and drove away.

'*Need to get my miles in* . . . What a dick,' he muttered under his breath as he resumed running, his pace quicker than usual.

◆ ◆ ◆

He was still processing the encounter with Millie as he arrived at headquarters later that morning. He replayed the meeting in his mind with little improvement. He thought about George starting secondary school, wondering where the time had flown and if he'd failed the boy as a father.

It was all well and good turning up for cricket matches and practice now and again, but Mark was there daily, likely knowing exactly how George felt about starting secondary school. It made him consider Rory and Tony Ellison's relationship. He tried to comprehend what was going on in the father's mind. No doubt he would be desperate to find his son, but deep down he must have considered that Tony was responsible for the killings, and as such must be carrying his fair share of guilt.

His mood hadn't improved by the time he arrived. He left the car carrying an untouched thermos of coffee, and saw Grace parking up. They exchanged pleasantries as they walked in together, any awkwardness about their night together put aside. Liam conceded he felt more relaxed with Grace than during his earlier encounter with Millie, and wondered what that meant – if it was a positive, or if his nervousness around Millie meant he still had feelings for her.

As he entered CID, Liam caught sight of Maya walking through the incident room with a cup of coffee. She saw him arrive with Grace, waiting until Grace walked away before tilting her head, a playful smile crossing her face. Despite the gentle teasing, Liam had appreciated her offer to talk. Kim aside, he didn't feel there was anyone else he could discuss the matter with and it would be good to get Maya's opinion on things, even if she seemed to be carrying a slight grudge against Grace.

The morning briefing brought three more names of girls Ellison had slept with. 'Seems he's been going through that college one by one,' said Quinlan, unable to hide a hint of admiration as he listed the names from Tess's college.

Maya added them to the whiteboard beneath Debbie's name, next to Tess and Carys.

'The list is getting out of hand,' she said, 'but they're all potential targets. Check in with them again today, reiterate the need to be careful and not be alone.'

Liam wondered how many more names would appear before the investigation ended, cutting his imagination off before it could picture others joining Tess and Carys.

He shared details of the book he'd skimmed last night by Tony's mother, Althea Marlowe.

'Remind me what you got for English A-level?' Quinlan said, already, in his mind at least, establishing himself as the team's joker.

Liam considered quoting the *King Lear* he still knew by rote from school but laughed it off instead. 'Admittedly, some of it went over my head,' he said, running his hand over his scalp, earning smiles from Grace and Maya. 'But she definitely had a keen interest in the Merry Maidens site and mentioned historical uses of red and yellow ochre.'

'Could Tony have taken on these obsessions after she died and distorted them?' asked Jack, who was sitting next to Quinlan.

'It's clear Tony has a strong interest in the subject,' Liam said, 'but we can't jump to conclusions yet. I've arranged to speak to one of Althea's former university colleagues today,' Liam said.

Quinlan went to respond but thought better of it as Maya assigned further duties and wrapped up the briefing, with Liam already heading out of the office towards Exeter.

Chapter Twenty-Three

Liam was pleased to be out of the office. It was taking some adjustment to be part of a larger team again, especially with the added complication of Grace being in it. The more tedious aspects of the job, such as the phone calls, the digital searches, and the general admin, were always good to escape, and he was content to be alone for a while.

The drive to Exeter was peaceful, though it gave him a little too much time to dwell on both the investigation and the night he'd spent with Grace.

He arrived at the main campus of Exeter University just after 1 p.m., navigating a labyrinth of corridors until he reached the English department, where he had an appointment with the Head of Department, Jessica Denholm, who had worked alongside Althea Marlowe during her time at the university.

Jessica looked almost startled to see him, glancing him up and down with a nervous laugh as she answered her office door.

'DS Kilshaw?' she said. 'Jessica Denholm. Please, come in.'

The office was more chaotic than Liam had anticipated. He could barely see the surface of the desk as he sat down opposite the academic. It was piled high with books, loose papers and writing pads.

'I thought everything would be digital nowadays,' he said.

'Oh, it is, mostly. But you can't beat the feel of a book in your hands. Or a pen, for that matter. You called about Althea?' said Jessica, crossing and uncrossing her arms, as if unsure what to do with them.

'That's right. You were colleagues?'

'We were in the same department, yes. She'd been there a couple of years more than me.'

'Would you say you were friends?'

Jessica tilted her head. 'Yes, I'd say so. Work friends, but friends, nonetheless. I didn't see her much socially, beyond staff get-togethers, the odd drink after work. We shared the same passions. Books, mostly.' She laughed, as if catching herself trying to steer the conversation. 'Particularly medieval literature. Why exactly is it you wanted to speak about her?'

Liam explained about Tony and the recent deaths in Cornwall.

'Oh my goodness. I didn't realise he was the boy who's missing,' said Jessica. 'She used her maiden name professionally so it never crossed my mind . . .'

'Did she ever mention her family?'

'Yes, of course. She was very proud of Anthony. Seemed like a happy family. I never met him, but I met her husband a couple of times at work events. They were a good match. I know he was devastated when she passed away. It was a slow death by all accounts. Tragic, must have been very difficult for all of them.'

Liam went into more detail about the stone circles and what had been found there. Most of it was in the public domain but Jessica placed her hand in front of her face when he mentioned the clay masks and the ochre doused on the victims.

'I was reading one of her books last night. She seemed very interested in stone circles. Particularly the Merry Maidens and the Hurlers,' Liam said.

'Yes, I recall that from her work.' Jessica glanced out of the window, distracted. 'Though it was only a minor part of her research. I think it was the legends she was most interested in. There are so many variations on those stories. People turning into stone for disobeying the Sabbath, such as the maidens and the hurlers. Althea was always intrigued by those details. Perhaps more by the tale itself than its origins.'

'We're still trying to locate Tony Ellison,' Liam said. 'This probably sounds absurd, but would you have any idea where he might have gone?'

Jessica frowned. 'I'm so sorry,' she said, sounding genuinely distressed.

'Was there anyone in the department she was particularly close to?'

'Not that I recall,' Jessica said after a pause.

Liam quizzed her some more but soon felt like he'd exhausted every angle for now. He stood, offering his hand before asking one more question. 'Have you ever come across an archaeologist by the name of Raymond Preston?'

'Preston . . .' Jessica repeated, testing the name. 'He wrote a book on mythologies, didn't he? A bit less academic than most . . .'

'That's him.'

'Yes, the name rings a bell, but I'm sorry, I can't recall meeting him. I can ask around if you like. Is it important?'

'Everything is potentially important. If you do think of anything that could help us, here's my card.'

Jessica blushed slightly as she took it. 'Please give my respects to Althea's husband, if you speak to him again.'

Liam nodded and thanked her once more before heading back to his car.

◆ ◆ ◆

He spent the journey back to headquarters once more considering the impact Althea's death may have had on Anthony Ellison. From what they could ascertain, it seemed that he had a decent relationship with his dad but Liam understood better than most what losing a parent could do to a child.

Not many days went past without Liam thinking of his father and the impact it had had on him, and his mother. No doubt Althea's death had affected the young Tony in myriad ways, and it wasn't a great leap to imagine that taking a darker turn, Tony taking his mother's interests and turning them into a twisted obsession.

Maya was waiting for him in the incident room when he returned. She was sitting with Jack, working through something on his computer. Liam updated them on his conversation with Althea's former colleague, and Maya told him about Carys's post-mortem. 'As we thought, all but identical to Tess. Cause of death was asphyxiation from the clay and ochre mix, which hardened in her airways.'

'The paralytic?' Liam asked, trying not to visualise Carys being manipulated into the prayer position, unable to move as the mixture was poured into her mouth.

Maya's face answered his question. 'Yep, blood tests are back as well. Traces of vecuronium mixture as before.'

Liam shook his head, wondering what processes Anthony would have gone through to distort the death of his mother into this type of behaviour. The link was obvious, and if Tony was the killer, it felt like it was only a matter of time before he struck again.

'I'm still working on the registered prescriptions of the drug but it's a long process. I've contacted local veterinary clinics as well,' said Jack. 'Nothing for the farm where Tony works.'

Liam doubted the killer had obtained the drug by legitimate means. Their elaborate MO suggested they planned everything meticulously, and it was unlikely they would be careless enough to leave a trace between them and the drug. But it had to have come from somewhere and it could be a potential opening.

The vagaries were frustrating. Liam spent the afternoon conducting more research on Althea. He noted the anniversary of her death was a couple of weeks away and wondered if that was a potential trigger for Anthony's actions.

He did his best to read through her published academic articles but they were even drier than her book, full of jargon he didn't fully understand. He skimmed through as best he could, stopping on any mentions of stone circles, ochre, or rituals, but couldn't find anything of value.

Althea's medical reports arrived late afternoon, and he checked through the file confirming she had died from pancreatic cancer. Anthony would have been nine at the time – the same age Liam had been when his dad had passed away.

Whereas Liam's dad had died fighting in war, Anthony would have witnessed his mother's deterioration over the last few months of her life. It would have been hard for anyone to go through.

Rory had told them it was during that period that Anthony had turned to reading the type of stories that had fascinated his mother. Liam understood the desire to escape the world. He'd seen it in his own mother, who'd turned to drugs and alcohol to dull her pain, and hadn't he diverted his obsessions into fighting and following in his father's footsteps in the armed forces?

'Boss, just got a call from Penzance nick.'

Liam looked up, having been momentarily lost in thought. 'What's that, Jack?'

'Sounds like a possible abduction. Teenage girl managed to fight the attacker off.'

'Name?'

'Katie Brookmeyer,' said Jack, catching Liam's attention.

'The same Katie Brookmeyer who's part of our investigation?' he asked.

'Yep, Tess Penrose's friend. She's at the station now.'

Chapter Twenty-Four

'Was she alone?' Liam asked, pulling on his coat.

'Yes. It happened not far from her house. She's having the forensic exam now. The details they gave me were piecemeal, but she may have drawn blood from the attacker,' Jack said. 'No ID on the attacker yet.'

'Okay. I'm heading over now. Check in with Katie's friends – the other two who picked Tess up that night. Evie and Janice. Where's DI Trent?'

'Budget meeting with Hargreaves. The rest of the team are on various call-outs. Do you need me to come with you?' Jack asked, sounding almost hopeful.

'No, that's fine. Hold things here. Let Maya know where I'm going.'

'Will do, boss.'

It was the wrong time of day to be heading to Penzance but he was used to the rush hour traffic.

The last time he'd seen Katie Brookmeyer had been the day Tess Penrose's body was discovered. He remembered her shock and disbelief as he'd interviewed her at the college. The tears and the hint of guilt as she explained how Tess had left the party with Anthony Ellison.

Whoever was behind the attempted abduction, the mode of the attack marked a shift from what had happened so far. Although dusk had fallen by the time they'd made the attack, it was still a risk trying to take someone in such a public place. So far, the killer hadn't made any obvious errors, and Liam considered the rashness of their actions. It was feasibly a sign of desperation, and suggested something had gone wrong in the execution of the plan. Either that, or the killer and Katie's would-be abductor in this scenario were not the same person.

Liam thought more about Tony Ellison as he made slow progress to Penzance. Tess had gone willingly with him from the party. And although they still didn't know how Carys had been abducted, she too had been one of Anthony Ellison's former lovers.

Did Katie's abduction mean she'd also slept with him?

Ted greeted him at Penzance police station reception, forty minutes later.

'She's just finished up,' he said, the weary look on his face suggesting both that he'd seen this all before, and that it never got any easier. 'She's with her mother.'

Ted handed him a document with Katie's initial statement and the forensic exam report. Liam let out a sigh as he read it, relieved to see there was no sign of sexual assault. Bruising to her forearms, wrists, and shoulder were all consistent with someone trying to force her into a van. Skin scrapings and fingernail samples had been taken, which if matched could prove pivotal.

Katie's statement described how she was attacked less than a hundred metres from her house. It had been dark, and the attack had naturally taken her by surprise. The van had appeared almost out of nowhere, screeching to a halt. She said she'd frozen as the driver got out of the van. He'd been wearing a black balaclava, and was holding something, possibly a knife, a scalpel, or even a syringe. He'd hesitated before reaching for her.

She reacted after a moment's pause. She'd been studying self-defence for the last three years and that instinct had taken over. She'd dug her nails into the attacker's neck and kneed him hard in the crotch. As he dropped, she screamed and ran. Seconds later, she heard the van pull away.

'I need to speak to her,' Liam said.

Ted nodded. 'No problem. Go get yourself a cup of muck and I'll set it up.'

Liam fetched a coffee from the kitchenette. The caffeine only made him more jittery, adrenaline having already done most of the work.

A few minutes later, Ted called him over and led him to the interview room. Katie was inside with her mother, who had brought her daughter a change of clothes. Katie looked younger than ever in jogging bottoms and an oversized sweatshirt, her face pale, her wide eyes dotted with red and unblinking.

Liam introduced himself to Mrs Brookmeyer and greeted Katie. 'I'm so sorry for what's happened,' he said. 'We need to move as quickly as possible if we're going to catch the person responsible. I'm afraid I need to ask you to go over it all again. Is that okay?'

Mrs Brookmeyer held her daughter's hand as Katie gave a small nod.

Liam let her recount the story in her own words. It matched the original statement almost exactly.

'You didn't see the attacker's face?'

'He was wearing a balaclava. One of those scary-looking ones.'

'Height?'

'Between five-ten and six-one. Average build, I guess,' Katie said, her eyes fixed on her lap, her mother still holding her hand.

'Do you have any idea who the attacker could have been, Katie?'

She shook her head, eyes reddening again.

Liam paused. He'd wanted Katie to reach her own conclusions, but he now had no option but to ask the question. 'Do you think it could have been Anthony Ellison?'

Katie didn't look up. Her mother glanced at her.

'Do you think it could have been him?' Liam asked again.

'I don't know,' Katie said, her tone sharpening. 'Like I told you, it was dark. He was wearing a balaclava. It could've been him, I suppose. Though why he would ever—' She stopped mid-sentence, glancing at her mother as if she'd said too much.

'Katie, I need to ask you something personal. Is that okay?' Liam said.

Mrs Brookmeyer frowned. 'What sort of question?'

Liam went to speak, but Katie cut in.

'I slept with him, okay? I slept with Tony Ellison.'

Mrs Brookmeyer looked stunned. Katie turned to look at her, her eyes narrowing in contrition. 'No one knows, Mum. I didn't tell Tess, or Evie, or Janice. It was just a one-night thing.'

'When did it happen?' Liam asked.

'About three months ago,' Katie said, her voice stronger now.

'So when I spoke to you last time, after Tess died . . .'

'Yes,' Katie interrupted, the word short and sharp. 'That's why I didn't want Tess to go with him. Not because I was jealous. Because I knew what would happen.'

'You knew what would happen?'

'I mean, he'd sleep with her, then never want to see her again. Like he did with me. Tess was always more sensitive. I just didn't want her to get hurt.' She blinked hard. 'I guess that was stupid, wasn't it? What would it have mattered if she'd suffered a broken heart? At least she could've recovered from that.'

Katie's last sentiment stayed with Liam as he called headquarters and arranged for a watch to be placed at the Brookmeyers' house.

Would it have made any difference if Katie had told Tess about her relationship with Tony? Would she have reconsidered going with him, and now be alive? He guessed it was something Katie might have to live with for the rest of her life.

He still wasn't convinced that Katie hadn't been jealous at the party but it was clear she'd known nothing good would have come from Tess leaving with Tony, though there had been no way she could have envisaged the tragedy that would befall her friend.

What was becoming clear, however, was the amount of women Tony had been involved with. They now knew of at least ten young women – six from Tess's college alone – who had slept with him.

Liam thought back to his own college years. He'd lost his virginity aged seventeen, not long before he'd joined the navy. He'd since had his fair share of lovers and one-night stands. He thought back on some of them with fondness, some with regret. He hoped he'd always treated the women with respect. Most of these one-night stands had been reciprocal in the sense that the other party hadn't expected anything more to come from the interaction, although in retrospect he suspected that hadn't always been the case.

Had there been times when the women he'd been with had wanted something more? There had been numerous occasions when numbers had been exchanged and he hadn't made contact, other times where he'd called back, his desire nothing more than sexual.

Tony must have known the effect he had on at least some of the young women he was sleeping with, and if the two men from the farm were to be believed he took some pride in his success. But for all that, Liam had yet to hear a bad word about him. Even Katie had been at pains to point out that her experience had been consensual. And although she sounded aggrieved that he'd subsequently wanted nothing to do with her, she'd been keen to keep their dalliance a secret even after Tess's death.

With the protection notice ratified by Hargreaves, Liam visited the other two young women who had been with Tess the night before her death. Both Evie and Janice were at home with their parents, Liam having to notify both families of the attempt to abduct Katie. He questioned both of Katie's classmates about their relationship to Tony Ellison, both denying ever having any encounter with him.

◆ ◆ ◆

Liam called Maya when he was back in the flat. The anthropologist had informed her that the remains found at the Merry Maidens site had belonged to a couple somewhere between the ages of thirty and forty-five. Their dental records were still being checked, the process laborious due to the fact that there was no national database. The age of the couple changed the approach, and the missing persons register was being investigated by the rest of the team for potential matches.

The bloods taken from Katie were being rushed through and hopefully a result would come tomorrow, though they would have to wait longer for DNA results and a potential match with Tony Ellison.

Liam spent the evening rereading the books by Raymond Preston and Althea Marlowe. He took particular interest in the chapters on sacrifice and the overt deterrent of breaking the rules resulting in such a horrific death. And even though he thought the ideas were strange and symptomatic of their time, he wondered – with everything that was going on – how much had actually changed.

While he ate, his mind drifted towards his impromptu meeting with Millie that morning. He'd felt like a giddy schoolboy running into her, and as he replayed the encounter he wondered if there was more he could have said. It was another relationship he'd managed to sabotage, and he wondered what Millie thought about him when she was alone.

He showered and went to bed and was about to sleep when Grace messaged him asking him how he was. It was nearly midnight and the day had taken its toll. He didn't open the message, instead putting his phone on silent and switching off the light.

Chapter Twenty-Five

He hadn't prepared properly. And that was his fault. His work may have been righteous. May even have been preordained. But it wasn't a fait accompli. That wasn't the way of devotion and sacrifice. He had to work hard, had to remain vigilant and smart.

She had been prepared for the attack and hadn't hesitated to defend herself. It was admirable. He'd seen the terror in her eyes, but that hadn't stopped her from fighting with everything she had.

At first, he'd been shocked by her ferocity, and that was what had defeated him. She'd screamed as she rallied against him, and though he knew he could eventually overpower her, he couldn't take the risk. He'd held on to her as best he could, but she'd slashed and clawed at him, and he feared that by the time he'd silenced her, aid would have come.

So he'd fled, running back to the van as she ran screaming towards her house.

The van was a necessity. Without it, he wouldn't be able to carry out the work. And a broken circle was no good to anyone.

He'd spent the evening meditating in Boscawen-Un – Carn Euny having been compromised – his blood trembling with the power of the circle as he waited for divine inspiration, the book never leaving his hands.

The list was obsolete now, but that didn't matter. There were other maidens out there. Others who had sinned, and who could rightfully take their place in the circle.

It was why he was now in Newquay. What better place to find someone worthy? It may not have been summer, but there was enough debauchery on show.

In some ways, there was too much to choose from. But he had to be careful.

He'd spotted the trio leaving the campsite early that evening, dressed as if it was the height of summer. He'd followed at a distance from bar to bar until they'd ended up here, a mindless place full of noise and light.

Doing his best not to stand out, he'd taken a seat in the corner. His rucksack nestled beneath the table, he sipped on a non-alcoholic drink, minding his own business, waiting for them to leave.

It was almost closing time when they finally left, giggling and squawking as they went. He reached beneath the table for his bag, his hand alighting on the book. He'd rushed the attack on Katie, but this was different.

He had the spray with him.

But still, he asked the book if it was the right thing to do. There were three of them, and although the spray would render them incapacitated, it would make things all that more difficult.

He closed his eyes. It was nearly complete, but time was running out. They would be coming for him soon, closing down his opportunities. If he took the three now, it would be enough.

Finishing his drink as they left the bar, he kept a safe distance, watching them enter a nightclub. It was a disappointment, but he could wait. They would have to go back the way they came and that was when he could strike.

He waited further down the high street, away from the cameras. He considered what could go wrong. He could be spotted by the police or some nosey do-gooder. Or the maidens might leave with new friends. He told himself there would be ways of dealing with both, but if he had to, he could wait until the next day.

They stumbled out two hours later. Arm in arm, they struggled to remain upright, stopping at a takeaway. Their piercing laughter poisoned the night air as they cackled and discarded their cheap food.

But as long as they managed to stay upright, it would all play to his advantage.

Finally, they left the glaring lights of the high street and took the turning he'd hoped they would towards the beach and back to the campsite.

He skipped further down the road, avoiding the CCTV camera, and crossed over. They were still giggling, their stumbling movements a strange dance of their own, as he rushed towards them, his hands ready on the spray.

Chapter Twenty-Six

Liam replied to Grace's text the next morning, apologising for not responding earlier. He went for a quick run before driving into headquarters, trying to clear his mind, but his thoughts rarely strayed from the investigation.

At the briefing, the team were allocated the names of Tony's former lovers to interview again. It was already impossible to put officers in place at all of the addresses they had, so it was important for them to stress the importance of security to each of the young women.

Liam had been in this type of situation too many times before. He felt like they were at once hoping the killer would not strike again, while waiting for something to happen.

The attempted abduction of Katie Brookmeyer had been rushed and ill thought out. If Tony was behind it, it begged the question of not only where he was but what his thought process was at present. Liam understood why the suspect may have dumped his conspicuous vehicle, but where had he got the van from, and what was he doing for money?

Questions he posed to Karl Sturridge and Malcolm Whitstable at Bosvellan farm later that morning. Both men were less belligerent than the last time Liam had spoken to them. News of the other murders had obviously reached them, and with Tony now missing and an active suspect, neither of the men cared to make any quips about their colleague's sexual exploits.

'Do you know where Tony could have got access to a white van?' Liam asked.

'The only van we have is that one there,' said Whitstable, pointing to a grey van gaining dirt on the forecourt of the farm.

'What about anyone connected to Tony who may have a van?'

'Can't say we see that much of the lad outside of work,' said Sturridge, who'd been the one to find Tess at the beginning of all this.

Liam ran through the names of Tony's lovers, checking if he'd ever revealed any details about them.

'He didn't mention names, did he, Malc?' Sturridge said.

Liam noticed his red beard was trimmer than the first time they had met.

'If he did, I don't recall them,' said the farmer.

'He ever speak about his parents?' asked Liam.

Sturridge scratched his beard, as the sun peeked out from behind the clouds. 'I know his mother died when he was young. He told me that once. He still has a dad, though, don't he? Mentioned him once or twice. As I said, we don't know that much about him.'

Liam thought about the abandoned SUV. 'What sort of wages do you pay him?'

'That important?' Whitstable said.

'If Tony is out there, he's living without his own vehicle or accommodation, and as far as we know he hasn't accessed any bank accounts. Is it possible he could have built up a cash fund?'

Sturridge laughed, receiving a frown of a rebuke from his boss.

'We pay cash in hand, but it's all accounted for.'

'Minimum wage,' Sturridge said. 'He was saving for uni.'

Liam left on better terms than the last time, though his opinion of the men hadn't changed that much. He wasn't sure to what extent their previous tales about Tony had been embellished, and how much of what Tony had told them had been the truth.

He did a quick tour around Katie's friends, stopping in on everyone in the local area Tony had supposedly slept with. Everyone was taking the threat seriously, and were only leaving their houses with friends or family members, but once more there was a sense of incredulity that Tony could be responsible for such crimes.

Disappointing news came in later that day: a report from toxicology stating that the limonite given to them by Reverend Frayne wasn't a match for the material found at any of the crime scenes.

Liam wasn't surprised. He hadn't really thought Frayne a likely suspect, and if the reverend was involved, he wouldn't have openly offered a direct match, but it was still another blow. He couldn't shake the feeling that they were dragging their heels, simply waiting for the killer to strike again – and another dead end made that possibility all the more likely.

In the afternoon, Liam collected George from school, deciding to wait in the playground with the rest of the parents instead of in his car as he usually did. He tried not to be obvious as he stood at the rear of the throng, doing his best to ignore the occasional glance sent his way. He tried to fool himself that he wasn't there for a glimpse of Millie, but had to concede seeing her again the other day had made her return to his thoughts.

As it was, George was released before the other classes were let out. He walked over to Liam, hesitating slightly before giving him a hug. Liam knew it wouldn't be long before hugs – in public, at least – would be out of the question. He was amazed to find himself on the verge of tears as he thought about how quickly the years were going. 'I think I need something to eat,' he said, giving George an extra squeeze before taking him for food.

After burger and chips, Liam drove them to cricket practice. With George practising in the nets, Liam took the opportunity to read through Althea's book once more. Liam had appreciated Cornwall's mythological past from an early age. A school trip to Tintagel Castle had sparked a brief obsession with all things Arthurian. He remembered watching a film on the subject, marvelling at the idea of Excalibur and the magic of Merlin.

Another legend that had taken hold in his young mind was of the giants of Cornwall – Comoran, in particular, whom he'd imagined pounding the streets at night as he'd been asleep.

Although Althea touched on these subjects, her book was more rooted in the reality of the time. She discussed how such stories and beliefs had shaped people's lives. Liam read through the chapters on stone circles once more, noting again her theory that the stones acted as a deterrent. Althea even compared them to the story of Moses and the Ten Commandments, arguing that both the stone tablets and the standing stones served, in different eras, as tools to enforce religious authority and control the masses.

He scanned through the ancient maps, comparing them to the modern versions on his phone, plotting the places asterisked on Tony's phone, and the locations where the three bodies had been found.

Something caught his eye, a potential pattern, and he was about to zoom in when his phone began to ring, Grace's name appearing on screen.

Liam felt a stab of guilt for not answering her text the previous night before he hit the green button on his screen. 'DI Hartley, to what do I—'

'I'll stop you there, Liam. Where are you at present?'

'Penzance, why?'

'Thought you'd want to know we have a missing persons development that could be related to the investigation.'

'Do we now?' said Liam, thinking about how easily Grace and her team had integrated, and what that meant for the department going forward.

'Campsite over in Newquay. Three teenage girls. From what we can tell, they didn't return to the site last night and their parents decided to call after being unable to reach them all day.'

'What ages are we talking?'

'Two are nineteen, one twenty.'

'Any link to the other victims?' Liam asked, under his breath, aware of his close proximity to the other parents in the sports centre.

'No, not directly. All three are on holiday from Cheltenham. Alarm bells started to ring when none of the parents could get hold of them.'

'When were they last seen?'

'Campsite manager says they were dressed up last night heading into town.'

'Does Maya know?'

'Yes, she said to call you.'

Liam tried to rationalise what he was being told. Three people missing at the same time was a new one on him, and unless Tony had travelled up to Cheltenham at some point, or met up with the missing women in the last few days, it was hard to see an obvious link. But with everything going on, it had to be a consideration.

'Okay, I won't be able to get there for another hour,' he said.

'You don't need to if you're busy. I'm here with Quinlan.'

'Someone has got to keep you guys in check,' Liam said with a smile, hanging up before Grace could give him a comeback.

Chapter Twenty-Seven

Liam waited thirty minutes for George to finish his net session. He spent the time liaising with Jack, making sure all the young women they had on Tony's list were accounted for. He was restless but he couldn't take George out of the session. Grace had things under control in Newquay, and at present they had no firm link between the missing women and Tony Ellison.

After George was finished, Liam dropped the boy back off at his mother's before making his way to Newquay, arriving at the Polgwyn caravan park just after 7.30 p.m. Grace was in the car park talking to an angry, gesticulating woman. He waited until they'd finished before approaching.

'What was that about?'

'We're trying to keep everyone on-site so we can question them. Easier said than done.' Grace quickly updated him. The missing young women – Nina Connors, Ruby Fletcher, and Erin Dunne, all from Cheltenham – were staying at the caravan park for a week. They'd gone out last night to celebrate Ruby's twentieth birthday and hadn't been seen since.

'What first alerted everyone?' Liam asked.

'Ruby's mother tried calling throughout the day. When she spoke to the other parents, they realised all three phones were switched off. From what we understand, it isn't like them not to be in contact.'

Liam didn't need to ask if Grace had checked the caravan but was tempted anyway, just to see her reaction.

'They're not sleeping in their caravan, if that's your next question,' she said with a smile. 'All the parents are on their way down.'

Grace walked Liam over to the small brick building at the centre of the park. 'Derek Vale, fifty-eight. Owns the site,' she said, pointing to a rotund man sitting behind a desk, his pale face lit by his monitor.

'They left at seven, all dressed up and already a bit giddy, according to him. We've got camera images of them leaving.' Grace handed Liam her phone, footage playing. The three women looked almost identical, with short figure-hugging dresses, long flowing hair and high heels.

'He's going through the footage again, but there's no sign of them returning,' Grace said.

Under usual circumstances, the current situation wouldn't have warranted this kind of response. It was plausible the girls had met some people, and were sleeping it off or still partying somewhere else. But with three deaths already and a killer at large, they had to be considered in danger.

Grace's colleague, Quinlan, pulled up as they were about to enter the caravan office. 'I've got sightings,' he said as he left his car. 'Looks like they ended up at a late-night bar. I've video from just after midnight. They were nearly the only people in there.'

Liam watched the video. The bar was almost empty, which was unsurprising for midweek off-season, but the girls seemed to be enjoying themselves, dancing and sipping drinks beneath the sprawling, flashing lights.

'They left just after one,' Quinlan continued, scrolling to another video showing the girls stumbling from the club. 'We tracked them to Bank Street, heading towards the beach. Nothing since.'

Maya arrived a few minutes later, the four of them using the caravan office as a makeshift incident room. They analysed the video footage as local officers were posted throughout the area – some in the town centre, searching the local bars, others sent further afield, to hotels, and other caravan parks.

The situation became complicated later that evening when the parents arrived from Cheltenham, demanding information. Liam arranged a caravan for them and they were each interviewed, repeating the same mantra that the girls would never be so irresponsible as to disappear without being contactable.

After speaking to Hargreaves, Maya received permission to search Towan Beach. Liam wasn't sure it was necessary. If something had happened last night, someone would've noticed during the busy day, but he understood the need to check, and it gave the parents some hope.

Dozens of torches lit the night-time sand as a grid search was conducted, a helicopter combing the area with spotlights. Liam kept glancing at his phone, hoping for news that the girls had returned safely, though as the hours passed it seemed increasingly unlikely.

The officers gathered by the edge of the beach, the torches off into the distance, the whirr of the helicopter loud above them.

The most frustrating thing so far was that none of the families had connections to Cornwall or knew of Tony Ellison beyond what they'd seen in the media.

'Maybe Ellison knows people in Cheltenham,' Grace suggested.

'He could've attended the Cheltenham Festival,' Quinlan offered. 'It was only a few weeks ago.'

'So, Tony Ellison goes to Cheltenham, sleeps with these three women, then waits for them to visit Cornwall to abduct them? I'm not buying it,' Maya said.

'Maybe he's panicking. The attempted abduction of Katie Brookmeyer wasn't like the methodical precision of the first killings. Could be he feels he's in too deep,' Liam said.

'Maybe he wants to get caught,' Grace added.

'Or he's grabbing as many as he can before he does get caught,' Quinlan countered.

Liam dragged his foot along the wet sand before addressing their shared fear. 'We need to consider what he'll do with them.'

There were sixteen known stone circles in Cornwall. Monitoring each was labour- and time-intensive but the killer clearly had an MO placing victims inside circles, trying to turn them to metaphorical stone. If the killer took them, we have to assume they plan to use one of these sites.'

'Fuck,' Maya muttered. 'Let's talk to the parents again, push them on any connection to Anthony Ellison. Get them to call the girls' friends. Find out if anyone has ever met him. Liam, call Rory Ellison. Wake him if necessary, but find out if Tony has been to Cheltenham recently. I'll speak to Hargreaves about getting people to monitor the stone circles.'

Liam called Rory Ellison before setting off for Truro. It was 4 a.m., and the PolSA had been called in to begin a full search of the area once the sun was up. Liam wasn't surprised Rory hadn't answered and wasn't looking forward to waking him.

The odds of Tony having any connection to the three women seemed slim. Liam considered the idea that the killer might be panicking, trapped in actions they couldn't escape, or that they subconsciously wanted to be caught. Both sounded plausible, and he wondered if Tony had planned all this from the beginning, or if he'd set out with Tess that night at the Merry Maidens and things had escalated beyond his control.

When he arrived at Rory's house, Liam switched off the engine. He checked his phone, but there were no messages.

All the lights in the house were off. Liam sighed, trying Rory's phone again, before ringing the doorbell. After two more rings, movement came from inside. Rory opened the door, bleary-eyed, frowning when he saw Liam.

'Have you found him?' Rory asked, panic animating his tired face.

'No, this isn't directly about Tony. Three young women are missing, and I need to know if Tony might have known them.'

Rory squinted, confused. 'What are you talking about?'

'Can I come in, Mr Ellison?'

Rory opened the door wider, letting Liam enter. The house was cold as Rory led Liam into the kitchen. 'I'll put some coffee on. I won't be getting back to sleep now.'

Liam wondered what Rory's mindset was like at present. His son was missing, yet he must realise the police considered Tony more suspect than victim. Did Rory feel the same? Tony was his only immediate family, but that hadn't stopped Rory from returning to work. If George was missing, Liam wouldn't be able to concentrate on work, but people had different reactions to such situations.

Rory sat at the breakfast table as they waited for the coffee to brew. 'Explain this again,' he said.

Liam detailed the events in Newquay, sharing the names of the missing women. 'Does Tony or your family have any connection to Cheltenham?'

Rory shook his head. 'I've never heard those names, and we have no links there. Can't imagine he's ever been. It wasn't close to any universities he looked at.'

'About sixty miles from Oxford,' Liam said.

'Still,' Rory replied, pouring black coffee for them both.

'What about Newquay?'

'Tony knows Newquay. He goes there weekends with mates sometimes. But you can't seriously think he's behind this. He doesn't have his vehicle. How could he abduct three women alone? The idea's ridiculous.'

'Ridiculous or not, there are three girls missing, as well as Tony. You can see the possible link, can't you?'

'My son would never . . .' Rory faltered. 'I don't know what you want from me. I just want you to find my son.'

Liam appreciated the man's frustration, but he also understood how people could live in denial, especially about those they loved. 'Just for a moment, let's say Tony is caught up in this somehow. Knowing what we do about his interest in folklore and mythology, where do you think he would consider going next?'

Rory squirmed, as if he'd tasted something unpleasant. He squinted, Liam imagining he was picturing his son responsible for these atrocities. 'The obvious place would be another stone circle, don't you think?' he said, after a short pause.

Liam told him about the officers now stationed at various stone circles. 'Is there anything more specific you can think of? Somewhere Tony has fond memories of, perhaps a special place he shared with his mother? Something she may have written about?'

The mention of Rory's wife seemed to make him turn inwards. He pulled his dressing gown tighter before pouring them both more coffee.

'She was always much closer to him than I was. They had a way of being with each other, an ease that wasn't there with me. I used to say it was like they had their own secret club. I guess my mind works differently to theirs. I'm all about facts, numbers and datasheets, as I've told you. Althea was always about the wondrous, and that was the side that rubbed off on Tony, which was probably a blessing. Or at least I thought it was.'

It was the first time Liam had heard him speak as if he believed it might be possible his son was involved in the killings.

'Were there any places they used to visit together?'

'They went everywhere together, that was the thing. I was always working. Still am, I suppose. They'd go on trips at the weekends. Various sites throughout the county, and further afield. Do you have any idea how many stone circles there are in the UK? And that wasn't even their only interest. Anything historic fascinated them, especially if that history was clouded in myth and legend. I never understood it, but it made them happy, so it made me happy too.'

Liam empathised more than he cared to admit. Though he shared interests with George – sport and surfing mostly – he was still something of an outsider compared to the relationship George had with Kim and Mark. It didn't make it easier that he accepted it was his own fault, but he could see where Rory was coming from. He pushed one last time for somewhere specific, but Rory didn't have any answers.

He thanked the man who looked lost and withered in his dressing gown, and returned to his car.

The sun was rising. A familiar tiredness crept over him and he entered a search for the nearest petrol station into the sat nav, keen for another caffeine hit.

Ten minutes later he pulled into a garage and made a coffee from the machine, wondering, as it coughed out the brew, how long the beans had been sitting there.

He paid and took his drink outside, sipping it as he watched the main road, currently devoid of traffic. Looking back to the forecourt, he caught sight of the CCTV cameras and wondered if at some point Tony had filled a white van with diesel and been caught on camera. Maybe one day there'd be an integrated system where facial recognition picked these things up from a central feed, but for now, collating footage from hundreds, if not thousands, of CCTV cameras countywide was never going to be a feasible approach.

Throwing the majority of the bitter drink into the dew-covered grass, he returned to his car and called Maya.

'Where have you been?' she said, answering.

Liam looked at his phone, which wasn't showing any missed calls. 'Poor reception. Just left Rory Ellison's place.'

'Well, you need to get over to a village called Lower Bostraze. I'll send you the coordinates. It's the nearest settlement to the stone circle at Tregeseal.'

'A body?' Liam said, adrenaline mixing uncomfortably with the recent injection of caffeine.

'Afraid so. Not confirmed yet, but it looks like it's one of the missing girls. Possibly Ruby Fletcher.'

Chapter Twenty-Eight

Lower Bostraze was a sparse patchwork of fields dotted with a few houses – including three holiday cottages across from where Ruby Fletcher's body had been found.

She had been discovered within the last hour by one of the tourists staying in the cottages, a woman who'd been out for a morning run. As the location was less than a mile from the Tregeseal stone circle, a member of the team had already been nearby and was at the scene within minutes of the call.

Liam had visited the place early on in the investigation, and recalled it from the books he'd read by Althea Marlowe and Raymond Preston. The circle was also known as the Dancing Stones. Like the Merry Maidens, the legend claimed the stones were women turned to stone for dancing on the Sabbath.

Maya's details had been piecemeal, and Liam had hoped that because the body hadn't been placed directly in the stone circle, the victim might not have endured what Tess and Carys had gone through.

That hope was dashed the moment he arrived and caught sight of the cordoned-off area where Ruby was arranged like the others: on her knees, hands contorted into a prayer position, her face a featureless mask of hardened clay.

Liam checked in with the first responder who confirmed he hadn't touched the body. 'Her ID was next to her. I bagged it wearing gloves,' said the PC.

Liam took the evidence bag, noting the shock of red hair on Ruby's photograph, which was a close match to that on the faceless corpse.

With the CSIs yet to arrive, Liam examined the scene as best he could from outside the cordon, careful not to contaminate anything. The signs were unmistakable. As well as the clay on the victim's face, more of the substance was on her hands and feet, with a dusting of limonite on her face and hair.

Maya arrived not long after with the CSI team. She lowered her eyes as she stepped out of the car. 'Do we have someone at the stone circle?' she asked.

'First responder's over there,' Liam said, nodding towards the uniformed officer.

'Better send him some back-up, in case the perp sees this as a chance to dump more bodies.'

Liam let out a breath. There had been a connection between the first three victims, however tentative, through Tony Ellison. But with Ruby's death, it suggested the killer might have widened their scope. Liam feared not only that Ruby's two friends would be found in the same fashion, but that the killer was now capable of targeting anyone of a similar age and that until they were caught, the body count would keep mounting.

The CSIs erected a tent around Ruby, shielding her from both the elements and anyone unfortunate enough to catch sight of her forced position.

Liam and Maya checked in with the other officers posted at the various stone circles across the county as they waited for the preliminary checks. No other bodies had been found yet, which was a brittle comfort.

The positioning of Ruby's body – away from but still near the circle – was further evidence the killer's ritual was becoming less rigid. Their approach seemed to be unravelling. Tess and Carys had both been placed at stone circles, presumably as a necessary part of whatever sick process the killer was going through.

But dumping the body here suggested the placement in the stone circle wasn't necessary and that the killer was making compromises due to the current situation. It also suggested that the killer was hurrying, and Liam wondered if they were working to some unknown timetable.

Tina was at the scene and gave him a shy look as she changed into her white coveralls. Liam fought a stab of guilt for not yet texting as he'd promised.

He walked to the perimeter as he waited for the body to be processed. The area was remote, desolate enough for the killer to have gone unnoticed during the night. They would've needed a vehicle to reach it, but all the occupants of the holiday cottages claimed not to have heard anything out of the ordinary beyond normal traffic noise.

The killer had clearly avoided the stone circle itself. But they'd placed the body somewhere it could be found. Which meant, at least in part, they wanted the attention.

Liam did a quick lap of the buildings, but unless he was prepared to walk a mile or so along the single track lane to the stone circle, there was nowhere else for him to go.

He arrived back in time to see Grace pulling up with Ruby's parents.

'What are they doing here?' he said.

'They insisted. Threatened to come on their own. We couldn't let them have access, but we couldn't stop them either.'

The mother shouted across the road as she left the car.

'I need to see my baby!' she cried, making a dash towards the scene.

Grace was forced to run after her.

'You're not going to be able to see her until the body's been fully processed,' she said softly.

But there was nothing she could say to stop the wave of anguish. Mrs Fletcher dropped to the ground. Her husband rushed to her side, glaring at Liam and Grace as he helped her up.

'Let's take her inside,' Grace said.

They brought the couple into one of the holiday cottages. Maya was already there, getting to her feet as they entered, shooting Liam a questioning look as Grace guided the parents to the living room.

'They insisted,' Liam said.

'We can't let them see her like that,' Maya replied.

Liam pictured the body. Ruby kneeling, hands contorted, limonite streaked through her hair, and the chilling covering over her face. No one wanted that to be Ruby's parents' last memory of their child but he understood why Grace hadn't said no.

After making tea, Liam and Maya left Grace and Quinlan with the parents and drove the short distance to the stone circle.

The first responder stood guard, looking like a scarecrow in the empty field, his only company the nine stones of the circle: the maidens, supposedly turned to stone.

The officer confirmed no one had been to the site since his return, aside from a couple of dog walkers. Liam and Maya moved silently from stone to stone, sweeping each plinth with forensic torches for signs of blood or ochre.

Sunlight burst through the clouds, causing Liam to squint. When he opened his eyes, he saw not stones but nine victims: Tess, Carys, Ruby, and six others, each on their knees, frozen in place, facing the centre of the circle.

He blinked the image away, his hand involuntarily moving to his chest as he imagined himself first beneath the sea, struggling for breath, and then within the stone prisons, his lungs filling with clay. 'I think I need some sleep,' he mumbled to himself.

'What's that?' Maya asked.

'You think he tried to bring the body here first?' Liam said, clearing his head.

'Can't be a coincidence he left the body so close to this site. Did PC Hayden record any vehicles overnight?'

'There was a steady stream,' Liam replied, showing her the officer's report on his phone. 'Most of the number plates were captured, but there were a couple he wasn't able to log.'

'You've sent this to Jack, I presume,' Maya said.

Liam shrugged. 'It's not my first rodeo, boss.'

They made a final circuit of the stones before returning to the cottages. Donning their white protective suits, they joined the CSIs inside the tent.

The lead CSI, Giselle, talked them through the findings. She pointed to injection wounds on Ruby's neck, the hardening clay on her hands and feet.

'You can see for yourselves, it's almost definite she suffered the same fate as the others.'

The clay mask had been removed to reveal Ruby's features, her mouth full of the hardened mixture that had traces of limonite on it.

Even with her being paralysed, it wouldn't have been a quick job, and in the dim light of the tent, Liam reluctantly conceded that Ruby did resemble the monolith the killer was trying to recreate.

'I'm afraid the parents are here,' Maya said.

'We'll do our best to make her presentable. I'll place a mask over her mouth and nose, and cover her with the top half of a shroud.'

They waited as the CSIs had fully documented the body and prepared it for transport, then wheeled her into the back of the van. Liam stood beside the gurney as the cover was pulled from Ruby's face. With the new mask in place, she looked almost peaceful, far from the grotesquery the killer had contorted her into.

'I'll take them back to the caravan park,' Grace said, as the parents walked over to see their daughter.

Liam nodded and looked away as the parents broke down once more.

◆ ◆ ◆

The afternoon briefing was held at headquarters with Liam, Maya, Jack, and Hargreaves. The Devon contingent of the team were with the parents. Jack went over what they knew, the crime board now so cluttered it had almost stopped making sense.

'We need to narrow it down,' Hargreaves said. 'We can't post officers at every stone circle. Realistically, with the threat this killer poses, they should be in pairs, and we don't have the resources.'

Liam understood. It was a lose-lose situation. They didn't have the manpower to cover every site properly, yet risked being accused of negligence if another body turned up at one of the unprotected locations.

'The killer must be holding the other two women somewhere,' Maya said.

'Could be the van,' Jack offered.

'Where are we on tracing those number plates?' Liam asked.

'We've got names and addresses for thirty-two vehicles. Uniforms are out now, locating the owners.'

Everything felt just out of reach. Frustrating at the best of times, but now they had two women missing.

Liam spent the afternoon scouring the case files, working through from day one until now. He read every statement, every witness report, so lost in the details, he barely noticed the light fading until Maya returned from Kian Burrell's post-mortem.

They held another quick meeting with Jack. There had been no developments. Newquay was still being searched. Witnesses from the night before had been urged to come forward. But they still had no idea what happened between the girls leaving the club on their way to the beach, and Ruby's body being found.

'Kian's post-mortem is similar to the first two victims,' Maya said, 'though not identical. Clay was applied to the hands and feet, but not with the same precision as with Tess and Carys. Cause of death was the same, though.'

Liam pictured Kian trapped in the boot of his car, maybe catching a glimpse of the killer as the substance was forced down his throat.

On the whiteboard, Jack had pinned a map showing the victim and abduction locations, transposed on to the version found in Tony Ellison's room. They all studied it in silence, as if the answer were buried somewhere in the alignment.

From what Liam could see, Kian's death had been almost incidental to the MO the killer was working to. He studied the map until it stopped making sense, and wondered where Tony Ellison was at that moment and what he planned to do next.

Chapter Twenty-Nine

The corridors felt narrow and claustrophobic, sterile with antiseptic, as Liam passed doors lined with photographs of the residents, each image capturing them in their past. The hum of a television guided him to his mother's room. It was 7 a.m. and she was sitting up in bed, staring blankly at the screen, the news looping endlessly.

She dragged her eyes away for a second, gazing his way but not acknowledging him, before turning back.

It had been over a month since he'd last visited. He used to make the pilgrimage every week, but something had shifted in him a few months back. It had taken years for him to fully understand how she'd treated him after his father died. And though he'd come to terms with the fact she'd chosen drugs and alcohol over him, and in doing so had marked a line in the sand between them, he still loved her in that way he guessed he always would. But the weekly visits had begun to feel pointless, a chore with no positive result, so he'd cut them back to once a month.

He thought the guilt would crush him, but sitting beside her now he was glad he hadn't come sooner. She didn't know him or understand what he was going through, and being here only stirred up the bad memories.

For a moment, he was a boy again, knocking on her bedroom door, opening it to find her face down in a pool of vomit on the carpet, an empty bottle on the sideboard, a rancid smell, which felt wrong to know, filling the room.

He shook the thought away and tried to recall something better, alighting on the same memory he always went to at such moments. His father alive, the three of them at the beach, his mother and father holding hands while he skipped towards the sea. He could still summon the feeling of contentment from that moment, a feeling he wasn't sure he'd ever had since.

He wasn't sure why he was here now. Maybe it was a distraction from the investigation, the relentless pressure of facing families who'd lost loved ones in circumstances he knew they'd never recover from. Maybe it was self-punishment, a reminder that what he'd endured was nothing compared to others.

'It's me, Mum,' he said, his voice barely above a whisper.

She didn't react.

'How have you been keeping? I guess they're treating you as well as they can.'

He didn't expect a response, and she didn't disappoint. He turned his attention to the television. The investigation was now national news. Photos of Ruby's missing friends appeared on the screen, an emergency helpline tagged beneath.

He glanced at his mother again. A line of saliva had begun to drip from her mouth. He flashed back to the victims and felt that panic in his chest as he imagined how they'd felt, unable to move or breathe. He looked at the lines on his mother's face, and for a second worried that she was suffering the same fate as the maidens – trapped within the shell of her body, aware and conscious of everything that was going on but unable to respond.

He wondered how long it would be until he was standing over the other two girls, how similar their faces would look, their throats filled with whatever substance the killer had used.

Being here did him no good. He said goodbye and was halfway out the door when he heard something behind him. A gurgling noise, faint and indecipherable, as if his mother was trying to speak to him. He turned to see her, but her attention was back on the television. 'See you later, Mum.'

Outside, the weather was calm but the grey clouds felt like a warning. As he drove, he played over the case notes he'd dictated, trying to spark a thought, something that would unlock what they were missing, but the words soon stopped making sense.

The full team was gathered at the incident room, bolstered by six additional officers stationed from across Cornwall and Devon. Maya delivered the briefing. The priority was obvious: find the two missing girls before the killer struck again.

As Liam had witnessed first-hand at his mother's care home, the investigation was now part of a national media campaign. Teams were heading to Cheltenham to speak to friends and relatives. The faces of the missing girls were everywhere. It would take just one sighting to change everything, but it still felt more likely that the next time they saw either girl would be as victims.

Duties were assigned, Liam volunteering to return to Penzance to speak to Danny Reeve and Raymond Preston again. It felt like a step backwards, but that was the nature of these investigations – constant circling, sometimes ending where you started.

Forty minutes later, he stood at Danny Reeve's front door, wondering what, if anything, he'd missed the first two times he'd been there.

'Oh,' said Danny Reeve. 'Wasn't expecting you. Just off to work.'

Liam couldn't help but be surprised. He was so accustomed to seeing the young man slouched in front of the television that it hadn't really occurred to him he might have a job.

'Where do you work?'

'The Boar's Head in St Ives. In the kitchen. Trying to save some money for uni.'

'Have you got a few minutes to talk?'

'Is this to do with those missing girls?' Danny said, not offering to let Liam inside.

'It is.'

Danny looked up and down the small street. 'Come in if you want, but I have to leave in five minutes, at the latest.'

The house was as it had been. The living room cluttered with discarded clothes and takeaway cartons. The only difference was that the television screen was off.

'How long have you been working there?' Liam asked, finding space on the armchair.

'Just a couple of months. I really do need to leave soon.'

'You've heard about the latest developments?'

'Of course I have. It's everywhere on the news. You can't still think this has anything to do with Tony, do you? Not that I think he'd be involved, but how the hell would he pull something like that off?'

'Until we find him, we can't rule him out,' Liam said, admiring the way Tony's friend still thought him innocent despite the evidence mounting against him. 'I know I keep pestering you, but you seem to know him better than most. Can you think of anywhere he might be hiding out?'

The time for coyness had long passed. Liam didn't mind asking the direct question, despite the confused look on Danny's face.

'He hasn't taken those girls. Of course he hasn't. Like I told you before, he used to flip between sofas, here and there. So I guess, if he's taken them anywhere, it would be one of his friend's places, but that's hardly realistic, is it? You're welcome to check here if you want.'

Liam understood the flippancy but didn't respond, leaving a pause so Danny could calm down.

'The three girls, including the one whose body was found – Ruby Fletcher – all came from Cheltenham. Do you know if Tony had any connection to the place?'

Danny pursed his lips and shook his head. 'Absolutely no idea. I don't recall him ever mentioning it.'

'Did he have family there?'

'I don't know. You're the police officer.'

'What about Newquay?' Liam asked, watching Danny closely, knowing agitation often led people to slip.

'What about it?' Danny said, folding his arms.

'Did Tony ever go there? Did you?'

Danny let out a sigh. 'We've both been there loads of times. We do a bit of surfing, and obviously we go for the nightlife.'

'Quite a long way to go.'

'It's not like the clubs in Penzance are bursting, is it? We'd stay the night. There's a couple of hostels that are dirt cheap.'

'When was the last time you went?'

Danny's arms stayed folded. He glanced up in recollection.

'New Year's Eve. Big night, as I'm sure you know. Fancy dress and all that.'

'Where did you stay?'

'Like I said, one of the hostels. I can't remember the name. I'll text you the details if you like.'

'Can you have a look now?'

Liam matched Danny's body language, folding his own arms.

Danny sighed again and started scrolling through his phone until he found an address. Liam jotted it into his own.

'Any other connections to Newquay? Anyone Tony knows there he might stay with?'

Danny shook his head, his arms folded once more.

'Look, I know you think you're protecting him, but if, as you say, he's not responsible, then he might be in trouble. Are you going to be able to forgive yourself if we find him in the boot of a car like that other lad?'

Danny's arms dropped. He leant back in his seat as if Liam had struck him. 'I'm not trying to protect him. He didn't do it.'

'Is there anyone in Cornwall we should speak to?'

Danny paused. 'There is someone I just thought of. An ex. Sylvie Waters.'

Liam sat forward slightly. 'Sylvie Waters? You didn't mention her before.'

'He's dated quite a few girls, hasn't he? You mentioned Newquay and she lives there. They used to date. Over a year ago, when he was still doing his A-Levels. She moved to Newquay last summer to work in a restaurant. She's been there since.'

'Why am I only just hearing about this, Danny?' Liam asked.

Danny raised his hands in mock surrender. 'Didn't occur to me. You've said yourself how many women he's been involved with. It's not my job to keep track.'

'Where does she work?'

'Sanham Hotel. Restaurant there.'

Liam thanked Danny, and left the young man where he was, doing a quick sweep of the small flat just in case he'd been bluffing.

Outside, the threatening grey clouds had yet to burst. He got in his car, case notes looping in his head. He couldn't recall Sylvie's name from the investigation, but as Danny had said, there were a lot of names connected to Tony.

The Sanham Hotel was not far from Towan Beach, where the three girls had gone missing.

Liam pulled up forty minutes later. He'd called Sylvie using the number Danny had given him, but got no answer. The receptionist at the hotel gave him a polite smile, her eyes flicking up and down as she asked how she could help.

'Sylvie Waters. Is she working today?'

'She's in the restaurant. Can I ask what this is regarding?'

Liam showed his warrant card. 'Police matter.'

'Take a seat,' said the receptionist. 'I'll see if she's free.'

'I'll come with you. This is urgent.'

Liam followed her through the restaurant. The receptionist approached a waitress, a young woman dressed in black, dark hair falling to her shoulders. They exchanged words and both glanced towards Liam before walking over.

The receptionist led them through to a small office behind the desk.

'Let me know if you need anything,' she said.

Liam and Sylvie sat down opposite each other. 'Sorry to drag you from work,' Liam said.

'You're doing me a favour. I was dealing with a really obnoxious table. Glad to get away,' Sylvie said. 'This is about Tony?' Sylvie had an oval face and large blue eyes, framed by heavy make-up she didn't seem to need. She looked older than the other young women he'd spoken to, carrying herself with a different kind of poise.

'Why would you think this is about Tony?'

'You'd have to be a hermit not to know what's going on. I know he went missing. Loads of people texted to ask if I'm okay. I'm surprised you didn't come sooner.'

'Believe it or not, I've only just found out about you.'

She laughed – a dry, flat sound. 'Doesn't surprise me. I imagine I'm way down the list.'

'You used to date him?'

'Yep. First boyfriend. First and only heartbreak.' Her smile was resigned.

'When did you split?'

'Last summer. After A-Levels.'

'Why?'

'You probably know. Tony's a lovely lad, but he gets a lot of attention. He wasn't grown-up enough to handle it.'

'He cheated?'

Sylvie shrugged. 'I don't blame him. Well, not now. I did at the time. He wanted us to stay together. I nearly agreed. But Mum said no and I knew it was the right call. He wasn't ready. That's why I took the job here. Out of sight, out of mind. It was hard at first, but I'm okay now.'

'When did you last see him?'

'New Year's Eve. They were dressed as Wombles, believe it or not. Him and Danny. I didn't know it was them until I made them take off their stupid masks.'

'How long were you with them?'

'Half an hour. They were already gone by that point. I left them to it.'

Liam could see she was uncomfortable with the questioning. Her hands were clasped and she was avoiding eye contact.

'You said you know what's going on. So you know two girls are still missing?'

Sylvie nodded but didn't reply.

'We think Tony might be involved. Is there anywhere you can think of that he might go? Anywhere he might be hiding them?'

Sylvie moved her head back. 'Tony wouldn't do that to anyone. I saw what they wrote about him, calling him a Lothario or whatever. But that doesn't make him a murderer.'

'He cheated on you,' Liam said.

'Doesn't make him a killer.' Her voice rose. 'You don't understand. He's gentle. Caring. Yeah, he sleeps around but I don't know many boys his age who wouldn't given the chance. Part of it's because he's insecure.'

'Insecure?'

'About his mum. I'm no psychologist, but I think he's scared of being abandoned. He cried when I broke up with him. I mean, sobbed. Begged me to stay. I nearly did. Told him maybe in five years if we were still single we could try again.'

It was the first time Liam had heard this description of Tony.

'He talked about his mum a lot?'

'Sometimes. Mostly he avoided it. But then it'd all come out at once. He loved her so much. They used to go on trips together to castles, stone circles. His dad took it badly when she died. Tony couldn't connect with him. They argued. He'd come and stay with me.'

'I know you don't think he's involved,' Liam said. 'But if he isn't, he could be in danger. Can you think of anywhere he might go? Anyone who might want to hurt him?'

Sylvie looked down, shaking her head. 'If I knew, I'd tell you. Everyone likes Tony. Even the lads. I just can't think of anyone who'd even think of doing something to him.'

Chapter Thirty

Liam was getting a little sick of people protesting Tony's innocence. He'd never in his life been blinkered during an investigation, and was still open to the possibility of Tony not being the killer. But it was undeniable that he had to be considered the prime suspect given the evidence they had against him.

He was known to have slept with at least two of the three female victims and had a keen interest in stone circles and Cornish mythology. And although Liam understood the loyalty being shown by family and friends, it was getting a little wearing.

Even Sylvie, who'd moved town because of Tony, had little to criticise beyond a need for maturity; an accusation that would apply to the majority of eighteen- and nineteen-year-olds.

Police presence in Newquay remained high. Bars and clubs, caravan parks and holiday homes were all being searched, owners and locals questioned. The search extended to farms and outbuildings in the surrounding areas, all in a desperate attempt to find those missing. But given the remoteness and cost of accessing certain areas of the county, it was impossible to cover more than a fraction of the potential locations where the two missing girls and Anthony Ellison might be.

Liam drove back to headquarters, where he met Maya in the car park. She still didn't seem herself. Her face was drawn, her tone clipped when he mentioned his meeting with Sylvie.

'Another woman he's fucked over and left,' she said as they walked into the station reception.

It was unusual for her to be so blunt and Liam was sure something beyond the investigation must be bothering her. Their friendship, always solid, had deepened during the Sennen murders investigation, but Maya tended to still keep things to herself. He found himself wondering if that was a failing in him. Maya knew all about his complicated history with Grace, the feelings he'd had for Millie, and the volatile relationship with his ex, Kim. Maybe Maya would have shared more, if only he'd ask the right questions.

'Don't you think it's strange?' Liam said as they entered the lift. 'Even after everything, it's all but impossible to get anyone to say a bad word about him.'

'He certainly weaved a spell on them, that's for sure,' Maya replied, her expression flat.

'It's not just that, though. No one thinks he's capable of this.'

She smirked, a gesture that rarely crossed her face. 'Where have we heard that before?'

The lift pinged open and they went to their separate desks.

Liam worked through the afternoon making calls and updating incomplete leads. His eyes kept drifting to the crime board, which was now more chaotic than ever.

Photographs of the four confirmed victims took centre stage: the three women who had metaphorically been turned to stone, and Kian Burrell dumped in the boot of his car like an afterthought.

Adjacent were the photos of the two missing women from Cheltenham, Nina Connors and Erin Dunne.

And finally, Tony Ellison as prime suspect in a column of his own, with smaller photographs of the other bit players surrounding him, including Raymond Preston, Danny Reeve, Rory Ellison, Reverend Frayne, Jerry Penrose and Kyle Sturridge among others.

Maya tapped him on the shoulder and nodded towards one of the interview rooms. 'Quick word,' she said.

Liam followed her across the incident room, noting a look from Grace, who had returned with Quinlan.

'Everything okay?' Liam asked as Maya waited for him to sit before shutting the door of the interview room. 'Is this where you ask for my badge and gun?' he added, trying to lighten the mood.

She ignored it. 'Bloodwork's in. Carys, Ruby, Kian, as well as Katie Brookmeyer. We're officially a priority case with forensics now, unsurprisingly.'

'What have we got?'

Maya sat beside him. 'That's the problem. There's no DNA match to Tony Ellison in any of them. Not even in the blood under Katie's fingernails.'

Liam closed his eyes, rubbing his forehead. 'That complicates things,' he said.

'It does more than that,' Maya replied. 'It means we could've been chasing the wrong person all along.'

Liam frowned. 'I'm not sure that's fair. We've always treated him as a potential victim as well. No match doesn't mean he isn't involved.'

Maya looked down. 'It means he didn't try to abduct Katie Brookmeyer. And unless we're talking about a coincidental second attacker, that seriously weakens the case against him.'

'Or he's working with someone else,' Liam said. 'Which would explain how he's pulling this off without leaving a trace.'

'It's crossed my mind,' Maya said.

Liam hesitated. 'Maya, is everything all right? You don't seem yourself.'

Maya sighed but didn't bristle at the question. 'I'm fine. Just tired.'

'So what next?' he said.

'We've got a DNA profile from whoever attacked Katie Brookmeyer. No match in the system, which means the next step is simple: we find out who it belongs to.'

◆ ◆ ◆

The following morning, Liam met Raymond Preston at a small café near the train station in Penzance. Preston had told him the night before that he'd be working at an archaeological site out towards St Levan later that day. He was already waiting when Liam arrived.

The café smelt of stale grease, more than one of the occupants tucking into mounds of fried breakfast. Liam ordered a coffee, Preston greeting him with the same unwavering smile as when they'd first met. 'DS Kilshaw, good to see you, despite the circumstances.'

'Thanks for making the time,' Liam said, accepting the offered coffee and nodding to the café owner in thanks. 'Where are you working today?'

'No stone circles, if that's what you're wondering,' Preston replied with a grin. 'There's some excavation work, nothing major. I'll be there all day. I've heard about the recent developments. Hard to believe any of this is happening.'

'You're telling me,' Liam said.

'What sort of warped mind takes the Merry Maidens legend and tries to make it real?'

Liam thought again about last night's revelation, that the DNA taken from the last three victims and Katie Brookmeyer were not a match for Tony Ellison.

The morning was the start of a renewed campaign, taking DNA samples from everyone remotely involved in the investigation.

Liam took a drink of the lukewarm liquid in his mug. 'As you know, we still have two girls missing. And Tony Ellison,' he said, showing Preston a picture on his phone, a map of the Penwith area with the body sites marked.

'Such a terrible thing,' Preston murmured, shaking his head. 'It's what they'll be known for now, isn't it? I imagine more people will visit them, knowing what happened there.'

Liam kept the image open, it slowly dawning on him that Preston was talking about the stone circles rather than the victims. He was right that this type of notoriety would probably drive tourists, and considered it for the first time as a potential motive.

'We're trying to work out where the killer might strike next. Obviously, it's a near-impossible task. But I was wondering if you had any insights.'

Preston leant forward, brow furrowed, bringing the phone closer. Liam let him, playing to his ego.

'The link between the Merry Maidens, Tregeseal, and Boskednan sites is fairly obvious – pointing to the sites where the three young women had been found. The story's the same, maidens turned to stone for breaking the Sabbath. It's only one of many legends, but the comparison holds. That's where the boy was found?' he added, pointing to the quarry site near to Boskednan.

Liam nodded.

Preston placed a hand to his mouth in thought.

Liam let the man think for a time before asking, 'Where do you think the killer might go next?'

'There are no more Maidens sites. I guess they could strike here.' Preston pointed to the Hurlers site in Bodmin.

Liam had already visited the triple stone circles on Bodmin Moor, with its hurlers turned to stone, twice so far.

'Maybe that's where you'll find Tony Ellison,' Preston said.

'Why do you think that?' Liam asked, taking back his phone.

'I'm no amateur sleuth, DS Kilshaw, but if the killer is placing female bodies at sites where maidens supposedly danced, maybe he's planning to place the male victims at the sites associated with men.'

It didn't explain the seemingly random disposal of Kian Burrell's body, but it did raise the possibility that the killer might be using different types of stone circles depending on the sex of the victims. It was also possible, thinking back to the ochre found at the Piper Stone, that both Tony, if he was a victim, and Kian had been killed at the stone circles and then removed, for whatever twisted reason the killer may have.

'Anywhere else?'

Preston tilted his head as if a thought had just occurred to him. 'You could try Trevowen.'

'Trevowen?'

'It's not technically a stone circle, but it is believed there used to be one there. It's nothing but a field now, but it is close to Boskednan. Might be worth a look.'

Liam took a note of the location. 'I enjoyed reading your book,' he said, as he finished his coffee.

Preston blushed. 'Really? That's lovely to hear. Perhaps you could leave a review online for me,' he added with a shy smile.

'I'll see what I can do. By the way, we're asking everyone involved in the investigation to voluntarily provide a DNA sample to help rule out the profiles we found on the bodies. Since you were at the site that first day, it'd be helpful if we could get a swab from you.'

'Is that really necessary?' Preston said, taken aback. 'It's not as if I touched the body.'

'We could do it now, if you like. I've got the kit with me.'

'I'm not sure I like the idea of my DNA being on file.'

'It wouldn't be on file. It's for this investigation only. Afterwards, it would be destroyed.'

Preston pursed his lips. 'You'll forgive me if I don't have much faith in your procedures.'

'You never struck me as a conspiracy theorist.' Liam reached for his coat. 'Listen, it's completely voluntary, like I said. But it would be helpful. You're not the only one I'll be asking today.' He handed Preston a leaflet. 'You can pop into any local station and have it done if you don't want to do it now. Takes a couple of minutes at most.'

Preston nodded slowly. 'Let me think about it,' he said, his earlier humour now faded.

Liam thought it a little odd that Preston had refused the DNA test but wasn't that surprised. There was a lot of misinformation out there, and people were more cautious than ever. Though when he tried to formulate a scenario in his head of Preston being the killer, it felt reasonably plausible. His love of stone circles was obvious, and there had been small discrepancies, including his having taught Tony Ellison, and the fact that he was always so hard to get hold of.

It made him wonder if all of Tony's friends and acquaintances had been right all along, and that they'd wasted too much time focusing on Tony Ellison.

He made a mental note to follow up on the archaeologist as he made the short trip to Danny Reeve's house. Tony's erstwhile flatmate wasn't home. Liam left a message requesting Danny attend a local station for a DNA test before then heading towards Bodmin, where he met Maya at the Hurlers stone circle.

She looked a little brighter than yesterday. 'None for me?' he said, nodding at the coffee in her hand.

'With your timekeeping, I thought it'd be cold by the time you got here.'

'I'll add that to the big book of DI excuses,' Liam said, drawing a smile from her as they walked across the field to the stones.

They'd decided to take another look at the Hurlers due to its similarities with the other three sites. There was a police patrol car on-site as he walked with her to the circles.

Liam told her about his meeting with Preston, the theory about the killer possibly using different sites for male victims, and the archaeologist's reluctance to provide a DNA sample. They both knew it didn't necessarily mean anything. A refusal wasn't an admission of guilt but it did put Preston a little more on their radar.

'Do you really think he could be involved?' Maya asked as they reached the first of the stones. Liam ran his hand across the granite, picturing the hurlers being turned to rock as the sun rose on the Sabbath.

Again, Liam thought about Preston as a suspect. 'He does love these stone circles.'

'Maybe pay him another visit later,' Maya said. 'It's a little red flag, at least.'

As they'd done before, they moved from stone to stone. The three rings of the Hurlers intersected one another and it was hard to keep count. Liam recalled reading in Preston's book that, like the Merry Maidens, some of the stones here were thought to have been repositioned or replaced over time.

As they reached the final stone, Liam found himself wondering when people had stopped believing in these old myths. Or if, in some quarters, they ever really had.

'It's not like we're actually going to find a dead body or anything, is it?' he said, half-laughing to himself as they walked back to the cars. 'Listen, boss, tell me if I'm out of line, but is everything all right with you?'

They kept walking. Maya didn't reply straight away and Liam worried he may have breached an unknown boundary before she eventually replied. 'Are you turning into my agony uncle now?'

Liam looked straight ahead. 'I just figured . . . you've listened to a lot of my shit in the past. Thought maybe it was my turn to return the favour. I'm trying to better myself here, you know?'

He was relieved to see a smile creep on to Maya's face. 'There's nothing really,' she said at last. 'Jane and I have split up.'

Liam feigned surprise. 'Jane?'

'Very funny.'

'So . . . what happened?'

'The usual. She thinks I'm never there for her. I work too much. Police cliché 101.'

'Been there,' Liam said. 'She's police, though, isn't she?'

'She's uniform, out of area. Has pretty regular hours, at least compared to me.'

'Well, as you know, I'm no relationship expert. But I think she's making a huge mistake.'

Maya stared at him. 'Just because I'm single now doesn't mean you can hit on me,' she said, deadpan.

Liam nodded. 'Understood,' he said matching her deadpan look as he got into the car.

The atmosphere at headquarters was tense. Everyone was running on fumes, the stress more about the missing people than the bodies already found. The investigation was in full swing. More and more DNA tests were being taken, and every viable lead followed, but it felt as if they were all just waiting for the inevitable phone call confirming that one of the missing women had been found dead.

Plainclothes officers had been stationed in and around the Hurlers site, and a number of other potential sites were being watched too.

The hope had to be that sooner or later the killer would make a mistake. With the exception of the attempted abduction of Katie Brookmeyer, everything the killer had done so far had been clean and calculated, but the potential for a slip-up was always there.

Liam left work at six and drove straight to St Ives where it was his turn to volunteer at the lifeboat centre, where he caught up with Phil. The coxswain was his usual morose self as the two of them worked on the *Mary Rose*, polishing the hull in silence for a while.

'So,' Phil said eventually, 'you any closer to finding someone for this?'

Liam, still scrubbing, found his thoughts turning immediately to Raymond Preston and his refusal to give a DNA sample. He wondered how he would cope if Preston was behind the killings after being under his nose for the majority of the investigation.

'Not quite yet, but you'll be the first to know.'

They worked through to eight, locking up before heading for a quick pint. It felt good to unwind, the tension in Liam's body loosening with every sip of cider, and for the briefest of times, the investigation slipped from his mind only to return with full force once he was back in his flat.

He couldn't shake the possibility of Preston being involved and he called the archaeologist to see if he'd made a decision on the DNA test. It was late but the call felt necessary, and he grew more restless when it went straight to answerphone.

Unable to consider sleep, he drove the short distance to Raymond Preston's remote address, a small village a few miles out of Penzance. He parked outside Preston's modest bungalow, which was surrounded by land cloaked in darkness, and tried his phone once more before knocking on his front door.

With no answer, he switched on his torch and took a short walk around the property's gated perimeter. Peering over the fence, he was surprised by the size of Preston's garden, which stretched into the shadows.

Adjusting the torch he alighted on something else, closer to the house.

It appeared to be a lone granite plinth, standing upright at one side, as if it had been plucked straight out of a stone circle.

Chapter Thirty-One

It wouldn't be long now. The circle was tightening.

He wasn't sure how much they knew, but they understood enough to have the special places guarded, albeit in a basic fashion.

Ruby had been a delight. He'd prepared her in the back of the van, the others forced to watch.

It was a shame he couldn't place her directly in the circle, but her proximity had been enough. It had made the job easier. He couldn't deny the sliver of pleasure that had given him, each of the voyeurs unable to move as they watched Ruby begin her transformation, knowing it was only a matter of time for them.

It had felt safe to leave them while he took a tour of the sites, searching for an opportunity.

All he needed was two more nights.

One to complete the circle, and one to finish it all.

It had been acceptable to leave Ruby close to Tregeseal, but for this next one, the maiden had to be in the circle.

Returning to the van, he told the others the plan. Their blank faces told him all he needed to know.

It would work.

After making the arrangements, he settled with the book, deciding that this time he would read some extracts aloud to his audience.

But not before he painted Nina's forehead with limonite, the beautiful yellow streak marking her as the next maiden.

Chapter Thirty-Two

For a moment, a vision of a body hidden behind the stone flashed in Liam's mind: an amalgamation of Nina and Erin, trapped within the stone, struggling for breath as the soil slowly filtered into their lungs.

It may have been irrational, but at this stage it didn't feel any more irrational than having a circle stone in your back garden without ever mentioning it.

He was tempted to climb the fence for a better look. It would be trespassing, and there was nothing illegal about having a granite boulder on your property. But it made him want to speak to Raymond Preston more than ever.

He walked further along the fence until he had a clear look behind the stone, relieved to see nothing but long grass. He tried Preston's number for the fourth time that day, before ringing Maya to tell her about the discovery.

'There's hiding in plain sight . . . and then there's *that*,' he said.

'Someone must've noticed it before,' Maya replied, not buying into any assumptions.

Liam reluctantly agreed. The stone wasn't exactly concealed. The neighbouring houses were in the distance but the garden wasn't hidden so it had to be common knowledge. His initial suspicions faded but he still wanted to speak to Preston, if only to find out why he hadn't mentioned it before.

'I guess I'm not getting permission to go into the garden,' he said.

'You guess right,' Maya replied. 'Maybe if you haven't heard from him by this time tomorrow, we can look at getting a warrant. But for now, we'd have no chance.'

'Got it, boss,' Liam said, hanging up.

It was the right call but only served to add to his continued frustration. There had to be more he could be doing and even though it was close to midnight, Liam wasn't prepared to stop working.

He drove the back lanes to the excavation site Preston was working on: Moorstone Reach near St Levan. As he meandered through the isolated roads that led to the site, he tried to make a case again for Preston being the killer. Despite the discrepancies, it didn't ring true to him, but that wasn't going to stop him getting proof one way or the other.

He passed the Merry Maidens on the way, his headlights catching an unmarked police car parked near the entrance, the only lingering sign of the horrors that had occurred there.

Another three miles on, he reached the field where Preston had said he'd been working. Like the stone circle, it was shrouded in darkness. He pulled off at the roadside and climbed over the hedge into the field, almost tripping over the rope marking the excavation perimeter.

Switching on his torch, he walked the boundary first before entering the larger field. A part of him braced to find another body but there was nothing there.

Back at the car, he called Preston once more, leaving another message, reiterating the importance of calling him back as soon as possible.

The moment he ended the call, his phone rang. He glanced at the screen, hoping it was Preston, half disappointed when he saw Grace's name.

'I hope this is a social call,' he said, answering. 'I haven't got the energy to go back to work.'

'You can relax, nothing to investigate tonight. I've barely seen you since the other night, thought it would be good to catch up,' Grace said.

'It's been a bit hectic,' Liam replied, before taking time to think about what he should say.

'Whoa,' she cut in, clearly pissed at him. 'I'm not chasing you, Liam.'

He winced, catching the defensiveness in his voice. The truth was, he *had* been avoiding her, though he wasn't entirely sure why. He enjoyed being with her, would happily see her again, but the reluctance came from somewhere deeper. Kim had always accused him of fearing commitment, of subconsciously pushing people away, and at times like this he thought maybe she was right.

'What are you doing now?' he asked, trying to change his own narrative.

'Just finishing up. Took the DNA sample from that lad we were chasing earlier.' She paused before continuing, her tone softening. 'I know it's late, but I was going to ask if you'd like to meet up. I don't fancy going back to the hotel room alone,' she added, her voice quieter than usual. A note of vulnerability he wasn't used to hearing from her.

'That sounds good. I'll be back at my flat in twenty minutes. I could make you a quick something to eat, if you like.'

'That sounds even better,' said Grace.

They drove to work in separate cars the following morning. Liam wondered why he'd avoided her these past few days. Being with Grace was a respite from everything, and already it felt like they were slipping back into something familiar, though he could only imagine the look on Maya's face when she found out.

They arrived at the station at the same time, so he gave Grace five minutes before following her inside.

A familiar ominous mood hung over CID. Most of the DNA tests had been completed, but one prominent exception remained. Liam had tried calling Preston again on the way in, growing increasingly concerned with the continued silence.

'Still nothing?' Maya asked, catching up with him in the kitchen area.

Liam shook his head.

'Do you think he's a legitimate suspect?' she asked.

His instincts told him Preston wasn't their killer. That wide-eyed, almost boyish enthusiasm for archaeology didn't square with the kind of person who could do something like this, but he wouldn't be the first killer to hide a darker side behind charm and intellect, and instinct alone wasn't enough to dismiss someone.

'I believe he's the only one to refuse a DNA test so far,' Liam said.

Maya nodded. She looked better than the day before – calmer, more rested – and Liam hoped their conversation at the Hurlers had helped, even a little.

'I'll head over to the excavation site today,' he said. 'Want to come?'

'Too much on here. By the way . . .'

Liam caught the teasing look on Maya's face. 'What?' he asked.

'Nothing really. Just that I happened to notice you and Grace arrived in the car park at the same time. And you both walked into the building five minutes apart. Almost like you were trying to hide the fact you were together.'

Liam shook his head, unable to suppress the smile tugging at his lips. 'You need to take a day off, DI Trent. And any more wild accusations like that, I'll be having words with HR.'

'Just an observation, DS Kilshaw,' Maya said, turning away before he could answer.

He risked a glance towards Grace and caught the faint upturn of her lips as she acknowledged him without making eye contact. It felt like being back at school. A quiet, blossoming teenage romance. He smiled to himself, grateful for the brief moment of lightness.

It would still be another couple of days before all the DNA samples were processed. The priority now was to stay proactive and visible. The last thing they needed was for the next breakthrough in the investigation to be another body, but they had no idea what, if any, timetable the killer was working to.

Liam read through the overnight reports. Officers were still stationed at the various stone circles countywide. Some saw it as a waste of resources, but Liam knew the backlash if something happened at a site they'd left unmanned would be worse.

He called Preston one last time before heading out, swearing under his breath when the cheery answerphone message played out.

The good mood he'd woken with after the night spent with Grace had evaporated by the time he reached the narrow stretch of the A30. The morning light was brighter now. As he passed the Merry Maidens, he caught sight of the nineteen stones and blinked away the vision of Tess Penrose's body that came to mind.

A few minutes later he pulled up outside the excavation site, relieved to see movement in the fields. The sun was out but the temperature was low, a gust of wind greeting him as he left the car. The excavation activity was spread across two fields. Liam kept his distance, the archaeologists continuing their work as if oblivious to his arrival.

Unable to spot Preston in the first field, Liam skirted the hedgerow towards the second. He tried to rationalise why Preston hadn't returned his calls, especially after emphasising the urgency. The only explanation he could come up with was that Preston hadn't checked his phone, which, although unlikely, was possible.

A loose vine whipped Liam's arm as he pushed through a gap into the second field, where another group of archaeologists worked, all crouched over damp soil, marked off with thin rope. A young woman stood to stretch, revealing Raymond Preston behind her.

Liam shook his head, irritated by the wasted time, as he moved towards the group. As he approached, each archaeologist looked up until Preston met his gaze. For a moment, Liam thought Preston might bolt, but instead the man rose, offering his usual broad smile.

'DS Kilshaw,' he said cheerfully. 'What brings you here?'

'Can we have a word in private?' Liam asked, barely acknowledging the friendly nod from the woman by Preston's side.

Liam led Preston away until they were out of earshot. 'Where's your phone, Raymond?' he said, unable to hide his irritation.

Preston looked surprised. 'I'm not sure. Probably in my bag.'

'When did you last check it?'

Preston shrugged, contrite. 'I'm sorry, I'm not good with phones.'

'But you knew I might need to speak with you again.'

'My apologies,' Preston replied, his smile becoming irritating. 'How can I help?'

'Start by explaining the stone monolith in your garden.'

Preston's eyes narrowed slightly. 'It's an abandoned artifact. It was going to be disposed of, so I took it for the garden.' The smile faded. 'Can I ask why you've been to my house?'

'Where were you last night?' Liam demanded.

'I don't think that's relevant . . .'

'I'll decide what's relevant. You weren't home last night, and you haven't been answering your phone. We have three missing people. So again, where were you?'

'This feels uncalled for.'

'Uncalled for?' Liam snapped. 'You're difficult to contact, refuse to give a DNA sample, and then vanish. Oh, and you have a stone circle monolith in your garden. How should I interpret that?'

Preston frowned, glancing back at his team. A woman in dungarees beneath a rain jacket was watching closely. 'I stayed at Janine's place,' he finally admitted.

'Janine?'

'Yes, Janine over there.' Preston gestured to the woman in dungarees.

'Will she confirm that?'

'Of course,' Preston said defensively. 'I've nothing to hide.'

'Then why refuse a DNA test?'

Preston shook his head, seemingly disappointed in Liam. 'Fine, let's do the test now, if you have it. Sorry if I've caused you so much trouble.'

Liam handed him the swab from his coat pocket, watching closely as Preston complied. It could be another two days until the result came back, and until then he would be keeping a closer eye on the archaeologist than before.

Chapter Thirty-Three

Out of earshot of Preston, Liam verified his alibi with Janine, who blushed as she confirmed the archaeologist had indeed stayed the night at her house.

'Do me a favour, Raymond, and leave your phone switched on,' Liam said, before traipsing back across the field to his car.

By the time he returned to the station, only Jack was in CID. None of the DNA results had come back yet, and the rest of the team were out following leads called in from the public.

Once more, Liam reread the case notes from start to finish, hoping to catch something he might have missed before checking in with Dr Thorne, the forensic anthropologist who'd been examining the bones found at the Merry Maidens for an update.

'We've expanded the dental records search,' the anthropologist said, 'but you know how long these things take.'

Liam hadn't handled many cold cases before. Dental record searches took time, and if you didn't have any possible indication of identity, it was close to an impossible task unless they struck lucky, and that was assuming records existed for the pair at all.

The team filtered back in as the afternoon passed, their tired faces mirroring Liam's own. Reacting to a crime was one thing, but the waiting drained everyone. They knew the importance of rest, but no one wanted to step away, fearing another body might turn up in their absence.

They took turns snatching sleep in the common room and spare interview suites. Liam and Maya checked in regularly with the officers stationed countywide as evening approached, their budget having been extended, response teams near each of the major stone circles.

Surveillance cameras watched roads nearby, each officer's bodycam active. On the whiteboard in the incident room, small screens showed images of empty roads, dashboards, and wildlife triggering static cameras.

It was hard not to feel despondent. So much effort for little reward. Liam watched a car pass the Merry Maidens site, unable to see the occupants clearly, as Maya ordered takeaway for everyone.

They ate quietly, phones and screens close by as they continued to wait.

Liam was helping clear away when a call came through from the Trevowen circle. It was far from the first call of the evening. Liam watched the bodycam footage of the stationed officer, which displayed nothing but vague shadows at present.

Trevowen was a scattered settlement of stone cottages and overgrown lanes, tucked between a stretch of moorland and a line of low hills. It wasn't on Tony's map but after Preston referenced it, and due to its proximity to Boskednan, they had a patrol stationed nearby with two uniformed officers.

'A vehicle's stopped near the field perimeter,' said one of the officers.

'Do we have visual?' Maya asked.

'Northwest field, opposite side. No cameras there. Watching through binoculars. Looks like a transit van. Driver's side door just opened, ma'am.'

'Can you approach?' Maya asked.

'Two-minute drive. On the move now. Hang on, someone's getting out. Large figure. Heading to the back of the van.'

The conversation began to catch the team's attention, eyes darting to the whiteboard screens despite the bodycam footage showing only the darkness.

'They're removing something,' said the officer, her voice urgent. 'Go, go, go. They've dumped something. In pursuit.'

Everyone had stopped what they were doing and were watching the scene unfold, the officer's bodycam now displaying the road from the viewpoint of the windscreen as they rushed towards the van.

'They're leaving. Should we follow the van or inspect the drop?'

'You inspect the drop, driver continue,' Maya said.

Jack pressed a few buttons so they could all see the images from the officer's bodycam, her heavy breathing echoing loud through the speakers as she left the patrol car and ran towards the dumped object.

'I've got visual on the van,' came the voice of the second officer who was in pursuit. 'Should I engage?'

'Pull up behind, lights on. How far's back-up?' Maya said.

'Six minutes,' Jack replied.

Maya cursed under her breath.

'Look,' Liam said, as the first officer slowed, the camera focusing.

'Something in the bushes,' the officer said, torch raised.

'Proceed carefully,' Liam instructed.

Jack updated on back-up progress as the officer edged closer, a white flash illuminating the screen briefly. Liam took a deep breath, fearing they'd soon see another victim.

'The van's slowing,' said the driver.

Liam and Maya glanced urgently at Jack.

'Forty-five seconds.'

Time felt like it was standing still. Officer one hesitated by the bushes as she waited for confirmation.

'I see the back-up lights,' said the driver. 'Van is pulling over.'

'Wait for back-up before approaching,' Maya ordered.

'And me, ma'am?' said the officer in pursuit.

'Continue,' Maya said.

The room collectively held its breath as the officer advanced.

'Whatever it is, it's dumped in the bushes,' she said, torch lighting her way. 'Hang on.'

The camera feed blurred, shifting lines of foliage crossing the screen before the officer stepped back sharply.

'Shit,' she muttered, torch beam steadying on the object. 'It's a bloody armchair.'

Liam turned from the feed, trying to control his anger. 'This can't be a coincidence,' he said.

Jack changed feeds, the second officer switching on his bodycam as he left the car and moved towards the stationary vehicle, where they could just make out the sight of the driver's leg as they began leaving the van.

Back-up arrived as three other officers joined him.

'Stay where you are,' the officer called, baton raised. Two others flanked him, another moved behind.

The driver's leg disappeared back inside as the officer edged closer.

'One male. Appears to be alone. Get out of the van, sir.'

The van door opened again. A man stepped out, his features blurry in the bodycam, hands half-raised. 'What the hell's going on? I stopped because I saw you following me. I don't know why.'

'Let's try to get a facial ID,' Maya said.

'What's your name, sir?' one of the officers asked.

'Farrow. Rick Farrow. What the hell is this?'

'Are you alone in the van?'

'I said I was. Will someone tell me what this is about?' He sounded confused and hadn't initially said he was alone as he claimed, but Liam wasn't buying it. Anyone local would've known the significance of dumping anything near a stone circle in the present climate.

'Tell him to open the back of the van,' Maya said.

The officer gave the instruction. The footage shook as he moved round, Farrow pulling open the rear doors.

'It's just furniture,' the officer said. 'We saw you dumping something two miles back.'

'All right. I'm sorry.'

'What was it?'

'An old armchair.'

'Why there?'

Farrow hesitated. 'Fly-tipping. You know how much it costs to get rid of this stuff?'

'So why just the one chair?'

No answer.

Jack shook his head after running facial recognition.

Grace pulled his details from social media and licensing databases. 'He's registered for waste disposal,' she said, an ID for Rick Farrow appearing on the screen.

'Then why dump it?' Maya asked, relaying the information to the officer on scene.

Farrow sighed. 'I know how it looks. I've got a big collection tomorrow. I needed space.'

'Keep him there. We're on our way,' Maya said, nodding to Liam.

They reached Trevowen twenty minutes later. The roads were quiet and there was no need for lights or sirens. Officer one was waiting at the roadside. They checked the chair before moving down the road to the patrol car.

Farrow sat in the back, cuffed.

'Anything new?' Maya asked the officer standing guard.

'Same story.'

'Let's get him out.'

Farrow groaned as he was ushered out of the van. 'Why are there so many people here? Do I need a solicitor? I thought fly-tipping was just a fine.'

'DI Trent. This is DS Kilshaw. You're Rick Farrow?' Maya said.

Farrow nodded, glancing between them, still trying to gauge the scale of the response.

'You're right to question it,' Liam said. 'Is there anything you can think of that might explain why we're here?'

Farrow frowned. 'No.'

'You follow the news?' Maya asked.

'Not really. Sometimes. I've heard about the murders, if that's what you mean.'

'Then why dump a chair on the edge of a field with a known connection to stone circles?' Maya said, not hiding the fury in her voice.

Farrow looked round. 'Jesus Christ. I just dumped a bloody chair. What stone circle? There's no stone circle here.'

Farrow seemed content to plead ignorance, but Liam still didn't believe him. 'Why that spot? Why just one item? Doesn't make sense to me.'

'I told you. I needed some space. I planned to dump a few things on the way.'

Liam looked towards Maya. 'I think we need to arrest him for the murders,' he said, under his breath, loud enough for Farrow to hear.

'What? No!' screamed Farrow. 'I was paid, okay? Some bloke messaged me online. Offered two hundred quid to dump something there at three a.m. Didn't care what. Just had to be that place, that time. I'm hardly going to turn that down, am I?'

Liam stepped closer. 'And that didn't strike you as strange?'

'It struck me as very bloody strange. Two-hundred-pounds type of strange.'

'And you never thought at any point how it would look, dumping something near a stone circle?'

'What bloody stone circle?'

Farrow's ignorance seemed genuine and Liam reluctantly accepted it. He hadn't known about the Trevowen site until Preston mentioned it, so it was understandable no one else had heard of it.

'Did he give a reason?' Maya asked.

'Said he had a grudge with the farmer who owns the land. That's all I know. Honestly.'

'Name?'

'Andy. Andy something. I can check my phone.'

Maya nodded to the uniformed officer who retrieved the phone from the van. Liam stayed close as Farrow scrolled through his messages.

'Andy W. No last name. Just a number.'

'Show me,' Maya said.

Farrow handed her the phone and they read through the short thread of messages. 'How'd he pay you?'

'Orbit. You know it, it's untraceable.'

Maya nodded. 'Take him in. I want that van stripped down.'

Liam followed her back to the car. Neither of them had to say it, but it felt like the fly-tipping had been a planned distraction. They returned to the location where the first officer was guarding the abandoned chair.

'How far to the Trevowen field?' Maya asked.

'There's an entrance four hundred yards down the road,' the officer said.

They drove towards the entrance, an old wooden gate tied to its post with rope. Liam shone his torch across the desolate field, which held no sign of any stone circle.

They opened the gate, and with torches in hand walked across the damp field, only able to see a few metres ahead.

The wind was up and howled across the desolate land. Preston had told them nothing was left of the stone circle beyond a few stumps but a few minutes in, something caught their eyes. 'There,' Liam said, as they broke into a run.

They stopped a few metres short of what they'd seen.

Breathless, Liam shone his beam on to the remains of a young woman, posed in a prayer position, her face obliterated by clay and dusted with fresh limonite.

Chapter Thirty-Four

The sun was rising by the time the CSIs began erecting a tent over the corpse, which had been identified as Nina Connors. Liam watched from a distance. In the morning glow, it was as if the killer had succeeded in their purpose. With the sun glinting off the limonite streaked across Nina's skin, her body still posed in prayer, it was too easy to imagine she was a statue, human turned to stone.

Liam ordered officers to the addresses of Danny Reeve and Raymond Preston. He wanted confirmation of both their movements from the night before. He followed up with a request for officers to visit the farm near the Merry Maidens site to speak to Kyle Sturridge and Malcolm Whitstable, as the list of Tony's former lovers were contacted one by one to confirm if they were safe.

Jack was already working on the transaction made on the Orbit app between Rick Farrow and the suspected killer. It was the closest they'd come to finding the person responsible, but the anonymity of the service made it unlikely they would be able to trace who had paid Rick Farrow two hundred pounds to dump an armchair anytime soon. Though, as Jack had said, a transaction had been made, which meant somewhere there would be a trail.

With the tent in place, the CSIs began documenting everything. The cause of death appeared to be identical to the others.

'Did it happen here, or was the body moved?' Liam asked Giselle, thinking of the time they'd wasted chasing Farrow's van when it was likely the body had been dumped on the field at the same time.

'I believe she has been moved post mortem. There's no sign of a struggle. The grass beneath her knees is compressed, but everything's a little too neat. The body and surrounding area is relatively clean. As if the clay had already hardened by the time she was placed here.'

'Drugged?'

'Puncture wound in the same place as the previous victims.'

'So, theoretically, it could have happened here?'

'Yes. If she was already incapacitated, the killer could have brought her to the site, arranged her, and then . . . you know the rest. I would estimate she has been dead for at least two hours.'

The field was already cordoned off, along with the path leading to the adjacent field where impressions in the ground suggested the killer had carried or guided Nina either alive or dead. Other CSIs were examining the trail, trying to determine footprints, while the nearest likely parking spots for the killer's vehicle were being analysed.

Maya walked over. 'Hargreaves is on his way to speak to the parents now,' she said.

She looked as frustrated as Liam felt. The killer must have been close by all along. If they'd had a second patrol car in place, they might have intercepted them.

'Whoever it is, they're getting more reckless,' Liam said, finding his mind still focused on Tony Ellison when he thought of the killer.

'Or more organised. They engineered all this just to make sure Nina's body made it to this field.'

'Makes you wonder why they didn't do the same for Ruby. Why proximity was enough for her.'

'We'll need to up security everywhere. This is only going to make the killer, or killers, feel invincible.'

'You still fancy Tony Ellison for this?'

'He's got the brains. And there could be a motive buried in that obsession of his. And with his mum dying so young . . .'

They both left unsaid what they were thinking about the final missing girl. Liam wondered if she would be the last or if the killer had no intention of stopping. There were nineteen stones at the Merry Maidens site and he feared that the number might be the ultimate goal, if there even was a stopping point.

They returned to headquarters late morning. Hargreaves had already spoken with Nina's parents and it had clearly shaken him.

'Budget's irrelevant at this point. Double patrols at all the sites,' he said during the briefing.

Liam thought of Erin Dunne's parents. They'd already lost two of their daughter's friends and were now living each second waiting for the same to happen to her. He wondered how they'd responded to the news of Nina's death, imagining a mixture of relief and guilt, twisted with fear.

After the briefing, he called Rory Ellison and explained the latest developments. He heard the shift in the man's voice, hope giving way to despair. 'What are you doing to find my boy?' Rory asked.

'Everything we can. Where are you right now, Mr Ellison?' Liam asked, Jack signing to him that they still hadn't obtained a DNA sample from the man.

'Plymouth. I know it must seem cold, me working, but I need to do something.'

'Not at all. I understand. We do need that DNA test from you. Would you be able to pop into the station in Plymouth today? It'll only take a few minutes.'

'Of course,' said Rory. 'I can get there after lunch, if that works?'

'I'll let them know,' said Liam, ending the call and returning to his view of the crime board.

There had to be something they were missing. It was obvious the killer had an obsession with mythology, stone circles in particular, but for now, that knowledge did little beyond providing them with an overwhelming number of potential kill sites.

The crime board and white screen were crammed with information. Victims, timelines, and the two remaining missing people taking centre stage.

The map found in Tony Ellison's bedroom appeared on the screen, now updated and superimposed with a new marker at the site where Nina Connors' body had been found that morning at the derelict Trevowen site.

That they now had to contend with sites that were all but theoretical, that might once have been stone circles, only sufficed to make their job that much harder.

Maya sat down next to Liam, placing a coffee in front of him. Such was his stress level, the simple gesture of kindness was close to overwhelming for him. 'Just trying to work out where they're likely to strike next,' he said, keeping himself in check as he voiced his concerns that the killer might be trying to match their toll of victims with the number of stones at the Merry Maidens.

'Whoever's doing this is good, but not that good,' Maya replied. 'Anyway, my feeling is this is all coming to an end. They're ticking them off one by one. If we don't find Erin first . . .'

'You think she'll be the last?'

'Let's try to make sure it doesn't get to that stage.'

Liam wasn't convinced by Maya's theory. The killer was taking great delight in murdering the victims one by one, each arranged with the same morbid theatricality. If Erin Dunne's body was added to the count, Liam doubted it would end there. The killer had got away with too much. He imagined the person responsible saw themselves as untouchable.

And if that was true, surely they'd try to get away with more.

His only hope was that this sense of invincibility would eventually lead the killer to make a mistake, and he prayed that happened before they found Erin.

'You look beat,' Grace said in the kitchen as he poured another cup of coffee.

Liam caught the familiar scent of her perfume, his thoughts going to their nights together.

'I feel it. Why do you look so fresh?'

Grace filled her tea mug with hot water. 'Charmer. DNA results are filtering back in, by the way.'

Liam didn't ask if there had been a match. If there had, the incident room would be in full reaction mode. As it was, everyone carried the same weariness, the tension etched into their features.

'We've managed to eliminate eight people from the list so far. Danny Reeve's one of them. Same goes for a few from the families of the Cheltenham girls.'

Maya walked over and interrupted them. 'Dr Thorne is here,' she said.

Liam blinked. He hadn't seen anything about an appointment with the forensic anthropologist on the schedule.

'I didn't know she was coming either,' Maya added. 'She's waiting for us in one of the interview rooms.'

Liam downed the rest of his coffee, lukewarm and gritty, before shooting Grace a look, as if to blame her for the building's terrible coffee.

'Was I interrupting something?' Maya asked as they took the lift two floors up.

'Your jealousy is becoming unprofessional,' Liam replied.

'In your dreams.'

Dr Aris Thorne had spread photographs and files across the oval table in one of the sixth-floor conference rooms. She glanced up as they entered.

'Thought it'd be quicker and more convenient to come to you,' she said in greeting. The air conditioning was on full blast and Liam rubbed at the goosebumps rising on his scalp.

Images of the eighth stone from the Merry Maidens site were laid out before them, alongside photographs of the two skeletal remains recovered beneath it. It felt like a lifetime ago they had found them.

'Do you have an identification for us?' Liam asked. It was the only reason he could think of for the unannounced visit.

'We received a second round of DNA testing back late yesterday. Partial familial match on the PNC. A man named Michael Holden, been in prison the past fifteen years, mainly for aggravated assault. Once we had his profile, I started digging through his relatives and found a name on the missing persons register.'

She handed them a photograph.

'Carl Holden. Aged thirty-five. Went missing five years ago. We got hold of his old dental records this morning, confirmed the match. He's our man,' she said, pointing to one of the skeletons.

'And the woman?'

'Still waiting on the dental confirmation, but his wife, Veronica Holden, was reported missing at the same time. I'd be surprised if it's not her. We should have a match within the hour.'

She paused, flipping to another page.

'According to the report, Mr and Mrs Holden were last seen heading off on a camping trip near Bodmin five years ago.'

Liam wasn't about to get his hopes up, but it was something to work with. They still had no idea whether the remains found beneath the Merry Maidens site were linked to the current murders or a grim coincidence, but he had to hope it was the former.

And even though he wasn't looking forward to delivering another death message, there was a flicker of optimism as he and Maya drove upcountry towards Tiverton, where they had an address for Carl Holden's parents.

They were already trying to locate the brother, Michael Holden. Unfortunately, the last known address upon his release from prison was in southeast London. Officers at the Met had been instructed to assist, but they were still waiting for an update from them.

Liam scanned through the man's file. He'd been put away at nineteen. A long arrest record even before that. Liam did some quick online checks, but beyond the odd newspaper report, there wasn't much. No links to Cornish mythology or anything connecting him to stone circles.

Still, the timing was impossible to ignore. Carl had vanished and Michael had gone to prison shortly after. And now, with Michael out, the killings had resumed.

'His brother looks like a nasty piece of work. Two counts of GBH in the last ten years. Did some real damage in a bar fight. Got five years on the last one,' he told Maya.

'When was he released?'

'Four months ago. The fight happened four months after Carl went missing.'

DNA was still being compared to profiles found at the recent murder sites. If there was a match, it would be the breakthrough they needed, but Liam wasn't holding out much hope.

The Holden family lived on a small farm at the edge of Tiverton. Liam had called ahead, and could only imagine what they were going through. Five years was a long time to have waited, and although sometimes there was a type of relief in finally having some answers, it was never going to be an easy conversation.

The sound of dogs barking greeted them as Liam pressed the doorbell. A woman in her early thirties answered, wearing jeans and a T-shirt, a tattoo of a rose snaking along her left arm.

'DI Trent and DS Kilshaw,' Maya said.

'Ellie Holden. I'm Carl's sister. My parents are through here. Have you found him?' Her face was unreadable, somewhere between hope and resignation.

'Let's speak with all three of you,' Liam said, stepping inside as two German Shepherds raced down the hallway, tails wagging furiously.

Ellie led them into a low-beamed sitting room. Her parents stood as they entered, each rising from separate armchairs to offer their hands.

'David Holden,' the father said.

'Sarah,' said the woman. 'Shall we cut to the chase? You're here to tell us you've found Carl. Please, just say it.'

Maya nodded gently and began explaining the discovery of the remains at the Merry Maidens site, giving them a brief overview of the current investigation.

David Holden remained standing, arms crossed as his wife collapsed back into her chair. Ellie moved to her side, her hand resting on her mother's shoulder.

'You're sure it's him?' David asked.

Liam nodded. 'We traced his dental records after a partial DNA match with his brother, Michael.'

David turned away at the mention of his other son's name, as if it left a bitter taste.

'What does this have to do with the other murders?' he asked. 'I've been watching the news. These girls . . . turned to stone? It sounds bloody ludicrous. What's Carl got to do with it?'

'And what about Veronica?' Sarah asked, her voice strained.

'We're still waiting on her dental records,' Liam said. 'But we believe the second set of remains belong to her.'

'I don't understand any of this,' David muttered, pouring a generous measure of what looked like brandy from a decanter.

'I know this is an extremely difficult period and you need time to process and grieve,' Maya said, stepping forwards. 'But we were hoping you might be able to help. Anything you can tell us about Carl or Veronica. Any interest they had in stone circles, folklore, anything like that?'

Sarah and Ellie exchanged a glance as David took a long drink.

'They were ramblers,' Sarah said, her voice strained. 'Loved the countryside. Coastal walks. Neither of them were into mythology or that sort of thing.'

'Any friends or other family who might've had that kind of interest?' Maya asked.

'I just can't imagine how this is connected,' Ellie said quietly. 'It doesn't make sense.'

'Have you spoken to his brother?' David asked, swirling his glass. 'I wouldn't be surprised if he had something to do with this.'

'We're trying to locate Michael now,' Maya said. 'When was the last time you spoke to him?'

David shook his head. 'We haven't spoken to that boy in years. Don't know how he turned out the way he did, but he doesn't represent this family. Not in the slightest.'

Liam studied the three family members and the obvious disconnection between the parents. 'So you're not in contact with him at all?'

They shook their heads in unison, almost as if it was a practised routine.

Maya stepped in. 'I know this is difficult to answer, but . . . do you think there's any way Carl and Veronica could've been targeted?'

'Targeted?' said David, drowning the rest of his brandy and refilling the glass, not once offering any to the others.

'The remains were found buried beneath a stone circle. It seems unlikely that it was a random attack. Is there anyone you can think of who would want to hurt either of them in such a way? Any enemies either of them may have had?'

'I don't understand what you're saying,' Sarah said. 'Why would anyone want to do this to them? To anyone?'

Liam shared the names of Tony Ellison and other people involved in the investigation but nothing prompted a response. The family were in shock, and the link to the murder investigation appeared to be spreading more confusion.

Liam handed his card to Ellie as they left. 'We'll have a family liaison officer with you shortly. If you think of anything, however trivial, please call me. Any time day or night. It could be the difference in saving someone's life.'

Ellie took the card and paused. Liam thought she might be weighing up whether or not to tell him something. 'I always knew this day would come. Is it wrong for me to be glad it's all over?' she asked.

'Of course not,' Liam said. 'You'll be able to grieve properly as a family now.'

Ellie hesitated again.

'Is there something you need to tell us?' Maya asked.

Ellie shook her head. 'Michael hasn't anything to do with this, you know, whatever you may think about him. He didn't have an easy childhood. Neither of them did.'

Liam nodded. 'If you need to talk privately, anytime okay?' he reiterated, thinking about the strange way Ellie's parents interacted with each other, and if the father's behaviour had any bearing on the troubled childhood she had suggested her brothers had endured.

Chapter Thirty-Five

Maya slept in the passenger seat as Liam drove back. He couldn't recall her ever doing so while working before, but he understood her exhaustion. This case was taking its toll on everyone. On more than one occasion he had to buzz down his window, using the cold air to keep himself awake.

At headquarters, his colleagues were pottering around as if half asleep. It was clear the whole team was at breaking point, and things were no clearer after meeting with the Holden family.

DNA results for Veronica Holden were confirmed later that afternoon, showing that she had been entombed with her husband, as expected. It meant another death message, Veronica having been survived by a father and brother who lived in the north-west.

As they waited for colleagues in the region to speak to them, Maya ordered the DNA profile for Michael Holden to be extended to all samples taken during the investigation so far. Not long after, a call came in from Manchester informing them that Michael Holden had been located.

'We don't have time to go there. We'll need to arrange a video link interview,' Maya said, as Liam watched on. 'They're going to bring him in,' she added, hanging up.

Liam felt like he was somewhere else. His tiredness was all-encompassing, but trying to rest now felt like a betrayal. Erin was missing, and such was the irrational behaviour of the killer at the moment, not to mention their growing confidence and possible sense of indestructibility, that Liam wouldn't be surprised if they were notified at any moment of more missing potential victims.

'Go,' said Maya, as if reading his thoughts.

'Go where?'

'Get some rest. You're no use to us running on fumes. Go to the communal space. I'll wake you when we have confirmation to speak to Michael Holden.'

Liam went to protest but lacked the strength. In truth, walking was all but beyond him. He wanted to curl up under his desk, but he forced himself up, his mind foggy, and stumbled out of the office, falling instantly asleep when he lay down on one of the mattresses in the darkened room.

His dream was fractured. Images of distorted angels and movable stone circles played against a background of rolling waves. He woke with a shudder, Maya's hand on his shoulder.

'Michael Holden has agreed to be interviewed via video link. Thirty minutes,' she said, handing him a coffee.

Liam sat up as Maya left. Sleep, however meagre, had invigorated him. The coffee was hot and strong and tasted so good he thought he might still be dreaming. He waited until he'd drunk it all before leaving, making a detour by the bathroom where he doused himself in cold water, noticing the tired lines beneath his eyes.

'Everything okay?' asked Grace, as he returned to the incident room.

'And why would you ask that?' he asked, noting the weariness in his voice.

'You look as tired as I feel.'

'So much for my super snooze. Where are we on the Holden video link?'

'Maya is waiting in Interview Room Four.' She smiled, Liam noting again the hint of vulnerability to her he hadn't seen since the time they'd first started dating.

Their rekindled affair had begun at probably the worst time possible. Both of them were so swept up in the investigation that it was difficult to give any thought or energy to anything else. But at least there was comfort in knowing she was there for him and, for now, he tried not to dwell on what would happen once this was all over and she was back in Exeter.

Jack was playing with the video equipment as Liam stepped into the interview room.

'I think they're almost ready for you,' he said, as the screen flickered to life. Two men glared out at them.

Liam recognised Michael Holden from the mugshots and photos they'd pulled from social media. He looked older than he'd imagined, his face drawn, his skin blotchy.

Maya went through the preliminaries, explaining why they were there to Holden and his solicitor. 'We're very sorry for your loss,' she said.

Holden smirked in response, as if the thought of a police officer being sorry about anything was anathema to him.

'When was the last time you saw Carl?' Liam asked.

'A few months before he disappeared . . . before he died,' said Holden.

'You weren't very close then?' Maya said.

'You know what brothers are like. We got on okay, but we'd taken different paths, as I'm sure you're aware.' Holden's tone was conversational, almost light-hearted.

'What did you think had happened to him?' Liam asked.

Holden bit his lip. 'Well, I didn't think he'd been sitting under a tombstone for the last five years, if that's what you're asking. My hope was he'd just disappeared, run off and escaped all the shit going on in his life. But deep down, I knew he was gone. I'm not claiming some sort of sibling connection, but Carl was much more of a family man than I ever was. He had a perverse loyalty to them, which I never understood. I knew he wouldn't just up and disappear.'

'Loyalty to your mum and dad?'

'I guess it was less about them and more about Ellie.' Holden scratched the back of his head. 'He would never have walked away from her. She meant everything to him.'

'So you thought something had happened to him?'

'As I said, not in this type of way.'

'Can you think of anyone who'd want to hurt him like this?'

Holden shook his head. 'He was an easy-going guy. Don't know what he got himself caught up in, but whatever happened it was out of character.'

He turned to his solicitor before looking back at the screen. 'That said, there is one person I can readily think of who would've done this.'

Liam sat up straighter as the solicitor shifted in his seat, a quizzical look on his face.

'I'm not saying he did it. Of course, he hasn't got the balls to attack people stronger than him.'

Liam was sure he was talking about his father, having seen enough during the Holden family interaction to make the assumption. But he waited for Holden to continue.

'I'm talking about that arsehole father. He made our lives a misery from the get-go. Every little failure in his life, he blamed on us.'

'What sort of things did he do?' Liam asked, thinking about how the parents had barely acknowledged one another, how David Holden had stood apart drinking brandy without offering anyone else a glass.

'He used to beat us,' said Holden with a scowl, a look of determination in his eyes. 'Nothing too elaborate, but the threat was always there. We lived in constant fear of his temper. If anything bad happened to him, it also happened to us tenfold.'

'How long did this go on for?' Maya asked.

'Until we were strong enough to fight back – at least, until I was strong enough. I stood up to that old bastard one day, and he never laid a finger on either of us again. Fucking coward. When I left, I told him if he ever hurt Carl I'd return and end him.'

His solicitor recoiled at the statement.

'Did he ever hurt Ellie?' Liam asked.

Holden shook his head, his face contorting. 'No. That would've gone against his twisted sense of what was right and wrong. Boys had to be boys, men had to be men. He never laid a finger on Ellie. And I think that's why . . . why Carl put up with it, why he remained loyal to the family when I moved away.'

Liam considered Michael Holden's criminal record, and how much of it could be attributed to his upbringing.

'Do you think your dad could really have done this?' he asked.

'As I told you, he was a coward. He has the temper, but he's mainly all bark rather than bite.'

Liam was glad they'd had the wherewithal to take DNA samples from the family earlier. 'Did you know Carl's girlfriend, Veronica?'

'She was the one with him? I met her once. Carl was up north at the time, visiting her parents, and they stopped in to say hello. She was a pretty thing. He seemed genuinely happy with her. First time I really remember him being like that.'

'Had he had girlfriends before?'

'Yes, but nothing serious as far as I'm aware. They seemed to be getting on well. She was very friendly. I was pleased for him.'

'You understand why we have to ask, but can you tell me where you were when Carl first went missing?'

Holden grinned. 'I was wondering when you'd get to the point. If you think I did this, you're wasting your time. Even discounting the fact I'm not a murderer, I'd never dream of hurting my brother. I was his protector. That's why I waited so long before I left that hell house.

'Anyway, I've answered all these questions before. I was in Manchester when I was notified about his disappearance, and I've barely been to Cornwall apart from a horrendous family holiday back when I was a kid.' He said the word 'holiday' with air quotes.

'You know about everything that's happening here at the moment, the people who've been killed, the people still missing?' Maya asked.

'I've read about it. Before you ask, I've no idea how Carl could've got himself involved in all of that.'

'Did he have any interest in mythology? Stone circles? That sort of thing?' Maya asked.

'God knows. Saying that, he was a big reader. It was his escape from all the shit going on with Dad. He'd lock himself in his room for hours. I guess it was his happy place.'

'What sort of stuff did he read?'

Holden shrugged. 'I don't really know. I think there were some horror books. Stephen King, James Herbert, Clive Barker, that sort of stuff. Maybe some fantasy. I really can't say.'

'Time is running out for us here, Michael. We really appreciate you speaking with us,' Maya said. 'Is there anything you can think of that could help us find the person responsible for killing your brother?'

'As I said, I just can't picture Carl making any enemies. Not to the extent that someone would want him dead.'

'You said you only visited Cornwall one time as a family?'

'Yep. Just that one holiday.'

'Why do you think Carl would've been in the area at the time of his disappearance? Did he go visiting there with Veronica?'

'It's possible. I really don't know.'

'Did he have any other links to the county?' Liam pushed.

Michael looked upwards. 'The closest I can think of him going to Cornwall, and I know it's not in Cornwall, obviously, was when he went to Exeter University.'

Liam turned to Maya. He'd read Carl's personal file. There had been no mention of Exeter University.

'I thought Carl studied history at the University of the West of England,' Maya said, picking up on Liam's confusion.

'He did. But a few years later, when he couldn't find a job, he decided he wanted to become a teacher. So he started teacher training college, or whatever they call it, in Exeter.'

There had been no mention of such a course in the file. Maya looked behind Liam to Jack, who nodded to the camera that he was leaving the room.

'We don't have any record of this,' Liam said.

Holden shrugged. 'Can't help you. Though maybe it's because he never finished. I think he was only there three months. He'd done some work experience at a local school and decided that was enough for him.'

Maya ended the interview, thanking Holden for his input.

Jack stopped them as soon as they left the room. 'He's right. Carl Holden was enrolled on a PGCE course, nineteen years ago.'

'Jesus Christ. How did we miss this?' Liam said.

'Isn't Exeter Uni where Tony Ellison's parents met?' Maya asked.

'And where his mother had been working when she died,' Liam said, glancing to Jack who looked like he had something to add.

'Already checked, boss. Althea Marlowe was working at the university when Carl Holden was on the course.'

Chapter Thirty-Six

It was too soon to jump to conclusions, but they now had a tentative link between the two bodies found under the eighth stone and the maiden murders.

'How many people go to Exeter University?' Maya asked.

'Approximately thirty thousand across the various campuses,' said Jack.

'So what we have is a victim at university at the same time as a potential suspect's mother,' Quinlan said dismissively.

'Nineteen years ago,' Liam added, the thought turning over in his mind. Nineteen, the same age as Tony Ellison.

It was a long shot, but worth considering. Maybe they had been looking at the wrong Ellison all along. Liam called the number he had for Rory Ellison.

It went straight to voicemail.

'Doesn't anyone answer their phone any more?' Liam muttered.

'We need to speak to him as soon as possible,' Maya said. 'Find out if he ever met Carl Holden, or more importantly, if his wife did. Where are we on the rest of the DNA results?'

'Still waiting,' Jack said.

'They're a priority now. I'll speak to Hargraves, but push forensics. I want all results back today.'

The new information may have been tentative, but it injected fresh energy into the team. Another thought occurred to Liam. 'Rory told me he was going to Plymouth nick after lunch to take his DNA test. He's away on work,' he said.

Jack typed away at his keyboard. 'Nothing's showing.'

It might not mean anything, but Liam called Plymouth, who verified that Rory hadn't turned up to take his DNA test.

A potential theory was forming in Liam's mind, but he didn't want to voice it yet. He thought back to the interview with Michael Holden. The revelation about their abusive father. And to earlier that morning when they'd met the family.

'I'm going to speak to Ellie Holden again. I'm pretty sure there was something she wanted to tell me.'

Maya nodded. Everyone in the incident room was now on their phones or at computers, gathering information or correlating what they already had.

'Hello?' said Ellie, her voice distant on the other end of the line.

'Ellie, this is DS Liam Kilshaw. We met earlier.'

'Yes, I remember, DS Kilshaw. How can I help you?'

'Where are you at the moment, Ellie?'

'I'm just out shopping. I'm supposed to be at work, but obviously the news about Carl has hit us all for six. My mum, in particular.'

'We spoke to Michael,' Liam said, wishing he could be face-to-face with Ellie to gauge her response.

'Oh,' she said. 'How is he?'

'He seems fine, all things considered. Has he not tried to contact you?'

'Michael doesn't have anything to do with the family any more, I'm afraid.'

'Do you know why that is?' Liam asked.

'What did he tell you?'

The urgency of the investigation meant there was no point holding back. 'He said he and Carl had a very difficult upbringing. That your father was abusive.'

The line went silent. Liam tried to determine what was going through Ellie's mind. Michael had said their father's abuse hadn't extended to Ellie, but Liam's experience in such cases told him that might not be true.

'It was tough on them both,' Ellie said after a prolonged pause.

'It must have been hard for you as well.'

'It was.'

'Did your father ever do anything to you, Ellie?' Liam said. He would've much rather been speaking in person, but there was no time for coyness.

'No,' came her simple reply.

'I really don't want to push you, Ellie, but I sensed this afternoon that there was something you wanted to tell me. Perhaps something you couldn't say in front of your parents?'

The line went silent again. Liam pictured Ellie in contemplation, as if she was plucking up the courage to tell him some terrible secret.

'It wasn't to do with my dad – at least not directly, I promise you. My dad never did anything to me. The way he treated the boys was terrible, and I'll never forgive him for that. But he never treated me the same way. He was sort of old-fashioned in that sense. He was cruel to the boys because his father had been cruel to him. I think it was the only way he knew how to deal with them.'

'And your mother? Did she ever try to stop it?'

'You can't blame my mother for what happened, DS Kilshaw.'

'No, of course not, but what was it you wanted to tell me this afternoon, Ellie? Some new information has come to light, and I think you may know something that will help us.'

'What information?'

Liam told her what Michael had said about Carl's brief spell at Exeter.

'That's hardly—' she began.

'I don't know for sure, Ellie. But I think something may have happened when Carl was at Exeter. Would I be wrong in thinking that?'

'What is it you think you know?' Ellie said.

'Look, I don't want to prompt you into anything. If there's something you need to tell me, do it on your own terms. But remember, there's a young woman missing. And a young man, for that matter. You might not think you know anything relevant but what you know could save lives.'

Liam waited. All he could hear was the faint breathing of Ellie through his phone. Eventually she broke her silence. 'I don't know if it's relevant or not. One time Carl told me something. He was drunk. We were at a party, at a friend's house. We were the last two up. He started getting teary about Dad and how he'd been treated growing up. I tried to console him, but nothing I said helped. I'd never seen him like that. It was like all the pain had caught up with him and he was finally letting it out. And all I had to do was listen. Then he told me something he'd never mentioned before.'

'What was that?'

'It sounds crazy, but he told me he thought he may have been a father. I asked him about it later on a number of occasions. He always denied it, claimed he'd been talking nonsense, but it always stayed with me.'

'Did you tell the police this when he went missing?'

'I thought about it. But I didn't think it was relevant. And I didn't want Mum to know. She was already in enough pain.'

'Tell me exactly what he told you.'

'It was in Exeter, like you said. He had an affair with a married woman. I think she was a lecturer. She broke it off with him, but he said he'd heard she was pregnant a few months later. He kept tabs on her over the years. The boy she had was about the right age. He never thought to confront her.'

'Why not?'

'She was married. They had a happy family. Though I guess that wasn't the real reason. It was probably because of Dad. Carl didn't think he deserved to have a child. He worried that if he did, he'd end up treating them the same way he'd been treated.'

'Do you happen to remember the woman's name?'

Ellie paused. 'It was something a bit strange but I'm afraid I can't quite remember.'

'Althea?'

'Yes, that's right. Althea, how did you know?'

'Thank you, Ellie,' Liam said. He hung up and informed the team of what he'd just been told.

'Carl Holden could have been Tony Ellison's father?' Maya said.

The incident room went silent as everyone tried to process this latest information.

'It does seem likely he was Tony's father, or at least thought he was,' Liam said.

'So you think if Tony found out, it sent him on this path to killing?' Jack asked.

'No, no,' Liam said. 'Let's think about this logically. Tony couldn't have killed Carl and Veronica. He would have been eleven at the time they died.'

'What then?' said Quinlan.

'What if Carl is Tony's dad and Rory Ellison found out? That would be potential motive for killing Carl and Veronica. And remember they went missing not long after Althea died. Logical trigger. From there, who knows what happened to Rory. Maybe he's been churning this over ever since. Tony is leaving for university in the autumn. That could have dredged up old feelings.'

'Let's get him in,' Maya said, clearly having heard enough.

Liam called Rory's work, placing the call on speaker for the rest of the room. 'Hello. I'm trying to contact Rory Ellison. Could you put me through or tell me where he is?'

'Can I ask who's calling?' said the woman who answered.

'DS Liam Kilshaw. It's a matter of significant importance.'

'Bear with me,' the woman said, her voice replaced by hold music.

Liam drummed his fingers, wondering how all this pieced together, and if Rory Ellison had been the person they'd been looking for from the start.

The music cut out.

'DS Kilshaw, I've just checked with his department. Rory Ellison is on compassionate leave. He hasn't been in for the last three days.'

Chapter Thirty-Seven

A warrant for Rory Ellison's house was issued within an hour, Liam and Maya heading the search team. They were still coming to terms with the information they'd gathered that day. Conversations were ongoing with Rory's colleagues, trying to locate him, and a nationwide wanted alert had been issued.

If Tony Ellison was Carl Holden's love child, as now seemed likely, then the working theory was that Rory had killed Carl and Veronica in some twisted form of revenge. They were still waiting on DNA profile matches to confirm the link between Carl and Tony, but until then, they had to work from the position that Rory wasn't Tony's biological father.

'He still raised the boy from birth,' Maya said, as they discussed the matter, moving from room to room in the detached property Liam had last been at when he'd taken the map from Tony's bedroom.

Liam had been thinking about nothing else. He considered his own fractured relationship with George, and how Mark had effectively been his son's main father figure. He knew Mark loved George as if he was his own, but no one could ever question the way Liam felt for his son.

If Rory was behind everything then it was yet to be determined what that meant for Tony. It couldn't be ruled out that Tony was involved somehow and Liam didn't want to consider what such an unholy alliance would mean.

He thought again about Althea Ellison dying around the time Carl and Veronica Holden had disappeared. He understood the twisted logic of him wanting to kill Carl Holden, and sometimes it was the first kill that triggered something in murderers.

They stepped inside Rory's office. A large oak desk dominated one side of the room, the walls lined with bookcases.

Liam scanned through the books, many of which were related to folklore and mythology.

'I wonder if it really was just Althea who was interested in all this stuff,' Maya said, scanning through the titles.

Together they went through the books title by title, hoping for something that would trigger an explanation.

Rory hadn't left any computer or documentation behind, though Jack was currently conducting a deep financial forensic search back at headquarters. As far as they knew, Rory didn't own any other properties, and there was nowhere in the current grounds where he could be hiding either Erin or his own son.

'There's a hatch through here, ma'am,' said one of the search team, pointing to a loft access point on the upper floor.

'Let's open it up,' Liam said.

The officer pushed at the hatch, pulling down folding metal steps. Liam was first up, crouching down as he manoeuvred his large frame through the gap, and switched on the light.

'You better come up, boss,' he said, peering through the opening to Maya who was already on the ladder.

The attic was the usual dumping ground most homes had, but what had drawn Liam's attention was the large, framed map of Cornwall hanging on the wall next to a water cylinder.

It was similar to the print in Tony Ellison's room but this one was an original oil painting. 'This looks much older,' Liam said, tracing his fingers over the rough paint on the canvas.

'It has the same marks as Tony's map,' Maya said, squinting at the faint smudges of pencil on the paint at the spots that had been asterisked on Tony's map. This particular painting was more localised, as if someone had zoomed in on the bottom half of Tony's painting, covering mainly the Penwith area of Cornwall.

Although he'd seen a similar image back at headquarters, seeing it now triggered something in Liam's mind. The pattern he'd been so desperately searching for was beginning to take shape.

He found some paper and gently traced the spots on the painting where the bodies had been found, including the latest one at Trevowen.

He made an outline for Maya's benefit, his hand moving from point to point, from the marks placed on the map by Rory Ellison.

It was close enough. The pencil created the vague shape of a circle.

Liam placed the pencil down. 'It looks like he's trying to make his own stone circle,' he said.

Chapter Thirty-Eight

Liam forwarded images of the map to Jack. With his help, they coordinated extra teams to all the locations that had been highlighted. Practically every working officer in the county was now assigned to the investigation.

Liam left the rest of the search team at Rory Ellison's house before heading off with Maya. They planned to go from site to site to check on how the searches were progressing, moving around the new circle in the vague hope that they might locate Rory.

They headed to the Merry Maidens site first. Maya was driving, Liam trying to read a copy of Althea's book in the passenger seat. He'd read it before but now he was looking at it with different eyes, searching for something that may have been important to her, something that could have triggered her husband's behaviour.

As they were driving along the back roads to the Merry Maidens, Jack called to confirm they had a familial DNA match for Tony Ellison.

'Carl was Tony's father,' Jack said.

'We should have made Rory come in for DNA testing sooner,' Liam said.

'We followed protocol. There was no way of knowing about this, so I don't want to hear it,' Maya said.

Liam nodded, but it was hard not to feel despondent. Although they had potentially uncovered Rory's pattern, they had no real idea where he would strike again. Liam had managed to trace a circle around the sites, but it had been far from exact. There were simply too many potential sites where a body could be placed. And that was before they took into account the more-than-likely scenario that Rory might not strike again that day, and may have already absconded.

Rory must have known sooner or later they'd be on to him. He hadn't been at work for over three days, so he would've had plenty of time to make an exit. Liam didn't want to admit it, but it was possible the man was anywhere in the world at this stage.

As for Tony Ellison, that was still unknown. It was hard to work out what his role in all of this was. It appeared that part of this, at least, was Rory attacking his son, but maybe they'd got that wrong as well. Maybe the relationship between Rory and Tony was more twisted than they realised, and that Tony was working together with his father. Maybe he had done so from the beginning.

'Any news?' Liam asked the officer on site.

'No sightings, sir.'

'I want a constant patrol of the circle,' Maya said, as the second officer joined them.

'Ma'am.'

'You really think he'll strike here again?' Liam said to Maya as the officers moved off, their torches making patterns across the field, at one point highlighting the missing eighth stone.

'This place obviously has some relevance to him, if he killed Carl Holden and his wife here as well as Tess.'

Jack and the tech team were still analysing the locations used so far, trying to decipher a logical step to determine where the next kill site would be. But as Maya said, if the killer was Rory, his actions were unpredictable. If he had killed Carl and Veronica, he'd done so five years before killing Tess. Unless there were other murders in between, something had triggered this new spate of killings.

Liam put the question to Maya.

'Maybe it's close to the anniversary of the first kills,' she said.

Liam thought of the maps found at the house. 'What if it's something to do with Tony? He's leaving for university soon. Rory's already lost his wife and now he's losing his son . . . or the boy he thought was his son?'

'It might explain why Tony's ex-lovers have been targeted,' she said. 'Though that could just be a jealousy thing.'

'Or a twisted statement. Maybe Althea cheating on him distorted his view of women and relationships, unleashed some latent prejudice that's caused him to act this way.'

It was all conjecture at this point, and the most important thing was finding Rory and Tony before anyone else died.

'Where's the next stop?' he asked.

Maya checked her map. 'Tregeseal stone circle,' she said, as another car pulled up, blocking the car park exit.

'It's Raymond Preston,' Liam said, as the archaeologist stepped out.

'DS Kilshaw. DI Trent,' Preston said as he walked over, his smile tempered by the solemnity of the situation.

'What brings you here, Raymond?' said Liam.

'I wanted to help. I may have spotted something,' he said, going on to confirm the pattern of the circle Liam had already identified, from the Merry Maidens to Boskednan, around to Tregeseal, and finally Trevowen.

'Good spot,' Liam said. 'Any idea why the killer would be creating their own stone circle?'

Preston moved closer, clearly pleased to be asked for his opinion. 'I've been considering that. Obsession, perhaps? I know I have a deep interest in these sites, but maybe someone else has a deeper one. You think Rory Ellison is responsible?'

Liam looked to Maya. The manhunt for Rory had reached the news outlets, but he still wasn't keen to discuss the investigation in this way with Preston. 'Would that make any difference?'

'I was thinking about where he might strike next, if he's continuing this idea of making his own circle, of course.'

'And?'

Preston couldn't resist a smile. 'I'm sure you know all the potential sites and I imagine you're here because you think he might strike at the same place again.'

'Get to the point, Mr Preston,' Maya said.

'I found something. I'd forgotten about it, actually, but then I got to thinking. Anyway, here,' Preston said, pulling a large tome from his satchel.

'*The Folded Path*, by Althea Marlowe. I haven't seen this before. Haven't even seen it referenced,' Liam said.

'No, it's a work of fiction. Self-published years ago. I managed to get a copy once. Completely forgot about it. I've just finished rereading it.'

'Any suggestion of where her husband will kill again?' Maya said.

Preston gave a nervous laugh in response. 'No. But there is a mention of a stone circle. This particular circle is fictional, but the location exists. And if my geography is right, it fits the pattern of the circle the killer is creating.'

Liam and Maya exchanged a look, Maya shrugging. 'Okay, Raymond, give us a brief overview.'

'*The Folded Path* reimagines Cornish folklore through the lens of the female experience, exploring themes of autonomy, silencing, and transformation. Althea wrote of threshold places where women throughout history had gathered or vanished.'

'Any women killed in stone circles?' Maya asked.

‘No. Not that simple, I’m afraid, but there is a final scene in the novel that Althea transposed to Treen. She called it the Listening Field, a stretch of open grassland where voices are said to echo back in someone else’s tone.’

Treen was less than a twenty-minute drive away. After some discussion, they decided to take Preston with them. It was the first they’d heard of both Althea’s work of fiction and her fictional mythological site, and Preston may have been holding on to more relevant information.

They parked at Treen car park, a grassy path leading towards Pedn Vounder Beach. The area was desolate. Maya kept the headlights on as they left the car, Liam retrieving torches from the boot. Preston, carrying the novel, pointed to a single track leading off towards the sand dunes, behind which came the distant rumble of waves.

Liam called in their position before Maya switched off the car, plunging them into darkness. He found a spare torch for Preston, and the three of them set off towards the location of the fictional stone circle.

Liam was reminded of a similar trek through Sennen at the turn of the year – he and Maya, hands bound, their lives in danger. He’d yet to read the passages Preston had described and couldn’t rule out the possibility this was all a ruse, that the archaeologist was in cahoots with Rory.

It was a gruelling climb, and Liam had to keep telling himself they weren’t wasting their time. He could taste the salt in the air as the sea came into view. Despite the circumstances, he had to concede that part of him was enjoying the experience, the darkened landscape lit by torchlight, the distant call of the waves.

‘There,’ said Preston, pointing to the jutting peninsula. ‘I believe this is the Listening Field.’

Liam wished he’d known of the book’s existence earlier. From what he’d seen of Preston’s copy, it was a poorly produced tome. He couldn't recall seeing a copy at Rory's house, but he wondered to what extent it was a blueprint for what Rory had done so far, and what he planned to do.

The coastguard had been put on alert, a helicopter already moving from location to location on the killer's circle.

Preston's foot caught in the sand as they moved across the field towards the cliff edge.

They shone their torches towards Althea's Listening Field, but the beams were only strong enough to guide them a few metres at a time. In the distance, Liam could make out shapes and shadows, but it was impossible to decipher anything clearly.

There had been no other sightings of vehicles in the car park, and no other visible route to approach the area, so if Rory had intended to use the site, he must have come earlier.

They kept a steady pace, Liam resisting the urge to run. He kept casting his torch over outcrops of rock, his mind forming patterns that weren't there, of people shaped into tangled figurines, circles of victims contorted into praying statues.

Arriving at the cliff edge, Liam shone his torch towards the rumbling sea, jets of water crashing into the rocks and spiralling into the air. 'This is it?' he asked, not hiding the accusation in his voice, even though he was relieved there was no body to find.

'It was this peninsula,' said Preston.

Liam stopped short of calling the man a liar, though he knew he'd be reading that passage as soon as this was over.

Maya edged closer to the cliff edge, shining her torch into the bristling waves below.

Liam could sense her relief, and her disappointment. They both knew this was only a postponement. The inevitable was still coming, and all they'd achieved was wasting time, possibly giving Rory the chance to strike elsewhere.

Back at the car park, Maya called it in while Liam checked in with the other teams.

'Give me another overview of this novel, Raymond,' he said.

It felt desperate to be asking for advice from a piece of fiction written by a woman who'd been dead for over five years, but he still thought there might be something in it. Rory's obsession was twisted, and there was no reason not to suspect it had been shaped by his wife's work.

'It's a mixture of fact and fiction, really. Very clever – perhaps a little too clever. It tries to interweave mythology and history with fantasy and magic realism,' said Preston.

'You're going to have to clarify that for me, Raymond. What's the basic story?'

Liam tried his best to follow what Preston told him. His tale of a modern-day woman who could effectively time travel when in close proximity to mythological sites like the Merry Maidens was a hard one to grasp. The novel meandered between present-day complications, a woman trapped in an unhappy marriage, and the same woman living in the Bronze Age when the stone circles were still in use. It was a trope Liam thought he'd encountered before, though he couldn't place where.

'I'm afraid I'm not much of a fiction expert,' said Preston. 'I understand the story, and the parallels to Althea's own troubled relationship are obvious, I suppose. To me, the book is a meditation on judgement and sin. Sacrifice. Rebirth.'

A breeze picked up, prickling the exposed skin on Liam's scalp.

'The sacrifice angle, I get. You said rebirth?' he asked, wondering why he was prolonging the conversation.

'Oh yes,' said Preston, as if Liam had reminded him of something. He picked up the book, reading the final pages by torchlight.

'The Merry Maidens. The Dancing Stones. The Nine Maidens. The Hurlers. These sites are clearly about sin and deterrent. The maidens turned to stone, same for the hurlers, even the pipers. It was a way for religious sects to control the masses. Something we've seen recreated throughout history. But there are other sites . . . yes, here, for instance.'

He handed the book to Liam, opened to the final chapter. Liam scanned the first few paragraphs but couldn't make much sense of it.

'Break it down for me, Raymond.'

Preston took the book back. 'It wasn't all moralistic warnings. There was beauty and hope too. The book ends with the lead character leaving her husband and returning to the old lands. She joins a commune, one that believes in feminine energy. They worship the moon. Their creed is more about transcendence than punishment.'

'Transcendence,' Liam said, as if trying the word out, just as Maya returned from her calls.

'What's this?' she asked.

'Raymond's telling me about Althea's novel. Apparently it ends with her joining a cult.'

Preston gave a short laugh. 'Can I see the map you were using?' he asked.

Liam showed him the updated map, a merger of the two found at the Ellison household, overlaid on a modern map of Cornwall, the hand-drawn circle marked in red.

'As I thought,' said Preston, almost to himself.

'Come on, Raymond, don't keep it to yourself.'

'No, sorry,' said Preston, shaking himself from his thoughts. 'Here, you see?' He pointed to a location. 'This is where the heroine ends up at the end of the novel. A place associated with transformation. A stone circle, of sorts. Though I'd call it an oval, really. But nineteen stones, like the Merry Maidens. Only these don't symbolise death and punishment. More . . . hope.'

Liam took the phone back off him, zooming in on the site he had highlighted: Boscawen-Un. An oval of nineteen stones with a prominent central leaning stone.

The site wasn't located on the imaginary circle they'd expected Rory to strike on again.

It was dead in its centre.

Chapter Thirty-Nine

Rory didn't know how long it would be until they arrived. All he could do was hope that they were concentrating on the circle he'd created. The connected stone circles where he'd sacrificed the maidens.

The real power lay in the centre of his circle. Althea's book, The Folded Path *had shown him that.*

Boscawen-Un was the centre of everything. It was where the heroine became reborn. Rory had known from the minute he read it that it was a message from Althea. It was where the final act had to take place. It was where they could become a family again.

The plan with Nina had worked perfectly, and even the bald policeman and his partner must have worked out the significance of the circle by now.

The circle was complete.

All he needed now was the centrepiece.

The last maiden who was currently transforming.

And finally, the pipers.

Rory had spared Tony from the worst of it. After killing Tess, Rory had kept his son – for he was his son, whatever anyone said – in a state of limbo. He didn't need to be conscious for everything that was happening. He only needed to be there for the final ceremony.

Rory had used the list he'd found in the boy's bedroom to continue the work he'd started five years ago, but not once had he made the boy watch. When he'd transformed Tess, Tony had been safely in the van, sleeping, and he'd kept him in a similar state ever since.

Still, it had been hard to look him in the eyes when he'd carried him to the field, the paralytic already in his system. He hoped Tony understood. He'd told him this was the way it had to be if they wanted to be with his mother for eternity. She may not have been a physical part of the circle itself, but in so many ways it was her creation.

Rory was sure he'd understood, even as he was pouring the liquid into his throat.

'We're going to be the Piper Stones forever, son,' Rory had whispered, before walking over to the other field and putting himself in position.

He checked the substance once more, sprinkling the last of the limonite over the top. He placed it into the funnel and set the timer, then covered his feet and hands with clay and injected himself.

Shuffling into a kneeling position, he placed the funnel into his mouth.

Within seconds, he was unable to move, the bottom end of the funnel sliding into his throat, the drug stopping him from gagging as the timer went off and the ochre mist began its slow descent.

Maya called Hargreaves at headquarters as Liam drove the three of them the short distance to Boscawen-Un, requesting the coastguard's helicopter make a pass over the site, which was dead centre of Rory Ellison's circle.

Liam recalled visiting the place before, though the sites were beginning to blur into one.

As the location wasn't on the mapped route of the circle, they hadn't stationed a patrol car there. And despite Preston's revelation about Althea's book, they were reluctant to shift resources as it could present Rory with an opening elsewhere.

Liam considered asking Preston what he thought Rory's endgame might be. It was likely they'd find nothing, as had been the case in Treen, but he'd heard enough about Boscawen-Un, about the way it had been used for worship and, more importantly, for sacrifice, both in Althea's novel, and in the past, to have a grim idea of what Rory might be planning.

The helicopter came into view about two miles out, its path all but guiding them to the turn-off from the A30, a narrowing farm track. Liam drove as far as he could before pulling over. 'Torches on again,' Maya said, as he cut the engine.

The wind had picked up since Treen. Liam handed Preston a torch as they set off down the dirt track towards the circle. Althea's weighty novel was clutched in the archaeologist's other hand like a holy relic warding off evil.

Liam remembered the narrow path from his last visit. It was a difficult traversal, even in daylight. Again, there were no vehicles parked nearby but there was a secondary route further along the A30 that Rory could have used.

It seemed absurd the degree to which they were dealing in maybes, but the investigation had been plagued by uncertainties from the start. If Rory wasn't there, it would be easy to accept. If one or more victims were waiting by the stones, he'd accept that too. Nothing could surprise him any more.

Static broke through their handheld radios. Liam looked up at the helicopter hovering above a spot roughly three hundred yards ahead.

'People sighted,' came the feedback. 'Three individuals. All appear to be static.'

Liam and Maya picked up their pace to a steady run, the narrow path and low light making anything faster too risky.

'Wait here,' Liam said to Preston, an afterthought as he and Maya pushed forward.

'Still no movement,' came the next update. 'The three figures are spaced in a horizontal line, spanning the width of the stone circle. Little to no motion.'

Liam tried not to replace the word *people* with *victims* as they reached the end of the path. The stone circle emerged into view, illuminated in patches by the sweeping helicopter light.

With the blades stirring the air above them, they stepped cautiously into the circle.

'It's them,' Liam said, stumbling over a low boulder as he made his way towards the centre.

At the heart of the stones, leaning against the large central monolith, was Erin Dunne.

Like the others before her, she was stuck in a false prayer.

Unlike the others, she was still alive.

Chapter Forty

Liam tore at the soft clay sealed over Erin's mouth and nose. She couldn't speak. Her neck was bent forwards, and as he gently lifted it, he noted her breathing was shallow at best.

'Can you move?' Liam asked, not surprised when there was no answer.

He wondered how long she'd been like this. The pattern had to be the same as the others, which meant she'd been paralysed and force-fed the clay-like substance, the drug stopping her from taking deep breaths, saving her for now, as her airways hadn't yet been completely flooded. But it also meant she was only moments away from suffocating as the substance hardened.

'We need to get her supine,' said Liam, easing her hands from the prayer position.

With Maya's help, they got Erin on her back, her neck slightly elevated.

Liam took his penknife from his jacket.

'What the hell are you going to do with that?' said Maya.

'It's her only hope. Once whatever's in her hardens, she won't be able to breathe.'

Liam had been in this position before, at least from an observer's point of view. He'd received extensive medical combat training in the SBS and had once watched a colleague perform an emergency cricothyrotomy. The procedure, beloved of TV and film, involved making an incision in the cricothyroid membrane between the Adam's apple and the cricoid cartilage, and inserting a makeshift tube so the patient could breathe.

In a medical setting, it was relatively simple. Out in the field, not so much. That night, they'd been under fire in the dark, and his colleague had misjudged the incision and hit a major blood vessel. Their fallen comrade had bled out before they could do anything else.

'I need a pen. A tube of some sort,' Liam said, trying to shake the memory. 'A thick one,' he added, almost to himself.

Maya found a pen in her pocket and dismantled it, handing over the outer casing as Liam passed a lighter flame over the blade. It was far from being sterile but it would have to do.

With Maya holding a torch to the area, Liam located Erin's cricoid cartilage. Holding the larynx steady with his other hand, he readied the penknife.

The whipping blades of the helicopter overhead did little to help his concentration.

Liam blocked out the noise, focusing everything on Erin, who was limp as a ragdoll.

'Ready,' he said, easing the blade through the membrane.

Erin's body shuddered.

'Pen,' Liam said, taking the outer casing from Maya and sliding it into the incision.

The split second of silence that followed felt like a lifetime.

Liam realised he'd been holding his breath as Erin's body twitched, and a rush of air came from the pen casing.

She was breathing.

The pain was unimaginable. Deep down, Rory had known it would be, but the mental strain of knowing what was happening to him and his body being unable to fight it was something he hadn't fully prepared for.

He tried to close his eyes as sorrow swarmed him. It may have been necessary but he didn't like the idea of Tony having to endure this, the pressure in his chest making him feel like he was going to explode.

If only he hadn't read that diary, the one Althea had kept hidden in her files along with her writing.

She'd loved him, that he understood. But she'd also loved someone else. Tony's biological father.

That first kill had been the hardest. Carl Holden had deserved to die. He'd destroyed Rory's family. Had taken his wife, and his only child.

With Althea dead, Rory feared Tony would find out about his biological dad and he couldn't risk losing him.

The act itself was simple enough, but it was the moral justification that had been hardest to straighten out.

Only when he'd buried the bodies – Carl's wife an unfortunate casualty – did it begin to make sense to him.

He was sure Althea would have appreciated the symbolism. It had brought a change in Rory he couldn't explain. It was a type of energy he'd never before experienced.

He realised he'd harnessed the power of the circle, and it changed everything.

Where once he'd dismissed Althea's work, he became obsessed with it. He was a man of science, but the more he read about the stone circles and the mythologies that went with them, the more he began to understand.

He devoured all of Althea's work, searching for the hidden clues that would bring her back to him, and when he eventually read her novel, he finally understood.

Everything went full circle. The maidens had belonged to Tony. Tony belonged to him and Althea. Even Carl had his place beneath the soil.

Soon, the clay within him would harden and he would join the others.

He and Tony would be reunited with Althea for eternity.

'Is she going to be okay?' said Maya, already reaching for her radio.

'If we get her medical treatment in the next few minutes.'

'Come in,' Maya said to the helicopter. 'Repeat.'

'Two more bodies. Arranged in similar fashion. East and west fields.'

'The pipers?' said Liam, his fingers pressed to Erin's weak pulse.

'I'll go,' said Maya, already moving through the circle to the first field before he could object.

'You can get through this, Erin,' Liam said, checking she was still breathing. They needed medics on site immediately. Whatever had been forced into her lungs had to be removed. The makeshift operation might hold for minutes, but no longer if the substance stayed in her airways.

'He's alive!' Maya shouted, reappearing through the stones.

'Who?'

'Tony.'

'The other figure?' Liam said.

'Over there. I'll sprint.'

'What the hell is going on?' Liam muttered, as his radio hissed. Paramedics had arrived and were making their way across the field. If his journey had been anything to go by, they would be some time. Time that Erin did not have.

In normal circumstances, he would have told the helicopter to take Erin out. But there was nowhere safe for it to land, and in her condition it was too risky to airlift her.

Liam wondered how much Erin was aware of. He tried to comfort her but her mind had to be in turmoil. She was trapped in her body, seconds from choking, unable to fight. Liam had seen hardened war veterans crumble under less duress. He just hoped that if she came through this, her mind would be able to adjust to the trauma.

'It's Rory Ellison,' said Maya, breathless as she returned from the other field.

Liam's body tightened.

'What do you mean? Is he like the others?' he asked, eyes scanning for any additional threat.

'I think he may have done it to himself. There's a tube and funnel by his side, and he's not in the same position as the others.'

'Is he breathing?'

'Yes, but he can't move.'

Liam was still supporting Erin's head.

'How long for the paramedics?'

'At least five minutes out.'

'I need to help Tony,' Liam said. 'All you need to do is keep this airway clear.'

They exchanged positions. If Rory had somehow administered the substance to himself it confirmed his responsibility for everything. It wasn't a surprise but it made Liam's decision that much easier.

He found a Sharpie in Maya's bag, snapped it open, and sprinted to the field where Tony was situated.

The young man was in the same kneeling position as the others, overlooking the stone circle beneath him. Maya had clawed away the clay from his mouth and nose. Liam wondered how much he'd known. Had Rory told him he wasn't his biological dad from the beginning, or had he lived in ignorance all this time, wondering why the one person in his life he should have been able to trust was doing this to him?

The skin on Tony's face was discoloured. Liam could see as much even in the relative darkness, the landscape lit sporadically by the sweeping beams of the helicopter's searchlights.

'Hold tight, Tony,' he said, placing his torch between his teeth as he lowered the boy to the ground.

Time was running out. His breathing was all but gone as Liam found the cricoid cartilage and made the incision through the membrane before inserting the tube.

Tony didn't respond, and for a second Liam froze before lowering his ear to the tube.

'Fuck, he can't draw a breath,' he murmured to himself. The paralytic must have reached his diaphragm.

Liam took a breath and forced it through the tube.

Tony's chest lifted. Liam repeated the motion. There was another slight rise and finally a gurgling noise.

'Come on, Tony,' Liam cried, breathing into the tube once more as the paramedics arrived.

'Bag valve, now,' he said, refusing to move until the medics had their equipment ready.

'We can take it from here, sir,' said one of them.

Liam stood as they began to work. 'You have another team?'

'On their way, sir.'

Liam had no option but to go alone. 'Do you have a spare airway kit?'

'Sir, I think—'

'Just give me it,' Liam demanded, taking the kit from the paramedic.

He returned through the stone circle, where Maya was with Erin.

'She's OK,' Maya said. 'Make sure that sick bastard doesn't die.'

Liam glanced towards the pathway, searching for a sign of the second paramedic team as he made his way to the adjoining field. Maya had said to keep Rory alive but beyond getting a few answers, which would no doubt prove worthless, Liam could barely see the point.

He supposed it was duty. Duty had plagued him since childhood, when he'd been forced to look after his mother during her increasing bouts of alcohol and drug misuse. It had continued during his time in the navy, the SBS, and now in the police. Most of the time, he didn't have a problem with it. He was disciplined and well-trained. He saw the need to follow orders and was happy to do so. But if his duty now was to keep a mass murderer alive – someone who had tortured and abused his victims, including his own son – he wasn't sure duty was something he cared much for.

Part of him wanted Rory to already be dead. It would take the decision to save a killer's life out of Liam's hands. But the man was clearly alive. He must have poisoned himself with the paralytic drug, then used the discarded funnel to pour the sludgy, ochre-tainted liquid down his own throat before it took effect.

To what end he would do this, Liam could only imagine. Maybe he saw some kind of honour in the act, or perhaps it was a twisted nod to his wife.

In some ways, it must have taken great mental strength. Not only was he willing to take his own life but he was willing to endure what his victims had.

Liam didn't care. It did nothing to lighten the way he felt about the man. 'What have you done to yourself, Rory?' he said, moving the man into a prone position.

◆ ◆ ◆

It couldn't end like this. The circle had been his obsession from the moment Althea had died, although it had taken the threat of Tony leaving for university for it to come to fruition.

Rory could feel the transformation within him. The heaviness of the substance fusing with his body. It hurt like the weight of the world was pressing down on him, but there was no sacrifice without pain.

So why was the police officer doing this?

He wanted to scream, to brush him away, but he couldn't move. The most he could do was listen, and he didn't like what the policeman had to say.

◆ ◆ ◆

Liam repeated everything he'd done before, the torch in his mouth as he opened the airway kit he'd taken from the paramedics. Like Tony and Erin, Rory couldn't move, but Liam could see the terror in his eyes as he held the scalpel and air tube towards the man's neck.

'What are you scared of, Rory? That I'll kill you or that I'll save your life?'

Rory held his gaze but there was no real decision to be made. Duty would win out. Liam wasn't a murderer and he wasn't going to let that change because of the monster in front of him.

'Just you keep still, Rory,' Liam said, thinking of Erin and Tony and all the other victims who hadn't survived as he made the incision, which was easier now thanks to the scalpel and breathing tube from the paramedics.

The tube was safely inserted and Liam checked Rory's breathing as the paramedic team arrived and took over.

Exhausted, he stumbled back to Maya, who was overlooking another paramedic team working on Erin.

‘You did a great job there, Liam,’ she said, as static blasted from the radios. The weariness was evident in Maya’s eyes as she responded. ‘Trent.’

‘Paramedic with Anthony Ellison. I’m afraid Mr Ellison went into cardiac arrest. We were unable to resuscitate him.’

Chapter Forty-One

The smell of freshly cut grass came to him, along with the distant taste of salt in the air. He took a deep breath, savouring the land, the deep scent of the mud beneath him, the more subtle tones of rain on the stones.

He pictured the stone circle. Not just the one he was in but the extended circle, the one he'd created with his offerings across the region, with his final resting place at its centre, beside his son.

A thick pressure pushed into his head as a noise disrupted his nirvana. An incessant beeping masking the sound of voices.

'Gives me the creeps. All he does is blink. Just thinking about what he did . . . best thing for everyone would've been if he hadn't survived.'

Rory wanted to open his eyes but they were glued shut. He tried to will himself back to the open country, but his subconscious began offering him titbits of unwanted information.

That last night at Boscawen-Un. The maiden. Tony. The funnel he'd created to seal his own fate.

'No, no, no,' he said to himself as the vision of the police officer came to mind. The man's giant dome of a skull, the violence of the scalpel in his throat as he'd forced air into his lungs – he had taken the glory from him, had stolen his right to complete the circle.

He went to scream, to sit up and fight, but it was all he could do to open his eyes.

'Good. You're with us, Mr Ellison. Do you remember me? Dr Evans.'

Yes, he remembered him. He remembered everything since the policeman had arrived at the circle uninvited.

The doctor had reminded him more than once how the poison in his system had gone awry, had left him permanently paralysed. Something to do with the clay impacting his chest and the lack of oxygen to his brain.

He remembered the policeman visiting him, gazing down on him as if he were God, telling him that Tony had died, that Rory had killed him despite their efforts to save him. And that the maiden had survived.

He'd had plenty of time to dwell on that. How his final kill had failed. How he'd imprisoned himself in a wrecked body and lost his only surviving family.

'Although he was never really yours, was he?' the policeman had said. 'I haven't heard anyone say a bad thing about that poor lad and you destroyed him. Why, Rory? Jealousy? Or did you simply hate him because he wasn't yours?'

Rory had tried to answer, tried to explain that what the policeman was saying was wrong. He'd loved Tony. He'd loved his mother. But the words were lost in his mind, the only noise leaving his lips a wretched gurgle.

'Any improvement?' he heard someone say, pain shooting through him at the sound of the voice.

The policeman had returned. Rory closed his eyes, tried to will him away but when he reopened them the man was leering over him.

'How you doing in there, Rory?'

Rory garbled a response.

'That's good to know. You'll be pleased to understand that your current condition won't exclude you from being prosecuted. You're going to pay for the heinous things you did, Rory. But that has nothing to do with you. That'll be for the victims. The people you killed. Their families. Including Tony's real father.

'Because you're already imprisoned, Rory, aren't you?' the policeman continued, under his breath but close enough that Rory could hear. 'I guess it doesn't really matter where you end up.'

He stared down at Rory for an imperceptible amount of time. Rory understood then that he was completely at the mercy of the policeman – and of everyone else for that matter.

Somehow, he'd got it all wrong. He'd known from the start that his interpretation of Althea's book had been subjective. Maybe he'd read too much into it. Or read it wrong.

He wished he could turn back time. He was glad Carl Holden was dead but Tony had never known about his biological father. Things had been difficult between them, but they'd had a bond. Maybe he should have let the boy go off to university. Ignored what he thought was his calling, his way of being with Althea again.

One thing he did realise, as the policeman disappeared from his sight: he was going to have an eternity to mull it over.

Epilogue

It was late evening when Liam left the hospital. He'd just been to visit Rory Ellison again. The doctors had confirmed what they'd long suspected: Rory would be permanently paralysed.

Two months had passed since the incident at Boscawen-Un. Since then, Liam's department had been working closely with the CPS to build a prosecution case. Today, they'd finally been given the go-ahead. Rory would be tried for the murders of Tess, Carys, Kian, Ruby, Nina and his son, Tony, as well as the attempted murder of Erin and the historic murders of Carl and Veronica. The fact that he was paralysed wouldn't change the approach being taken.

Although no other outcome would have been acceptable, it was still a relief. The case had captured the public's imagination. Liam had grown tired of reading the wild theories online. Some suggested Rory had acted out of jealousy towards Tony's lovers. Others connected his crimes to the ideology in Althea Marlowe's books. There were even claims that Tony had been working with his father and that Rory had turned on him when he sensed the police were closing in.

Rory hadn't given any evidence yet, but plans were in place for him to communicate using eye-tracking technology. Eventually, they would speak to him.

Liam had his own theory about the truth. He suspected even Rory wouldn't know it fully. But he was certain of one thing: Tony had no part in the killings.

That afternoon, he took George to cricket practice and forced himself to switch off completely from the investigation. They went for burgers afterwards on the wharf, Liam enjoying the time together more than ever. He didn't see the boy as often as he'd like but it was a joy to watch him grow. He was bright and funny, always willing to share his thoughts, and Liam hoped that wouldn't change.

'I saw Miss the other day,' George said, wiping ketchup from the corner of his mouth.

'Miss?'

'Miss Foster. You do remember her?'

'Oh, Millie. Well, she is at your school.'

'No, I saw her at the beach when I was with Mum. She came over to speak to us. It was mortifying.'

Liam laughed. 'Is there a point to this story?'

George took another bite of his burger. 'Could be. I heard them talking when they thought I wasn't listening.'

'Do I want to hear this?'

'Miss said she'd split up with her boyfriend.'

Liam took a sip of his soft drink, unsure how to respond. He was a little surprised George had so much insight and wondered how much he understood, and if his son had noticed on the days he'd decided to collect him from the school playground rather than waiting for him in the car.

'I think we should get you home, Mr Eavesdropper,' he said.

The tide was in as they walked back to the car, the sky a glorious blue as seagulls swooped on anyone naïve enough to be eating out in public. Liam took in the sight and smell of the water, deciding he might find a beach later for a late-night surf.

His gradual recovery from his PTSD meant he could now face the waves without too much trouble, his breathing exercises on hand for when thoughts wandered.

Back at his house, he walked George to the front door. Kim was a little surprised to see him as he usually waited in the car until George was inside. 'Everything okay?' she said.

'All good. You?'

Kim nodded, a familiar smile on her lips, as if she knew something he didn't.

Liam said goodbye, resisting the urge to ask Kim about Millie. He felt foolish for even considering it, and was disconcerted with himself for letting George's mention of her affect him so much.

The thought was still with him later as he carried his board from the car park down to Gwithian Beach. Grace and her team had left a couple of weeks after the discovery at Boscawen-Un, though Liam suspected discussions were still going on in the background about a potential merger of the CID teams.

He'd seen Grace a few times since, having sent Tina a text to politely say he wasn't interested in developing things.

Grace had stayed over in St Ives, and he'd made a few trips to Exeter. They were still taking things slowly, but Liam sensed a shift in their relationship and wasn't sure if it was because of the distance, or if Grace was expecting something more from him. Sooner or later he would need to make more of a commitment, but the way he'd reacted when George had mentioned Millie made him think that things between him and Grace might not work out.

The waves rumbled as he reached the shoreline, the slight breeze pushing at his board as he made his way across the sand. He thought about Tony Ellison, and the former lovers he'd left in his wake, and reminded himself that Grace deserved honesty from him, and that he had to sort out the way he felt soon.

Easing the board into the water, he doused his head in the surf before paddling out to the breakers, his mind now blissfully only focused on catching the next wave.

◆ ◆ ◆

The next evening was the summer solstice. Liam met Maya at the Merry Maidens stone circle.

The road was littered with vehicles and they had to walk half a mile to reach the destination. Insects buzzed as they made the walk, the humidity causing Liam to sweat.

'Odd coming back here like this,' Maya said as they reached the field, a large crowd already gathered.

'Rather this than for any other reason,' Liam replied, nodding to Raymond Preston, who was part of the throng, his leather satchel over his shoulder, holding hands with his companion from the archaeological site.

Neither Liam nor Maya wanted to impose, so they kept to the rear of the congregation, which for now was gathered around the edge of the circle. Many were dressed in yellow, some had decorated their skin with limonite or similar yellow-coloured ochre.

The eighth stone had been put back in place, and with the sun glinting down on the stones, it was a beautiful sight.

Liam caught the eye of Danny Reeve, both acknowledging one another with a respectful nod of the head before Liam returned his gaze to the circle.

The sun strained his eyes, and as he blinked, his mind played a merciless trick on him, conjuring images of the victims kneeling in front of each stone – from Tess Penrose through to Tony Ellison, each caught in the prayer position, their faces covered in clay.

He shook the image away as music started from the Piper Stone.

The evening had been the idea of Phillipa Penrose and Reverend Frayne. A replication of the event that had taken place near St Michael's Mount, it was an attempt to take something back from the tragedies inflicted on the community by Rory Ellison. It was a celebration of those murdered, a remembrance aimed to take the power away from the killer.

The family members of the deceased were all present, each carrying an image of their loved ones. Even Ellie Holden was there, carrying photographs of her brother Carl, Veronica, and the nephew she'd never met – Tony Ellison.

Liam hoped that these were the images the family members recalled when they thought of those taken from them.

The ensemble stopped at the circle, each family member placing the photos of their fallen loved one on one of the stones, and dousing the granite with limonite.

Finally, Erin Dunne stood, helped from the wheelchair she was still temporarily using as she recovered from her ordeal. The crowd fell silent as she placed flowers against the stones, marking the memory of her friends.

Frayne didn't speak, and Liam was glad of the fact. It was enough to watch everyone gathered, taking what they could from the ceremony.

Liam felt Maya's hand on his back, and he nodded.

The crowd began singing as Liam and Maya returned to the car. Liam found that he finally understood what Frayne had been getting at – that dousing the stones with limonite, and returning to the place where the terrible series of events had taken place, was empowering.

And despite everything that happened, Liam felt a surge of optimism he hadn't felt in years.

ABOUT THE AUTHOR

Photo © 2019 Lisa Visser

Following his law degree, where he developed an interest in criminal law, Matt Brolly completed his Masters in Creative Writing at Glasgow University. He is the *Wall Street Journal* and Amazon bestselling author of the DI Blackwell novels, the DCI Lambert crime novels, the Lynch and Rose thrillers *The Controller* and *The Railroad*, and the standalone thrillers *Zero*, *The Running Girls* and *The Alliance*. *Broken Circle* is the third in a new series set in Cornwall, featuring DS Kilshaw. Matt lives in London with his wife, their two children, and a golden retriever called Herbie. You can find out more about him at www.mattbrolly.com or by following him on X: @MattBrollyUK.

Follow the Author on Amazon

If you enjoyed this book, follow Matt Brolly on Amazon to be notified when the author releases a new book!
To do this, please follow these instructions:

Desktop:

1) Search for the author's name on Amazon or in the Amazon App.
2) Click on the author's name to arrive on their Amazon page.
3) Click the 'Follow' button.

Mobile and Tablet:

1) Search for the author's name on Amazon or in the Amazon App.
2) Click on one of the author's books.
3) Click on the author's name to arrive on their Amazon page.
4) Click the 'Follow' button.

Kindle eReader and Kindle App:

If you enjoyed this book on a Kindle eReader or in the Kindle App, you will find the author 'Follow' button after the last page.